Best known as a writer of crime fiction, his work translated into more than twenty languages, John Harvey is also a dramatist, poet, publisher and occasional broadcaster.

The first of his twelve Charlie Resnick novels, *Lonely Hearts*, was named by *The Times* as one of the '100 Best Crime Novels of the Century'. The recipient of honorary doctorates from the universities of Nottingham and Hertfordshire, in 2007 he was awarded the Crime Writers' Association Cartier Diamond Dagger for Lifetime Achievement.

'John Harvey has saved the best for last.' Jon McGregor

'A troubling tale that succeeds not only as a murder mystery but as a memorial to an epic struggle.' *Mail on Sunday*

'Harvey's gritty, downbeat tales of Nottingham copper Charlie Resnick are some of the best recent English crime novels.' *Sun*

'If only every series of crime novels could end with such grace and style.' John Connolly

'Masterful, poignant and true.' Jill Dawson

Praise for John Harvey

'Just when you thought Harvey couldn't get any better, up he pops with yet another brilliantly constructed, coolly written, chillingly sharp and utterly contemporary procedural.' *Daily Mirror*

'Sharp plotting, great characterisation and a powerful narrative; it's as good as they get.' *Observer*

'As ever, John Harvey's writing is cool, light, and beautiful. His combination of darkest emotion, present-day concerns, and simple human wanting, where everything isn't tied up neatly at the end, and pain goes on beyond the end of the novel – because it always does – is flawless.' Stella Duffy

'Harvey's fleshed-out characters and sure grasp of the complex emotional underpinnings of society generally, and individuals in particular, make him a favourite among crime writers and readers alike.' *Daily Mail*

'Quite possibly Harvey's most authoritative in years: visceral, engaged and yes, unputdownable.' *Independent*

'In John Harvey's sure and practised hands, police procedural novels achieve new heights in grainy reality . . . The writing is thrilling and atmospheric.' *Guardian*

'An impassioned, at times heartbreaking story about love and violence and the breakdown of contemporary society and it confirms Harvey as one of our most accomplished writers in any genre.' *Sunday Telegraph*

'Everything is just as it should be in a classic modern British crime novel.' *Times Literary Supplement*

'A powerful, uncompromising, perhaps brave book, vividly mapping Nottingham's meaner streets with a gritty realism. As the body count begins to rise, Harvey's complex characters and terse, essential prose raise uncomfortable questions about policing and society.' *Financial Times*

'This is one of John Harvey's best novels, which means it's one of the best, full stop.' *Crime Time*

'Harvey is as good as they come; a writer of consummate elegance and deft characterisation, never wasting a word in what amounts to a master class in crime writing. Gripping and heartbreaking in equal measure, this is a must-read for anyone craving a beautifully written and literate page-turner.' Mark Billingham

'John Harvey's roll continues; no one in Britain is writing better crime fiction.' *The Times*

'John Harvey never writes a dull page and the pacy dialogue and momentum of the investigation from one smooth and plausible villain to another ensure that this novel is compelling from the start.' *Times Literary Supplement*

'Reading John Harvey is like settling under the wheel of a masterfully engineered, classic car . . . crime fiction at its best.' George Pelecanos

'A large gallery of credible characters with familiar hang-ups and minor joys populate the novel and supply it with the invigorating breath of life in Britain as we know it today . . . Harvey makes it all look effortless but this is first-class craftsmanship.' Maxim Jacobowski, *Guardian*

'Immaculately engineered . . . fast, fluent and exciting, with a pace and assurance that never lets up.' *Literary Review*

'A bloody good writer who understands clean, spare and beautiful prose.' Mo Hayder

'John Harvey is one of my favourite writers. Whenever he has a new book out it goes to the top of my reading list. And I haven't been disappointed yet.' Peter Robinson

'Harvey reminds me of Graham Greene, a stylist who tells you everything you need to know while keeping the prose clean and simple.' Elmore Leonard

Also by John Harvey

In a True Light
Nick's Blues
Gone to Ground
Far Cry
Good Bait

The Elder Novels
Flesh and Blood
Ash and Bone
Darkness and Light

The Resnick Novels
Lonely Hearts
Rough Treatment
Cutting Edge
Off Minor
Wasted Years
Cold Light
Living Proof
Easy Meat
Still Water
Last Rites
Cold in Hand

Short Stories
Now's the Time
Minor Key
A Darker Shade of Blue

Poetry
Ghosts of a Chance
Bluer Than This
Out of Silence: New & Selected Poems

As Editor
Blue Lightning
Men From Boys

For more information about John Harvey visit
www.mellotone.co.uk

John Harvey

darkness,
darkness

arrow books

Published by Arrow Books in 2014

1 3 5 7 9 10 8 6 4 2

Copyright © John Harvey 2014

John Harvey has asserted his right, in accordance with the Copyright,
Designs and Patents Act, 1988, to be identified as the author of this work

First published in Great Britain in 2014 by
William Heinemann
Random House, 20 Vauxhall Bridge Road,
London, SW1V 2SA

www.randomhouse.co.uk

Addresses for companies within The Random House Group Limited can be
found at: www.randomhouse.co.uk/offices.htm

The Random House Group Limited Reg. No. 954009

A CIP catalogue record for this book
is available from the British Library

ISBN 9780099590958

The Random House Group Limited supports the Forest Stewardship
Council® (FSC®), the leading international forest-certification organisation.
Our books carrying the FSC label are printed on FSC®-certified paper.
FSC is the only forest-certification scheme supported by the leading environmental
organisations, including Greenpeace. Our paper procurement policy can be found at
www.randomhouse.co.uk/environment

MIX
Paper from
responsible sources
FSC® C016897

Typeset in Times by Palimpsest Book Production Limited,
Falkirk, Stirlingshire
Printed and bound by CPI Group (UK) Ltd, Croydon, CR0 4YY

For François Guérif

darkness, darkness

1

The snow had started falling long before the first car departed. It fell in long, slanting lines, faint at first, then thickening. It gathered in corners and against the sides of buildings, funnelling between the broken brick and tile and rusted car parts that littered the back yards and paltry gardens. Covering everything. The sky a low, leaden grey, unrelenting.

By the time the cortège pulled away from the small terrace of houses, there was little to see in any direction, flakes adhering fast to the windows, all sound muffled, the dull glow of headlights fading into the surrounding whiteness.

Resnick was in the third car, sharing the rear seat with a solemn man in a threadbare suit he took to be one of Peter Waites' former colleagues from down the pit. In front of them sat an elderly, pinch-faced woman he thought must be a relation – an aunt, perhaps, or cousin. Not the one surviving sister, who was riding in the first car with Waites' son, Jack. Jack home for the funeral from Australia with his teenage sons; his wife not having taken to her new father-in-law the one time they'd met and grateful for the ten thousand or so miles that kept them apart.

That last a confidence Jack Waites had imparted the night before, when he and Resnick had met for a pint to chew over old times, Jack once a young PC, stationed at Canning Circus under Resnick's command.

'He was never the easiest bloke to get on with,' Jack said, 'the best of times. My old man.'

Resnick nodded. 'Maybe not.'

They were drinking at the Black Bull in Bolsover, the local pub in Bledwell Vale long boarded up; the village itself now mostly derelict, deserted: only a few isolated buildings and the terrace of former Coal Board houses in which Peter Waites had spent most of his adult life still standing.

'You should've lived with him,' Jack Waites said. 'Then you'd know.'

'You didn't come out of it so bad.'

'No thanks to him.'

'That's harsh, lad. Now especially.'

Jack Waites shook his head. 'No sense burying truth. It was my old lady pushed me on, got me to raise my sights. God rest her soul. He'd've dragged me down the pit the minute I got out of school, else. And then where'd I be? Out of work and drawing dole like every other poor bastard these parts. That or working in a call centre on some jerry-built industrial estate in the middle of bloody nowhere.'

Less than twenty-four hours back and you could hear the local accent resurfacing like rusted slippage in his voice.

No sense arguing, Resnick raised his glass and drank. There was truth, some, in what Jack Waites was saying, his father obdurate and unyielding as the coalface at which he'd laboured the best part of thirty years until, after strike action that had staggered proudly on for twelve months and come close to tearing the country apart, the pit had finally been closed down.

Resnick had first met Peter Waites in the early days of the strike, and somehow, despite their differences, they'd gone on to become friends. Waites' one of the strongest voices raised in favour of staying out, one of the loudest at the picket line, anger and venom directed towards those who would have gone back to work.

'Scab! Scab! Scab!'

'Out! Out! Out!'

Recently made up to inspector, Resnick had been running an intelligence gathering team, its function to obtain information about the principal movers and shakers in the strike, assess the volume of local support, keep tabs, as far as possible, on any serious escalation. Right from the earliest days, the first walkouts, the Nottinghamshire pits had been the least militant, the most likely to drag their feet, and Peter Waites and a few others had shouted all the louder in an attempt to bring them into line.

Around them, tempers flared: fists were raised, windows broken, things were thrown. Resnick thought it was time he had a word.

'Bloody hell!' Waites had exclaimed when Resnick – battered trilby, raincoat belted tight; wet enough outside to launch the ark – had walked into his local and sought him out. 'Takin' a bit of a risk, aren't you?'

'Know who I am, then?'

'Not the only one wi' eyes in their backside.'

'Good to hear it.' Resnick stuck out his hand.

The men, five or six, who'd been standing with Waites by the bar, watched to see what he would do, only relaxing when he met that hand with his own.

'My shout then,' Resnick said.

'Shippos all round in that case,' said the man to Waites' left. 'Skint, us, you know. Out on strike. Or maybe you'd not heard?'

'Fair enough,' Resnick said.

One of the miners spat on the floor and walked away. The others stood their ground. Some banter, not all ill-humoured, and after another round bought and paid for, Waites and Resnick moved to a table in the corner, all eyes watching.

'It'll not work, tha' knows.'

'What's that?'

'You and me, heads together. Makin' it look like I'm in your pocket. Some kind of blackleg bloody informer, pallin' up with a copper. That what this is about? Me losing face? 'Cause if it is, your money's gone to waste an' no mistake.'

Resnick shook his head. 'It's not that.'

'What then?'

'More a word of warning.'

'Warning!' Waites bristled. 'You've got the brazen balls . . .'

'The way things are going, more and more lads coming down from South Yorkshire, swelling your picket line . . .'

'Exercising their democratic right . . .'

'To what? Put bricks through folks' windows? Set cars alight?'

'That's not happened here.'

'No, maybe not yet. But it will.'

'Not while I've a say in things.'

'Listen.' Resnick put a hand on Waites' arm. 'Things escalate any more, pickets going from pithead to pithead mob-handed, what d'you think's going to happen? Think they're going to leave all that for us to deal with on our own? Local? Reinforcements enough from outside already and either you back off some or they'll be shipping 'em in from all over. Devon and Cornwall. Hampshire. The Met.' He shook his head. 'The Met coming in, swinging a big stick – that what you want?'

Waites fixed him with a stare. 'It's one thing to walk in here, show your face – that I can bloody respect. But to come in here and start making threats . . .'

'No threat, Peter. Just the way things are.'

Light for a big man, Resnick was quick to his feet. Waites picked up his empty glass, turned it over and set it back down hard.

As Resnick walked to the door the curses fell upon him like rain.

The church interior was chilly and cold: distempered walls, threadbare hassocks and polished pews; a Christ figure above the altar with sinewed limbs, a crimped face and vacant, staring eyes. 'Abide with Me'. The vicar's words, extolling a man who had loved his community more than most, a husband and a father, fell hollow nonetheless. A niece, got up in her Sunday best, read, voice faltering into silence, a poem she had written at school. The former miner who'd ridden with Resnick in the car remembered himself and Peter Waites starting work the same day at the pit, callow and daft the pair of them, waiting for the cage to funnel them down into the dark.

Resnick had imagined Jack Waites would bring himself to speak but instead he remained resolutely seated, head down. With some shuffling of feet, the congregation stood to sing the final hymn and the pall-bearers moved into position.

As they stepped outside, following the coffin out into the air, it was the dead man's voice Resnick heard, an evening when they'd sat in his local, not so many years before, Waites snapping the filter from the end of his cigarette before stubbornly lighting up.

'Lungs buggered enough already, Charlie. This'll not make ha'porth of difference, no matter what anyone says. Besides, long as I live long enough to see the last of that bloody woman and dance on her grave, I don't give a toss.'

That bloody woman: Margaret Thatcher. The one person, in Peter Waites' eyes, most responsible for bringing the miners down. After the strike had been broken, he could never bring himself to say her name. Not even when he raised a glass in her hated memory the day she died.

'Says it all, eh, Charlie? Dead in her bed in the fuckin' Ritz.'

Resnick's feet, following the coffin, left heavy indentations in the snow.

A blackbird, unconcerned, pecked hopefully at the frozen ground close by the open grave. Out beyond the cemetery wall, the land offered no angles to the sky.

As the coffin was lowered, a small group of men who'd kept their own company since before the service began to unfold a banner, the red, black and gold of the NUM, the National Union of Mineworkers.

'What's all this?' Jack Waites said angrily. 'What the bloody hell d'you think you're doing?'

'What's it look like?' one of the men replied.

'You tell me.'

'Honouring a comrade.'

'Honouring be buggered! Not here, you're bloody not.'

'Dad,' Waites' eldest said, pulling at his sleeve. 'Dad, don't.'

Waites shrugged him off. 'Wanted to honour him, should've done it when he was still alive. Out of work thirty years near enough, poor bastard, after your union helped bring the industry to its bloody knees . . .'

'Don't talk so bloody daft.'

'Daft? Course you bloody did. You and Scargill, arrogant bastard that he was, delivering up the miners on a sodding plate and you were all too blind to see.'

'I'd watch my mouth if I were you,' another of the union men said, showing a fist.

'Yes? Where is he now, then, Scargill, tell me that? In the lap of luxury in some fancy flat in London while your union pays out more'n thirty thousand a year for his rent, and has done since God knows when. And my old man, all that time, scraightin' out a living

in some one-time Coal Board house as was fallin'
apart round his ears. And you want to raise a fucking
banner in his honour . . .'

'Jack,' Resnick said, moving towards him, 'let it be.'

'I can only thank Christ,' the union man said, spitting
out his words, 'your father's in his grave, 'cause if
he weren't, hearing you'd make him shrivel up and
die of shame.'

'Fuck off!' Waites said, his voice shaking. 'Fuck
right off, the lot of you!' There were tears in his eyes.
Both his sons had turned aside.

The union men stood their ground before backing
away and resting their banner against the cemetery
wall, some small distance off; the snow falling only
fitfully now, sad moultings curling slowly down.

Resnick weighed a handful of earth carefully against
his palm, then opened his fingers and let it darkly fall.

2

Bledwell Vale, like a number of other villages across the north of Nottinghamshire, owed its existence to the spread of coal mining and the railways towards the end of the nineteenth century, rather than to any deeper history. In 1895, the company that owned the local pit bought a tract of land and wasted little time in building four facing rows of terraced houses, twelve to a row, each with gas lighting and running water and with earth middens and ash pits in their back yards. Soon enough after the miners and their families had moved in there was a Methodist chapel and a school. Allotments. A Miners' Welfare. A branch line to the colliery. A pub.

Between the wars, the earth toilets were replaced by water closets and gas lighting switched to the more modern electric. Then, when the industry was nationalised after the Second World War, all the properties were taken over by the National Coal Board and modernised again, with indoor bathrooms and toilets.

Brave new world.

Although the most profitable of the Nottinghamshire pits were not on the initial list of closures that set off the Miners' Strike in March of 1984, Bledwell Vale colliery was deemed to be played out. Less than six months after the strike had grudgingly ended and the men had gone, still defiant, back to work, the colliery was closed down for good.

Or ill.

By the time of Peter Waites' death, only one of the initial terraces was still standing, the allotments long overgrown, the station platform so weeded over as to be virtually unrecognisable; both school and chapel had been plucked clean of any lead or solid timber that could be reused or sold. Unlike some other communities – Arkwright Town, for instance, close over the border into Derbyshire, where fifty or so new houses were built to replace those being knocked down, and people simply moved their belongings, lock, stock and barrel, to the other side of the main road – for Bledwell Vale there would be no rebirth, no new life, no second chance.

The earth was still dark and new on Peter Waites' grave, the flowers at his headstone not yet blown, when the first of the diggers and the bulldozers moved in.

And so it was, on the morning of the third day, clearing away the debris from the terrace end, the unsuspecting operator of the JCB discovered, buried beneath the rear extension, what, even to his untutored eye, were clearly human remains. A human skeleton, otherwise undisturbed.

Resnick padded out to the bathroom in bare feet; Dizzy, his one surviving cat, winding its way between his legs. The animal waiting then, patiently, until Resnick had stepped back out of the shower, rubbed himself dry, dressed, and made his way downstairs. Previously the fiercest, most persistent of hunters, who would return from a night prowling the nearby gardens with field mice, shrews, an occasional rat – once, a young rabbit – all of them deposited at Resnick's feet with pride, Dizzy had become domesticated, virtually housebound, slowed down by arthritis and following Resnick from room to room; whenever he was out, waiting for him to return.

'Happens to us all,' Resnick said, bending to stroke the cat behind the ears. 'Eh, you sad old bugger.'

Never much of a cinema-goer, early in his retirement Resnick had taken to watching films of an afternoon, careful to leave the room during the adverts for stair-lifts and health insurance, lest they cause his anger to run over; returning with a fresh cup of tea – coffee now more strictly rationed – to watch Columbo solve the crime in the final reel, or John Wayne, in some aged western, walk heroically into the technicoloured sunset. His favourite of these – he had managed to watch it three times between Christmas and Easter – was *She Wore a Yellow Ribbon*, towards the end of which, Wayne, as Captain Nathan Brittles, is riding off into unwanted retirement when the army send a galloper after him, begging him to come back and take up a position as chief of scouts with the rank of lieutenant colonel.

Only in the movies.

For Resnick himself, resuscitation had been less glamorous.

A phone call that had come as he sat, sandwich lunch over, listening to Monk at the piano, prising every strange angle possible from the melody of 'Smoke Gets in Your Eyes'. An abrupt young HR person from force headquarters informing him that, following his previous enquiry, there was now a vacancy, part-time, for a civilian investigator based at divisional HQ – Central Police Station on North Church Street in Nottingham city centre. Which was where, for some months now – three days a week at first, then four, now practically full-time – Resnick had been busy interviewing witnesses, taking statements, processing paperwork, all the while forcing himself to remember he no longer had any real status, no authority, no powers of arrest.

From time to time, an officer pursuing an investigation would stop by and filch some fact or other from his memory, go so far as to ask his advice. For the rest, he kept his head down, got on with the task, however menial, in hand. Whatever kept the stairlifts at bay.

Currently, he was providing the underpinning to an incident in the city centre, a late-night fracas in which a twenty-two-year-old student had been seriously injured. Coming across a loud and potentially violent argument between a local man and his girlfriend, the student, asking the girl if she needed assistance, had attempted to intervene. Whereupon the pair of them had turned on him, and, joined by their mates, clubbed the student to the ground and given him a good kicking, with the result that he was currently in Queen's Medical Centre in a coma. So far, two men and one woman had been charged with inflicting grievous bodily harm, charges that could escalate if circumstances changed.

That day, Resnick was due to re-interview some of the dozen or so witnesses who had come forward, each with a slightly different view of what had happened, a different opinion as to who had been responsible.

Biting down into his second piece of toast, he looked at the clock. Another five minutes, ten at most, and he should be on his way. Unless the weather was truly dreadful, his habit now was to walk from where he lived into the city centre, the twenty or so brisk minutes down the Woodborough Road enough to get the circulation going, perk up the old heart, keep his limbs in good working order.

'Exercise, Charlie, that's what you need,' a divisional commander had insisted, buttonholing Resnick at his retirement do, a Pints and Pies night in the Masson Suite at Notts County's ground on Meadow Lane. 'Mind and body . . .' Poking a finger against his chest. 'Body and bloody mind.'

Five years younger than Resnick, the poor bastard had dropped dead a short month later, a cerebral aneurysm cutting off the blood to his brain.

The clock now showing 8.07, Resnick paused in buffing his shoes to turn up the volume on the radio. Newly appointed, the local police commissioner was answering questions about the effects of a further twenty per cent cut in the force's budget.

'Isn't this going to leave the people of the county without adequate protection?' the interviewer asked. 'Make them more vulnerable? Lead to an increase in burglary and other crimes?'

'Not if I have my way,' huffed the commissioner.

'Which is?'

'Making more positive use of existing personnel, the resources at our disposal. Hoiking some of the time-servers out from behind their desks and putting them back on the front line.'

Good luck with that, Resnick thought.

Checking he had everything he needed – wallet, spare change, keys – he remembered he'd left his reading glasses upstairs beside the bed, a biography of Duke Ellington he'd been making his way through, a few pages each night before falling asleep.

Glasses recovered, he made sure the back door was locked and switched off the kitchen light; the radio he left on, deterrent against burglars, company for the cat. Stepping outside, he closed the front door firmly behind him and turned the key. Pulled his coat collar up against the wind. Rain forecast later, spreading from the west.

'Bit late this morning, Charlie, not like you.' Andy Dawson, the DS in charge of the investigation, was waiting just inside the main entrance, manila folder in hand. Resnick had stopped off at the coffee stall in the Victoria Centre Market for a double espresso and to hell with the consequences.

'New witness,' Dawson said, 'just come forward.'

'Took their time.'

'Holiday booked in Florida. More important than some poor sod on life support. Be here around ten.'

He passed the folder into Resnick's hand. An old-school copper who'd joined the force not so long after Resnick, he didn't trust anything unless it was committed to paper. Preferably in triplicate.

'By the way, Charlie, Bledwell Vale – didn't you used to have a pal up that way? Lad of his in the force for a spell?'

'Used to is right. Why d'you ask?'

'Knocking the whole place down, thought maybe you'd heard. Not before time, either. Any road, seems they found a body. Back o' one of the houses. Poor bastard been down there a good while, they reckon, whoever it were.' He shrugged. 'Thought you might be interested, that's all. Post-mortem's set for tomorrow afternoon.'

Resnick nodded and pushed open the interview-room door. Dust and stale air. He opened the window out on to the street and sounds of traffic travelling too fast along Shakespeare Street towards the Mansfield Road.

Poor bastard been down there a good while, they reckon, whoever it were.

Too many dying, Resnick thought. Too many dead. There was a good chance he might know who this particular poor bastard might be.

3

All too aware that his short-term memory was going – he was quite capable of making the short journey to Tesco Metro and, by the time he'd arrived, forgetting what he had set out for thirty minutes earlier – as yet, Resnick's long-term memory still thrived. Without hesitation, he could call to mind the names and faces of every officer who'd worked with him at Canning Circus and after; every senior officer – good and bad – he'd served under from the morning he pulled on his first uniform until the moment he retired. He could reel off the cream of the Notts County side promoted to the top division under Neil Warnock in '91 – Steve Cherry, Charlie Palmer, Alan Paris, Craig and Chris Short, Don O'Riordan, Paul Harding, Phil Turner, Dave Regis, Mark Draper and Tommy Johnson – and, further back, the full personnel of the Duke Ellington

Orchestra he'd travelled across country to see and hear at the Free Trade Hall in Manchester in November 1969 – the same year, a raw recruit, he first started pounding the beat. And he could remember the name of the woman who'd gone missing at the heart of the Miners' Strike, 1984: Jenny Hardwick.

He recalled seeing her on two occasions, the first relatively early on in the strike, a community meeting at the local Miners' Welfare he'd attended in some vain hope of de-escalating an increasingly acrimonious and violent situation.

Tensions between striking miners and the police, between the families of men in villages like Bledwell Vale who continued, despite intimidation, to turn up to work and those who jeered and taunted them every step of the way, were stretched to breaking point and sometimes beyond. When Resnick attempted to speak at the meeting, he was shouted down, despite angry appeals from Peter Waites that he should be heard.

Waites had introduced him to Jenny afterwards, along with several others. It was Jenny who'd stood out. Dark haired, medium height, her features sharp rather than pretty – bright, quite intense, blue-grey eyes – she'd not been shy of giving Resnick a piece of her mind.

The second time was an open-air meeting in Blidworth, late enough in the year for her breath to be visible on the air when she spoke. Earlier there'd been talk of hardship and want; cutting their losses and accepting, maybe, whatever deal the Coal Board was currently offering. But when Jenny Hardwick spoke she had little truck with conciliation: aiming her words at the wives and mothers present, telling them in no uncertain terms it was their duty as women to persuade any of their menfolk still working to down tools and join the strike.

Buoyed up by cheers of encouragement, she was just hitting her stride when one of the working miners, the dust from a day's shift still etched into his face, had lurched towards the platform, yelling at her to shut her bloody trap and get back home where she belonged.

'This is where I belong,' Jenny Hardwick had responded. 'And this is where I'll stay till this strike is over and the miners have won!'

Amongst jeers, head down, her heckler had limped away, leaving Jenny to relish the applause.

Resnick never set eyes on her again; scarcely heard tell of her until almost the year's end, when rumours came through from one of his undercover officers that she had disappeared. Done a runner, some reckoned, and perhaps no great surprise; she and her husband on opposite sides in the dispute and hardly speaking – at least that was what folk said. Eventually, when, after too long an interval, she was officially reported missing, an inquiry was launched, local, low-key.

There were other things more urgent, more pressing. Nothing was found. No sign.

Fucked off and good riddance, her husband is supposed to have said in the local pub. But he'd been well into his cups by then, not to be taken too seriously.

The kids, three of them, all under eleven, had stayed with their dad for a while, then gone to live with their nan on the North Sea coast near Mablethorpe: ice creams when they behaved, donkeys on the beach, fresh air; on a good day you could even glimpse the sea itself.

A few scattered sightings, none verified, aside, there was no clear indication of where Jenny might have gone, where she might be.

Until now? Resnick wondered. Until now?

He would keep his own counsel, keep shtum: wait and see.

The work at the autopsy was painstaking and slow: no matter. After all those years beneath the ground, no need to hurry now at all. From the size and shape of the hips and pelvic girdle, they assessed the gender; from the thigh bone, the height; from the shape and size of the skull, the ethnicity; from the incomplete fusing of the collarbone and the absence of any spikes around the edges of the vertebrae, they assessed the age.

According to the forensic pathologist's report, the skeleton was that of a female Caucasian between the ages of twenty-four and twenty-eight, approximately 1.65 metres or five feet, five inches tall: it had been beneath the ground in the region of twenty-five to thirty years.

There were signs of two separate fractures of the radius, the lower arm, the first of which had most likely taken place in childhood. Also, and more tellingly, there was evidence of considerable damage to the back of the skull, the pathologist confirming this to have occurred when the woman was still alive, rather than post-mortem, live bone breaking in a different way from dry.

A blunt-force injury, the pathologist concluded, most likely the result of being struck by a heavy object at least once, if not several times, and, in all probability, the cause of death.

Even so, supposition and circumstantial evidence aside, no clear identification was yet possible. Forensic examination of the teeth showed evidence of root canal treatment and a porcelain crown, but Jenny's dental records were hard to come by. Of the three dental surgeries in the immediate and surrounding area, one had closed down fifteen years before, the building now privately occupied, with no indication of whether any records had been placed in storage or destroyed; one had moved across the county to the other side of

Retford, their records, since the awkward process of transferral, only complete as far back as 1998; the third surgery was still operational, though now part of a wider consortium that welcomed private patients and promised, in a glossy brochure, teeth whitening, invisible braces and porcelain veneers, all the things that modern cosmetic enhancements can do to provide a perfect smile.

'Oh, no,' the receptionist said when asked. 'Thirty years ago? No, I shouldn't think so. All our records are computerised.' Anything that much older than herself, her expression suggested, was difficult to imagine.

One of the partners, Chinese, an impeccable accent, public school and then the University of Buckingham, was more accommodating. Everything relating to the previous practice had been boxed up and was in storage in the basement. Of course, there could be no guarantees . . .

After several hours of searching they found a faded file, smelling of mildew and damp to the touch: a set of dental records barely legible, amongst them an X-ray showing several fillings and some root canal treatment on the first molar in the right half of the lower dental arch.

A match.

The name and address at the top of the file in neat but badly faded ink: Jennifer Elizabeth Hardwick, 7 Station Row, Bledwell Vale, Notts.

Jennifer Hardwick.

Jenny.

Lost and then found.

It gave Resnick not one shred of pleasure to learn that his educated guess as to the identity of the body had been correct. Far rather Jenny Hardwick had followed the bright lights as some had suggested, fetched up in another town, another city – another country, even – with a new identity, new family perhaps, a new life.

Hauling his mind back to the task in hand, he double-checked the list of witnesses against the statements already processed; made a note of those he thought might usefully be seen again. The couple who'd been holidaying in Florida had provided what at first had seemed like positive identification, a brace of photographs taken from across the street on their mobile phone showing one of the accused kicking the student in the head as he lay against the kerb; the range and focus, however, were such that any competent barrister appearing for the defence would challenge them successfully in court. Meanwhile, the family were discussing with medical staff at the hospital the prospect of their son's life-support system being switched off.

Where Jenny Hardwick was concerned, the coroner would have been informed and arrangements made for an inquest to be opened and then adjourned while an inquiry would be set up to investigate the circumstances of her death; that responsibility, Resnick imagined, passing either to the cold case unit based out near Hucknall, or the now regionalised Serious Organised Crime Unit, comprising officers from four counties – Notts, Leicestershire, Derby and Northants – its local headquarters a brisk walk away through Forest Fields and down into Hyson Green.

Either way, it was no concern of his.

4

Anxious not to wake him, Jenny started to squeeze slowly out from beneath the weight of her husband's arm. She was almost free when, with a grunt, he turned his face towards her, mouth open, the stink of beer stale on his breath. Lifting his arm quickly then, and sliding away to the edge of the bed, she pulled the T-shirt she wore as a nightgown briskly up over her head.

'Where you offta?' he asked blurrily.

'Nowhere. Go back to sleep.'

'Whatever time is it?'

'Five, somewhere round there. A quarter past.'

'Come on back, then. Come back to bed.'

'I can't. You sleep.'

Falling back with a grunt, he closed his eyes.

The boards were cold beneath her feet.

She pulled on jeans, sweaters, one over another, a pair of thick socks. She could hear footsteps passing by outside, muffled voices, the first of the men setting off for the pithead, the day's picket.

By the time she'd found her boots and pulled them on, her husband was beginning to snore. In the back room, all three kids were still fast off, the youngest, Brian, making small sucking sounds around his thumb; Mary, the girl, clinging to a ratty old bear by its one remaining ear. Colin lay on his back, mouth open, snoring lightly, a perfect version of his father in miniature.

Jenny went quickly down the stairs and out of the house.

Frost glistens on the tops of the cars parked further along the street. Her soft grey breath swirls on the air. Ahead of her a door opens and a man steps out, his face illuminated for a moment by the light from the hall – no one she knows. A dozen or more of the Yorkshire pickets have been billeted in the village for a week now, others in the villages around; some are camping out, it's said, in the fields close by. Since the police had begun blocking the roads and turning back vehicles heading south, the strategy had changed; stopping the movement of coke and coal, forcing the Notts pits to close, still a priority. Over fifty per cent of Nottinghamshire miners, closer to sixty, are as yet refusing to support the strike, continuing going into work. Despite any arguments Jenny has so far been able to muster, her husband still one of them.

There are more bodies now, falling into step around her, men mostly but a good scattering of women; faces amongst them she recognises, local, faces she knows from evenings in the pub, the Welfare, the gates of the school.

A woman with a scarf wound close around her head veers in her direction, touches her arm.

'Jenny, that you?'

'Either that or me ghost.'

'Not seen you out before.'

'No, well, thought maybe it was time.'

'Your Barry . . .?'

'Don't ask.'

It is the best part of a mile from the village, the road winding gradually uphill; forty or fifty of them by now, others joining, stragglers; a few in cars, but mostly on foot. Up ahead, the pithead lights show clearly, and beneath them, in silhouette, a line of uniformed police stretched across the entrance, shoulder to shoulder, waiting.

Voices around Jenny rise louder the closer they come and she can feel the anger growing around her. Men calling out, laughing some of them, joking, laughing but angry all the same. One or two more she recognises clearly now; Peter Waites from the strike committee raising both arms aloft, stepping out in front, leading.

'Maggie, Maggie, Maggie! Out, Out, Out!'

'Maggie, Maggie, Maggie! Out, Out, Out!'

They are almost up to the police line now and she can read the expressions in the officers' faces: wary, some of them, the younger ones, afraid almost – she hadn't realised they'd be so young, still wet behind the ears – others cocky, chock full of themselves, eager for it all to kick off; but most of them blank, staring out over the heads of whoever is confronting them as if they aren't there.

A shout goes up from the back, followed swiftly by another: the first of the buses carrying the men reporting for work is coming. As if at a signal, the line of police begins to move forward, pushing the crowd back, and for the first time Jenny realises just how many there are, how many reinforcements waiting behind.

'Hang on!' a woman standing close beside her says. 'Hang on to my arm!'

The front line of police divides, forcing them back to either side, making a passageway for the buses to pass through. People around her are pushing back, thrusting her forward, an elbow sharp in her side, and from somewhere the first stone.

To a great cheer, a policeman's helmet goes flying.

'Scab! Scab! Scab!'

'Out! Out! Out!'

As the first bus draws near, fists pummelling against the windows and the shouting rising to a crescendo, spittle running down the glass, the faces of the men inside remain immobile, staring forward, her husband's not one of them, not one she can see.

'Judas! Fucking Judas!'

Three busloads altogether and nothing they can do to stop them.

'Bastards! Blackleg fucking bastards!'

As soon as they pass through, the gates are closed behind them: the tension seeping slowly away, like water through muslin. A last stone, thrown in the direction of the retreating phalanx of policemen, falls nowhere near. All the energy draining from her body, Jenny turns aside. What have they achieved? They've achieved nothing.

She knows there is neither use nor ornament to that way of thinking.

'Maggie, Maggie, Maggie . . .'

Back home, her children will be waking.

5

Catherine Njoroge was Kenyan by birth, her family having migrated to England when she was eleven, uprooted by the violent disturbances that followed the re-election of Daniel arap Moi to the presidency. After excelling at school, where she'd acquired the most English of accents – now given some character after time spent living in the East Midlands – she had gained a 2.1 in politics and history at the University of Nottingham, missing a first by 0.3 of a percentage point. Uncertain what to do next, which path to follow, Catherine had wavered for several months before joining the graduate recruitment programme of the Nottinghamshire Police. Her parents had been less than happy.

Her mother was a doctor, her father a lawyer, and they had hoped their daughter would be looking for job opportunities in the professions. The civil service, perhaps, or politics itself. Diplomacy. There was even the possibility of following her father into the law. Something worthy of her talents and reflecting the family's place in the community. Worthy in a wider sense, also. Her father, especially, had always drilled into her an awareness of her responsibility towards others, those less fortunate, less privileged than herself.

'It's your fault, Daddy,' she had said, smiling through his disapproval. 'You shouldn't have brought me up with such a strong sense of duty.'

Now here she was, at thirty-three, a detective inspector in CID, promoted to that rank eighteen months previously. Just recently she'd been transferred to the East Midlands Serious Organised Crime Unit, physically no more than three-quarters of a mile from where she'd previously been stationed, but a move away from officers with whom she'd got used to working to a more disparate group drawn from four counties, a different environment, a new chain of command.

Her immediate superior was a Leicestershire man, Martin Picard, a detective chief inspector no more than two years older than Catherine herself and sincerely dedicated to his own advancement. In command of the unit, and the subject of Picard's not infrequent sniping, was Andrew Hastings, a detective superintendent with a total of some twenty years' experience, fifteen of those in Nottingham.

Running a relatively high-powered, prestigious unit was both a testimony to the regard in which Hastings was generally held, and a tribute to the years he'd spent in careful service. Never the most dashing of senior officers, nor the most publicity conscious, Hastings was viewed, above all, as well organised and reliable, if, to all intents and purposes, a little dull. Exactly what was needed to steer what some still saw as an experiment, foisted on all four forces by the need to economise as much as by the sharing of expertise.

Two days after the identification of Jenny Hardwick's body, Hastings summoned Martin Picard to his office.

'Major inquiry, this, Martin, media interest by the shedload already – lass's body being found way it was, down there thirty year near as damn it. Just up your street, I'd've thought.'

'Why us?' Picard asked, cautious. 'More the cold case unit, surely?'

'Maybe. But with things kicking off around the strike again the way they are – all this talk about the IPCC taking another look at how it were policed – them upstairs are getting their bollocks in a right shemozzle. Handled by us, makes it look like we're taking it more serious. Less likely to drop bloody ball.'

Picard could appreciate that, the cold case unit, in his eyes, a bunch of superannuated has-beens who switched on *New Tricks* each week, thinking it was the biography of their own sad little lives.

Even so, he wasn't convinced, and it showed.

'What's up?' Hastings asked. 'Thought you'd be snapping my hand off for a go at this.'

Picard shook his head. 'All the same with you, I'd like to give it a bit of thought.'

'Think on, then. Just don't take too bloody long.'

The way Picard saw it, if the Independent Police Complaints Commission did get the go-ahead to follow up their investigation into the Hillsborough disaster with a detailed look at the Miners' Strike – Battle of Orgreave and all – things could start getting decidedly dicey. Especially if, as was rumoured, they were given new powers to compel any or all police officers and staff involved to testify under oath.

What would come crawling out of the paperwork then, he could only imagine. Not a lot that was blameless and shiny, he thought. Go looking for dirt and dirt's likely what you'll find. So no matter he'd been barely going to school when the strike had started, if the police came out of things badly, chances were, carrying out an investigation in the same area, he'd end up well and truly tarred with the same brush.

Anyone other than Hastings, he might have thought he was being dangled over the shit on purpose, but Hastings, he was sure, didn't have a Machiavellian bone in his body.

Or did he?

Maybe he was a lot cleverer than he looked.

No, Picard thought, I'll pass. Pass the job on to somebody else.

Catherine Njoroge was at her desk, scanning the reports thus far in on the death of a seventy-two-year-old man who'd been found wandering close to his home with what turned out to be severe injuries to head and body. Three days later, he'd died in hospital. His sons, twins, both of whom had lived with him in the same house, both unmarried, had been arrested and questioned: so far, 'No comment' was the most either of them had said.

'Patricide,' Picard said, glancing down over her shoulder. 'That the word?'

'We don't know that yet, do we, sir?'

'Course we bloody do. Anyway, let it go, no longer any concern of yours.'

She looked up at him, surprised.

'Open and shut, after the old man's cash, something of the sort. Let that team of yours handle it. Ex-team. You've got bigger fish to fry.'

Catherine closed the file.

'Jenny Hardwick,' Picard said. 'Know the name?'

Catherine nodded. 'That's the woman whose body was found, north of the county. Reported missing – what was it? Eighty-four? Nothing heard of her till now.'

'Right. Not till she turned up more or less in her own back yard.'

Catherine cleared her throat; the beginnings of a cold. 'Sorry, but I'm not clear what you're saying. I'm going to be assisting you in the investigation?'

Picard smiled. Picture perfect, Catherine thought.

'More than that,' he said.

She took a breath. 'Why me?'

'Here long enough to get your feet under the table, feel your way around. Time to get stuck into something more than a walk in the park, show us what you can do. Live up to all those references. Commendations.'

Catherine bridled, bit her tongue.

'Andrew and I discussed it, of course. Something for me, he thought, potentially high profile, media interest. Only natural, I suppose. But I thought, no, why not Catherine? Time to get that light out from under its bushel.'

The smile again, slimier than before.

You bastard, she thought. I can see what you're up to. You either think this is going to fizzle out in a mess of false trails and dead ends, or else it's going to blow up in someone's face. Mine. No way you'd be delegating this otherwise. Designed to fail.

'Thank you, sir,' she said. 'I appreciate it. The vote of confidence. Just as long as you're sure.'

'Of course.' He held out a hand. 'I'll be keeping a watching eye, naturally. You'll report directly to me. That way, if there's anything you're uncertain of . . .'

'Thank you, sir.'

'Look around, pick your own team. Someone experienced, not go amiss. Couple of young DCs, keen enough to do the legwork. B Division, you might look up there. Local knowledge, that kind of thing.'

'Yes, sir, thank you,' she said again, the words 'poisoned chalice' ringing in her ears.

It was a good hour before she thought of Charlie Resnick, languishing now, she believed, in the bowels of Central Station. Not so many minutes more before she gave him a call.

6

The first time Catherine Njoroge had encountered Resnick she had been newly made up to sergeant and assigned to the City Division's Robbery Squad, where he had recently been made senior officer in charge. Something of an unlikely move for him it had seemed, sideways at best, Resnick, for a good number of years, having run the CID team out of Canning Circus, dealing with major crimes up to and including murder. But the force, not for the first time, had been in the throes of reorganisation, and though, rumour had it, Resnick had been offered a further promotion that would have kept him in the thick of things, for whatever reasons, he had declined.

'Charlie?' one of his contemporaries had told Catherine when she'd enquired. 'Seen writing on bloody wall. Seen the future and it's bright young things like you with university degrees comin' out their backsides, not the likes of him an' me. Dinosaurs, that's what we are. Least that's what top brass think. Charlie's just takin' hisself out the firing line afore they stick him in front of it blindfold.'

'Charlie,' said another. 'Cosyin' up with that young woman out of Homicide, lucky sod. Someone to look after him in his old age.'

It hadn't worked out that way. On her way home late from a meeting in London, Lynn Kellogg had been shot and fatally wounded outside the house she and Resnick latterly had shared. Catherine had been attached to the team that had investigated her murder.

Whenever she had seen Resnick around that time, he had seemed like a husk, empty and dry, scoured out. Only more recently, on the few occasions they'd met, had the life seemed to have bled slowly back into him, the light behind his eyes fired with the occasional spark.

'Charlie,' she said when she called, 'you wouldn't have time for a coffee, I suppose?'

They sat, cradling takeout cups from the Pelham Street deli, on one of the benches overlooking the Old Market Square. The square remodelled like so much else now, redesigned. *A fluid and relaxing public area whose organic form echoes the classic formality* . . . To Resnick's eyes, they had stripped it of whatever had made it interesting – the flower beds, the fountains, the bandstand – and left a vast flat open space without character or distinction.

But the toddlers splashing their way in wellies across the shallow, flowing water terrace at one end of the square seemed happy enough, despite the cold. And the people, young and old, sharing the benches that spread out in either direction, were content, apparently, to sit there and eat their lunch, chat, or simply stare. Crotchety, that's what he was getting. Even Lynn had said that. Old before his time.

'You okay, Charlie?' Catherine asked.

'Fine, why?'

'You seemed lost in thought.'

There had been a brass band Resnick was remembering – years back now – youths mostly, a scattering of old heads to keep them in line. The conductor standing out front, occasionally taking up his cornet to solo. The odd march, a bit of light classical, songs from the shows. Two youngsters, the only ones not in uniform, a boy and a girl, had sat huddled together in the back row; the pair of them scanning the music, waiting their turn. At the crucial moment, instruments to their lips, the wind had whipped the girl's music from its stand, and she had sat there, numbed and silent, while the lad had scrabbled for it on the floor.

'Some Enchanted Evening.'

Resnick, soft bugger, had sat watching, tears in his eyes.

'It's nothing,' he said. 'Not important.'

'And the job? How's the new job?'

Resnick forced a wry smile.

'I was wondering if you might fancy something a little more challenging?'

He looked at her. 'Such as?'

'A woman's body found, long buried . . .'

'Bledwell Vale, you mean?'

'The inquiry, it's gone to our unit. I'm SIO.'

'Congratulations.'

'Picard handed it to me on a plate.'

'He'll have his reasons. Good ones, I don't doubt.'

Catherine's turn to smile. 'I'm going to need help, Charlie.'

'I'm not sure . . .'

'Real help. I think – I don't know why – but I think they might just be hanging me out to dry.'

'Who, Picard?'

'Picard, Hastings. Who knows? It's all politics, anyhow. All that stuff coming to light about the Miners' Strike. The IPCC.'

'Maybe what they want's a clean pair of hands.'

'And if it all goes tits up, I'm the one takes the blame.'

Resnick grinned. 'Tits up – Kenyan expression, is it?'

'Fuck off, Charlie.'

He laughed and drank the last of his coffee. There were trams criss-crossing at the foot of Beastmarket Hill. From just beyond the square, on Angel Row, he could hear the usual saxophone player doodling over a soundtrack of 'Winter Wonderland'.

Busk early for Christmas.

'Let's walk,' he said.

They made a strange couple for anyone with time to notice. Resnick tall, though with the beginnings of a stoop that threatened to take an inch from his height; bulky still inside that grubby raincoat, a man, one might think, who liked his food, a glass or two of ale. Who spent too much time behind a desk, sitting in a chair. Fifteen, twenty years before, he would have looked much the same.

Catherine Njoroge was tall also, not so far off Resnick's height, and she walked with a certain stateliness, accentuated by her long neck, the way she held her head. She wore a black trouser suit, trousers with a slight flare, boots with a low heel; her hair tied back with purple ribbon; a silver ring on her right hand aside, no accessories, no ornamentation; almond eyes.

'Who else,' Resnick asked, 'have you got on board?'

'Just you so far. Assuming you say yes.'

'God help us then.'

'Charlie, come on. Don't start doing yourself down.'

'You think they'll wear it? Picard and Hastings. Me tagging along.'

'I don't see why not. As far as they're concerned, you're going to be doing the same as you do here. Interviewing witnesses, taking statements. Just travelling a bit further to work, that's all.'

'And as far as you're concerned?'

They stopped short of the pavement edge.

'You were there, Charlie, weren't you, during the strike?'

'Running an intelligence gathering team, yes. Out of Mansfield. Half a dozen officers in the field, undercover, mix and mingle – letting on they were local, journalists maybe – not that that made them all that welcome. All the while keeping their eyes open, eyes and ears. Cameras, sometimes, those little video recorders. Anything useful – a new face giving instructions, passing on orders, plans for a new picket – we'd pass it along to headquarters. From there, on down to London. Special Branch, the NRC.'

She looked at him questioningly, not recognising the acronym.

'National Reporting Centre, Room 1309, New Scotland Yard.'

'You were running spies, then, Charlie. Espionage.'

'I was doing what I could to stop this part of the country breaking apart. Civil bloody war. At least, that's what I thought.'

'And now?'

He didn't answer. They turned left along Cheapside,

a trajectory that would take them back past the Victoria Centre and so to the Central Police Station.

'There was a lot of what we did that wasn't right,' Resnick said eventually. 'A lot we should've done differently or not done at all. And a great deal of what happened locally, well, that was taken out of our hands. Not much of an excuse, maybe, but there it is. But I met some good people, no mistaking that. Either side of the picket line. Helped bury one of them not so long back.'

'You feel all right about going back up there, though? After all this time?'

'Find out, won't we? Soon as you get the go-ahead.'

7

Cat and mouse, that's what it was, except a sight more serious. Striking miners from Yorkshire, the more militant areas like Barnsley and Doncaster in particular, targeting the more northern of the Notts pits at first – Harworth, Welbeck, Bledwell Vale – and then, when they'd succeeded, temporarily at least, in persuading large numbers not to cross the picket line, moving their attentions further south – Warsop, Thoresby, Shirebrook; Sherwood, Rufford, Ollerton. All of this activity in the purview of Resnick's intelligence team, the information they passed on meshing with that from other sources, including, increasingly, the tapping of telephones, before being rationalised into the Nottinghamshire force report that would be sent each morning to the NRC in London.

From that, and reports from other areas concerned,

a briefing would be prepared for senior officers from ACPO, the Association of Chief Police Officers, and F4, the division of the Home Office with a responsibility for public order.

Areas were designated as Peaceful, Hostile or Violent.

Up-to-date charts were kept monitoring police involvement, serious injuries and arrests.

There were twenty-five pits in Notts in all and not many more than two thousand or so police to ensure that those miners who wanted to report for work – still a majority, if a wavering one – could do so and the pits remain open.

It was never enough.

By early March, not long after the strike had started, some three thousand officers from nearby forces had been brought in to help, many of these in small, specially trained Police Support Units – PSUs – with experience of using riot shields and batons. Army camps were commandeered to provide temporary housing.

Realising that issuing instructions by telephone was no longer safe, union officials organising the picketing began sending out orders in sealed envelopes, often switching their targets at the last moment. Even then, there were ways and means of obtaining information; one of Resnick's team had a grubby arrangement with a driver who would pass on details as to where the pickets were heading in exchange for a few back-handed fivers.

Another of his men was adept at infiltrating groups of striking miners in this pub or that, joining in with the general bad-mouthing of the bastard police and picking up bits and pieces of useful gossip in the process.

Diane Conway, a detective constable recently attached to the team, was a dab hand at merging with various sets of miners' wives at the pithead, one time standing alongside those loudly cheering their men as they went into work under police escort, at another swearing and spitting and generally fulminating against the scabs who were no better than vermin.

Never entirely happy with what he was responsible for, the means he was using, Resnick kept telling himself the rule of law had to be upheld – and reminding himself of a conversation he'd had with a fellow Notts County supporter on the terraces at Meadow Lane, a miner from one of the local collieries who was continuing to turn up for work.

'Not a Notts strike this, Charlie, not national, either. Local, that's what it is. Yorkshire. Scargill calls a national ballot and the majority votes to come out, I'll come out along with the rest. But until that time, I believe it's my right to work and your job to make good and sure no one stops me. And I'll tell you one thing more – if they'd come down from Yorkshire and the like and been prepared to argue, make their case, things'd gone a lot better for 'em than now. But come chargin' in like they've done, mob-handed, yelling scab, scab, scab in us faces, puts your back up, no mistake. And some I know, as might've joined strike, set 'emselves dead against it instead. Now let's hope to Christ Pedro Richards' legs don't give out and he keeps tabs on that bloody winger of theirs, 'cause if not we're bloody buggered.'

It was mid-March, mid-week, towards the end of an otherwise unexceptional day, when Resnick received a telephone call from one of his team, out at Ollerton.

'Kicking off here, boss, and no mistake. Couple of hundred pickets, if not more.'

'I thought they'd been stopped,' Resnick said. 'Clumber Park.'

'They're here now. Walked it across the fields some of them. Come round back roads, whatever. Out to stop night shift clocking on. Determined. 'Bout same number of our lads facing 'em down. All sorts getting thrown. Bricks, bottles, bits of wood. Nastier by the minute. As many of the locals cheering shift on as there are shouting scab, maybe more.'

Resnick could hear the swell of noise, of ragged shout and counter-shout rising up behind.

'Keep your head down,' Resnick said, but the connection had gone.

He didn't hear anything more till several hours later. One of the Yorkshire pickets, a young man named David Jones, had collapsed under a hail of missiles when he and some others had been trying to chase off a group of local youths who were attacking their cars in the main street where they'd left them parked.

First reports suggested he'd been struck in the chest by a brick and, after receiving first aid at the spot, been taken to the casualty department at Mansfield Hospital.

'Get yourself down there,' Resnick said to Diane Conway. 'Get down there now.'

She rang back at 12.25; Jones had been pronounced dead at eleven minutes past the hour.

Never a religious man, Resnick found himself, nevertheless, offering up a quick prayer that things wouldn't escalate further; a prayer for a young man he'd never known, never met.

When the news spread, striking miners sped to Ollerton by all means possible; more police reinforcements were called. At three in the morning, the president of the Yorkshire NUM, Jack Taylor, arrived with Arthur Scargill, and Scargill climbed on to the roof of a car and called for calm. When he asked for two minutes' silence out of respect, Resnick was relieved to be told later, those police present were quick to take off their helmets and bow their heads.

At the post-mortem, the Home Office pathologist

said that Jones had died as the result of a 'crashing impact of considerable force'; a 'massive but short and sharp' compression to the chest, most likely as the result of coming into contact with an immovable object.

The chief constable ordered an immediate independent inquiry, to be led by a senior officer from another force.

That inquiry was still ongoing.

A vein at the side of Resnick's temple would start to pulse each time the phone rang unexpectedly, for fear it was announcing another needless death.

8

'Leaving us then, Charlie. So rumour goes.'

Andy Dawson was half-leaning against the door jamb, one size twelve boot angled behind the other, sucking on one of the extra-strong mints he'd become addicted to since finally stopping smoking six months before.

Resnick nodded. 'Helping out, that's all. Background. Interview or two. Not much more'n I do here.'

'Murder investigation, Charlie. Not any old murder, either. Woman's body as lay buried near thirty year. Headlines in *Post*, front page. Least it was till Forest sacked their manager again.'

'Like I say, just helping out. What's the news from Queen's?'

Dawson shook his head. 'Lad's still in a coma.

No decision, either way. Happen by the time you're back . . .'

'Aye.'

'Well, you've left everything in order, I don't doubt. Any wrinkles, I'll know where to find you. Oh, and while I remember, Martin Picard, he wants to see you, later this morning. His office. Radford.' Dawson winked. 'Be sure to give him my best.'

It was common knowledge the two men could stand neither sight nor sound of each other, Picard slithering up the greasy pole towards the top, while Dawson hovered uneasily near the bottom, waiting by the sign marked Exit.

Resnick walked up Waverley Street, skirting the edge of the Forest, site of the annual Goose Fair, and crossed Gregory Boulevard close by the New Art Exchange building – all smart grey brick and glass – on to Radford Road. Purpose-built, sixties, from the outside the police station looked to have scarcely changed since, a young copper on the beat, Resnick had spent six months there, finding his feet. Community policing, that's what they called it now, and, more often than not, it was done from the inside of a car. In those days it meant walking the streets alone, eyes open and helmet cinched tight, wary of what the next corner might bring.

'Respect,' old-timers like Andy Dawson would say, 'that's what we had in those days. Not like now.'

Resnick remembered it differently. Blues parties where the sweet smell of ganja knocked you backwards the minute you walked in; hard-faced young men from the Hyson Green flats who'd stare you in the eye, then piss on your shoes and tell you it was raining.

Now it was kids of little more than twelve or thirteen, as like to stick up a finger, telling you to fuck off to your face, before pedalling away at the same insouciant speed, whether to deliver a wrap or two of crack cocaine or pick up a carton of milk for their nan from the local corner shop.

So much had changed; so much remained the same.

Martin Picard met him just inside the main entrance: grey suit with a faint blue stripe, pale blue shirt, neatly knotted tie. Hair recently cut, brushed and combed: the very model of a perfect detective chief inspector on the rise.

Not for the first time, Resnick felt shabby and old.

'Coffee, Charlie, that's your thing, as I remember.'

There was a cafetière on his desk, china mugs. Little else. Laptop, mobile phone. A single file, grey, open; pages highlighted here and there in green or red, annotations in the margins.

'Your involvement, Bledwell Vale, Charlie, a good thing. Approved it straight off. Local knowledge, that's important. But what I'm hoping, a little more than that, keep an eye on things, make sure they stay on track.' He eased back a little in his chair. 'Bright, of course, your Ms Njoroge, no denying that. Keen to get ahead. Be a shame to see her overreach herself here, make more of this than it is. You know what I mean.'

He smiled conspiratorially, drawing Resnick in.

'I'm not sure,' Resnick said, 'that I do.'

'Come on, Charlie, what is it after all? Woman dead and buried more years than she lived, whoever's responsible either dead themselves or eking out their days in some nursing home with Alzheimer's or dementia or both. In the grand scheme of things, no big deal, no big deal at all. Weren't for the force here running scared there's going to be an inquiry into how they policed that bloody strike, it'd never come to us at all. Something for the deadbeats in the cold case unit to be falling over their pension books about.'

He leaned forward, elbow on the desk. 'The investigation, thorough of course, but low-key. No call to go stirring up more than you need. Nothing surfaces after a good week or so, no strong leads, be prepared to step away. Case remains open, after all this time, no skin off anyone's nose. Not be the first.'

He gestured towards Resnick's mug. 'Top-up?'

Resnick shook his head. Despite looking promisingly full and dark, the coffee tasted thin, empty of flavour, flattering to deceive.

Catherine Njoroge had spent the morning tidying up the last of the work in which she'd been involved, making sure the necessary files and information were in the right hands. Neither twin had so far felt the need to speak, though she doubted they could maintain that silence for very much longer. And then, if they were guilty, singly or together, which, on balance, she assumed they were, all her team – her ex-team – would have to do would be to sit back while one accused the other. That was the way it usually worked.

Though the investigation into Jenny Hardwick's death would continue to be based there at Radford Road, with the necessary computer access to HOLMES 2 – the Home Office Large Major Enquiry System, which was used for the coordination and exchange of information in all major crimes – there would be a forward post in Worksop, in the north of the county, divisional headquarters for the region. After a trail of emails and several abortive calls, Catherine had finally got to speak to the divisional commander and received his blessing: an incident room would be set up in the police station on Potter Street, with a detective sergeant to act as action allocator and receiver, and the assistance of at least one member of the civilian support team as necessary.

When she'd asked if other personnel would be available, the commander had been less forthcoming: experienced officers were at a premium, staffing levels across the county, as he was sure she appreciated, were in decline.

Catherine continued to plead her case and finally it was agreed. Two young DCs, Alex Sandford and Robert Cresswell, not much more than novices, would be attached to the inquiry, along with Detective Sergeant John McBride. The commander would look forward to meeting her when she arrived.

Hearing Resnick was in the building, Catherine intercepted him and suggested lunch. 'The café at the New Art Exchange, Charlie – you ever been?'

Resnick had not.

'You'll like it. It's tasty and cheap.' She smiled. 'No obligation to look at the art if you don't want.'

They sat at a table midway between the counter and the glass frontage, Resnick looking out past Catherine's shoulder towards the passing traffic on the Boulevard, the constant footfall. When first he'd got to know this part of the city, the only faces not white would most likely have been Caribbean; a dozen or so years later they would have been from the Indian Subcontinent – Pakistan, India, Bangladesh – or, like Catherine, from some part of Africa. Now they were likely to have come from countries Resnick, for all his Polish background, would have had difficulty placing on a map. Moldova. The Republic of Macedonia. Turkmenistan.

Georgia, until relatively recently, had mainly existed for him as a province of Ray Charles' mind.

The older you got, he'd read somewhere, the more threatening multiculturalism was meant to become.

But, while he didn't exactly embrace it, the odd incursion from the Eastern European mafia aside, he didn't think he found it at all threatening. Over the years, it had certainly done wonders for the food.

His curry with chicken and sweet potato, aubergine and okra was seriously spicy, seriously good, and Catherine was making short work of her dahl soup with fresh coriander and roti bread.

Not only tasty, as she had said, but inexpensive too. As far as Resnick was concerned, a perfect combination. Which reminded him, he had to remember to check with Catherine about travelling expenses.

'How was your session with Picard?' she asked.

Resnick paused, a piece of sweet potato midway to his mouth. 'He wants me to be a steady hand. A moderating influence, something of the sort.'

'Moderating what, exactly?'

'Oh, I don't know . . .' Grinning. 'Your natural exuberance, perhaps. Any temptation you might have to go chasing headlines, reaching for the stars.'

'You are joking?'

'Not exactly.'

She shook her head. 'Picard, Hastings, all the top brass, the last thing they want is anything stirring up the past. Far happier, all of them, for it all to have stayed dead and buried. Jenny Hardwick, everything.'

She broke off another piece of bread and scooped up the last of the lentil mixture from her plate. 'Picard, he wouldn't have been involved in any way, policing the strike?'

Resnick shook his head. 'Too young. Hastings, it's a possibility, but, no, even then I doubt it.'

'But you were.'

'As you know.'

'Sending out your spies.'

'Your words, not mine.'

'Reporting back to HQ. What was it? The NRC.'

'That was the job.'

'And now?'

'Am I going to be reporting back to Picard? Hastings? Telling tales out of school?'

'Are you?'

'You really need to ask?'

'No, no, Charlie, I'm sorry. It's just . . . after what you said, your meeting, I just needed to be sure.'

He held her gaze. 'If you're not, I'll walk away now. No offence taken.'

'Charlie, no.' For a moment, she covered his hand with her own. 'Forget it. It's fine. Pre-investigation nerves. Besides, I was the one who asked for you, remember?'

Before leaving, they walked round the main gallery: an exhibition of work by women photographers from the Middle East.

What caught Resnick's attention, and what he kept going back to, was a portrait of an elderly Iranian woman, holding a framed photograph of her son, killed in the Iran–Iraq war. The young man's portrait held out towards the viewer, and behind it, the woman, his mother, stony-faced and staring directly at the camera: proud, accusing, a memory she won't let go.

9

The police station was brick built, solid, municipal, set back from the road; small rectangular windows arranged neatly across the first two floors in rows, more generous use of glass beneath the sloping roof above. A short flight of steps led up to the entrance on the left, white railings, a canopy, reinforced glass doors; the Nottinghamshire Police crest fastened to the wall.

They'd driven up to Worksop in a pool car, Catherine at the wheel. Traffic on the motorway no better nor worse than usual, the day's early promise of sunshine and brighter skies faded now into a neutral grey. Alongside, Resnick was content to sit and stare, this road a road much travelled, back in the days of the miners' strike and after.

There'd been a woman, a woman he'd met during

the strike, a social worker, and Resnick, not that long divorced, had, after some hesitation, entered into a brief and heady affair; an affair that had left him shaken when, almost as suddenly as it had started, it was over. Even now, all these years later, the sudden unexpected thought of her made him shudder as if touching, inadvertently, a length of bare electric wire, as if touching skin.

'You all right, Charlie?'

'Yes, why?'

'You jumped, that's all. Like someone had stepped on your grave.'

'Perhaps they had.'

North of the Chesterfield turn-off, they swung eastward on the A619, finally joining the Mansfield Road before entering the town.

The room they'd been allocated was on the top floor, at the rear. A view out over the car park towards the Priory and a swathe of open space beyond. Desks, chairs, a single computer, two telephones, printer, dust in the corners, last year's calendar on the wall. Behind the door a flip chart rested uneasily on an easel, the A1 sheets curling upwards at the bottom edge. Catherine gave a little shake of the head. What she'd hoped for was an interactive whiteboard, that at least; what she'd got was this.

John McBride had picked them up at reception; the

divisional commander was at force headquarters at Sherwood Lodge and hoped to catch up with them later.

McBride was in his late forties, hair prematurely grey; an accident when the vehicle in which he'd been in pursuit of – a stolen four-by-four – had overturned, leaving him with a slight but permanent limp and an air of grievance against the world in general. More so if Partick Thistle had lost the previous weekend.

'The lads, I'll let them know you're here.' Though it was years since he'd spent any length of time back home, the faint barb of a Maryhill accent still underscored his voice.

When they were gathered, McBride planted himself in the most comfortable of the chairs, the one with the leather arms, padded, the window at his back. Daring Catherine to order him to move, give over the seat to her. His place, his manor; he was at home here, uppity bastards from the south of the county were not.

The young DCs, the lads, they didn't count.

Alex Sandford was whippet-thin, a steady runner of half-marathons, training, when time allowed, for the real thing; his ambition the London Marathon in three years' time, two if he were lucky, New York the year after that.

The older of the pair by just a couple of years, Rob Cresswell had joined the force after trying university and dropping out after a single term. He'd had spells following that on a supermarket management team and in automotive sales, but now he seemed settled, as if something had finally clicked. Maybe.

Introductions over, Catherine instructed Sandford to move the flip chart to a more central position, armed herself with marker pens and folded back the cover sheet to expose the plain page beneath.

'Let's make use of this since it's here.'

In strong red she wrote the initials JH at the centre.

'Jenny Hardwick, disappeared just before Christmas, nineteen eighty-four, aged twenty-seven, her body only recently discovered, at the rear of number twenty Church Street, just a few streets away from where she lived on Station Row. Cause of death, blow or blows to the head. Close to thirty years, a long time. Before, I dare say, either you, Robert, or you, Alex, were born.'

'And you, boss?' asked McBride with something approaching a grin.

'A toddler,' Catherine said. 'Not that it's any great concern of yours.' But she said it with a smile.

McBride neglected to smile back.

'So,' Catherine said, 'the first thing we need to do, build up as clear a picture as we can. People who knew her at the time, family, friends. She had a husband, Barry, now in his sixties, still alive, living in Chesterfield. Three children, Colin, Mary and Brian, all in their thirties. The first two we have an address for, for some reason not Brian.' As she was speaking, she was adding names to the page with blue pen.

'All right, Alex,' she said, wanting to draw the attention away from McBride and get the others involved. 'After that, the immediate family, where are we going to look? Who might we want to speak to next?'

Sandford reddened slightly, fumbled his first words. 'Neighbours, ma'am, any close friends.'

'And?'

'And the place, ma'am, the, um, location. Where the body was found.'

'Exactly. Good. Who was living there at the time. And more. The rear extension beneath which the body was buried, when was that added – around the same time or later? Whoever did the work, are they still in business? Perhaps who was living there did it themselves?'

She added two large question marks in purple.

'The lassie was officially reported missing,' McBride said. 'Surely there'd have been an investigation at the time? Official?'

Catherine nodded. 'I was just coming to that. Charlie, you were stationed up here then, close anyway. You know more about this than me.'

McBride muttered something beneath his breath that went unheard.

Briefly as he could, Resnick explained how his unit had functioned during the strike.

'So, naturally,' he said, 'we heard bits and pieces about what might have happened. Gossip. Rumour. She was having an affair. He knocked her around. None of it, far as I could tell, based on much more than people's fancy. Nothing that, without some corroboration, we should believe.

'And John's right, there was a missing person's inquiry. Low-key. Local. In the light of what we know now, not near searching enough. But what you have to realise, amongst all that was going on – the levels of disruption, the extent of police involvement, the sheer numbers involved – one person gone missing, like as not done a runner – it was small beer at the time.'

'This inquiry,' McBride chipped in. 'You said just local . . .'

'Keith, Keith Haines. Village bobby, more or less. Lived right there, Bledwell Vale. Least till the strike took hold. Had his windows smashed in so many times, moved a safer distance away. Here, into town. After that, you can imagine, going round asking questions, with all that was going on, not easy. But the impression I had at the time – second- or third-hand at best, mind – he did what he could.'

Catherine looked across at McBride. 'There'd have been a report. We could track it down.'

A faint smile on McBride's face. 'We could try.'

'And Haines himself? Charlie, do you know?'

Resnick shook his head. 'Mid-thirties then, my best

guess. So sixties now. He could still be somewhere around, but . . .'

'Could be six feet under,' McBride said.

'We need to know,' Catherine said, adding his name with a flourish. 'We need to know a great deal.'

McBride started to say something more, but thought better of it. Coughed and cleared his throat instead. Let the woman run the show as she sees fit: for now, at least.

'Sergeant,' Catherine said, 'something you'd like to add?'

'No, boss.' Close to a growl.

'Right, then. Charlie and I are off to Chesterfield, talk to Barry Hardwick. You can organise things here? Get Alex and Rob on the move?'

'Manage that, boss. Do my best.'

Rather than drive straight off, Catherine motioned for Resnick to wait, took a packet of cigarettes from her bag and lit up, resting one elbow on the car roof. Resnick hadn't even known that she smoked.

'What is it with him, Charlie?'

'McBride?'

'Too young to be outranking him, is that the problem? Or just too black?'

'Maybe that's just the way he is.'

'With everyone?'

Resnick shrugged.

'Am I just being oversensitive? Is that it?'

'I wouldn't say that.'

'Don't say a lot, do you, Charlie? Not if it means taking sides.'

'I didn't know there was a side to take.'

'No, you're right.' Stepping away from the car, she took one last drag at her cigarette before grinding it out with the underside of her shoe. 'If there's a problem it's mine. Mine to deal with. One way or another. Now let's go and look at that famous spire.'

Glancing back up at the building she glimpsed McBride at one of the upper windows, looking down.

It was just starting, lightly, to rain.

10

The spire could be seen from a distance, through a mist of rain and low, faltering cloud. Seated atop the parish church of St Mary and All Saints, in the very centre of the town, it twisted as much as forty-five degrees from the perpendicular, leaning almost ten feet away from its true centre.

'Story goes,' Resnick said, 'this blacksmith from Bolsover was shoeing one of the Devil's cloven hoofs, drove the nail in so hard made the old Devil jump right over the church, grabbed hold of the tower to stop himself falling and twisted it into shape you see now.'

'Is that the best you can do?' Catherine said, laughing.

'All right, how's this? Young girl getting married in the church, comes down the aisle dressed in white from head to toe. Turns out it's not for show, lass'd never as much as been kissed. News gets round, there's a genuine virgin about to get wed, right there in Chesterfield parish church, the old tower's so surprised, twists itself into a state to take a look.'

'Charlie, come on.'

Resnick was laughing, too. 'Stayed like that ever since, waiting for the next virgin to come tripping up the aisle. Till that happens it'll not twist back.'

Catherine shook her head. 'And the real reason? I suppose there is one?'

'Some say it was down to using unseasoned timber, some due to an overloading of lead tile. Truth is, no bugger knows for certain.'

'Not so much different to us, then.'

They were about to pass close to the church itself and turn into Saltergate. The rain, never strong, had more or less stopped. Hardwick's address was a few streets along, past The Barley Mow.

'Any luck,' Resnick said, 'we're about to put that right.'

After knocking on the front door several times, ringing the bell, they tried the neighbours to either side. An elderly woman appeared at one of the upstairs windows, lined face, tightly permed hair.

'Is it Barry you're looking for? Because he usually gets back round about now.'

'From the pub?'

'Bless you, no. The allotment. Rain or shine, up there every day.'

Five or so minutes later he came into sight, astride an old boneshaker of a bike: donkey jacket – likely the same one that he'd worn all those years ago at the pit – cloth cap, boots, trousers tied fast at the bottom with string. Still a big man, he looked fit for his sixty-odd years, agile enough as he swung his leg over the saddle and lifted the bike up over the kerb, leaning it against the wall.

'Police, is it? Been expecting you for yonks now, ever since inquest were opened an' adjourned. Just some spotty-faced kid round taking a statement, stuff about Jenny, family history, what did I know about her disappearance. Knew bugger all, didn't I? Same as you lot, I reckon.'

Turning back to the bike, he began unfastening his fork and spade from where they'd been tied to the crossbar.

'Leave anything worth pinching up there an' it'll get nicked.' He looked for a minute from one to the other. 'Don't suppose you're here to tell me when her body'll be released for a proper burial either?'

'No,' Catherine said. 'I'm afraid not.'

He held her gaze a moment longer. 'Aye, well, you'd best come inside.'

The house was small but tidy: boots lined up in the narrow hallway; pots on the draining board in the kitchen, waiting to be put away; not what you might expect, Resnick thought, from a bloke living on his own. If that's what he was.

'I'll set kettle on,' Hardwick said, shedding his outdoor clothes. 'Best take a seat through there.'

On the narrow mantelpiece above the hearth was a framed photograph of Hardwick, his arms around three children, two boys and a girl, all happy, all smiling. Alongside, a young woman on the day of her wedding, the same girl grown, Hardwick beside her in his hired suit, beaming with pride.

No pictures of Jenny to be seen.

The tea, when it arrived, was dark and strong, as if he'd waved the milk at it, Resnick thought, and no more. Sugar decanted from the packet into an empty cup for the occasion. Hardwick helped himself to two spoonfuls and, after a momentary hesitation, added a third.

'Thirsty work. This time of year, specially. Not that I'm complaining, mind.'

'Keeps you busy,' Resnick suggested.

Hardwick nodded. 'Time hangs else.'

'You live here on your own?' Catherine asked.

'Lad comes over a time or two. Colin, the oldest. Stays the night, sometimes the weekend. Side of that, just me, aye.'

'You keep it nice.'

A smile rounded Hardwick's face. 'Margaret, lives

a couple of doors down, she lends a hand. I see she's not run short on fruit and veg, she pops in here couple of times a week, bit of dusting, hoovering, irons the odd shirt. Suits us both down t'ground.'

He supped some tea.

'Colin,' Catherine said. 'We have an address in Derby.'

'That'd be right.'

'And Mary, she's in Ireland?'

'Aye, settled long since.' He glanced round towards the photograph above the fireplace. 'Met this chap when he was over working, went back with him. Galway. Just outside. Kids now, two of them. Boy and a girl.'

'And Brian?'

Hardwick shifted in his chair. 'Brian – you have to understand – he was always a bit wild, school an' that. Sent home from lessons, getting into fights. I think . . .' He looked down. 'When Jenny . . . disappeared . . . I think he took it hardest. Him being the youngest, maybe, I don't know.'

He wiped a large hand down across his face.

'Truth is, I've not seen Brian since the wedding, our Mary's wedding. We had this bust-up – he'd been drinking, goin' on and on about Jenny, about his mum, how it was all my fault, her leaving.'

'That's what he thought had happened?' Catherine said. 'Jenny, that she'd left, left home?'

'Course, that's what we all did. When dust had settled, like. When we had time to think.'

'And he blamed you? Brian?'

'Yes.'

'Why would he do that?'

Hardwick looked at her. 'He just did.'

'But why? I assume he must have had a reason?'

'I told you, he'd been drinking. Most of the day and into the evening. Of course he'd blame me – what else was he going to do?'

'It was irrational, then?' Catherine said. 'The drink talking. No truth in what he was saying? That somehow you'd driven her away?'

Hardwick took his time in answering.

'Back then, back then I thought, I reckon we all thought, most of us any road, it were the man ruled the roost, went out, earned the bread, brought it back home. Every man to his castle, right? Then, with the strike, when that happened, somehow going out to work, going down that bloody pit day after bloody day, shift after shift, it weren't enough. And there were women, just lasses some of 'em, up on their hind legs telling us we was wrong. What we were doing, what my old man'd done before me, working every God-given hour to put food on't table, it were wrong.'

He looked quickly up and then away.

'I couldn't fathom it out. Not as if we were on

strike, not Notts, not the pit where I worked, but all of a sudden I was being called blackleg, scab, all sorts. And Jenny, the way she'd look at me . . .'

He faltered into silence.

'You argued about it?' Catherine suggested. 'Fought?'

'Nay. Not really. At first, maybe, but then not over-much. If we'd argued it through more it'd maybe not've been so bad. Instead she just looked at me like I were some insect'd crawled up out of ground. Despised me in the end, that's what she did.' A slight shake of the head. 'Not as I could've blamed her, not altogether. Not a lot of love between us by then, truth be told. And I dare say I was drinking more than I should.'

'She didn't approve?'

'I liked a pint or two, always had, but no more than the next man. But after she turned agin me it got worse.' Another shake of the head, firmer this time. 'I'd've not stuck wi' me either, if I'd had the choice.'

'So you thought that was why she'd left you? Because of the drinking, and the difference of opinion about the strike?'

'What else?'

Catherine gave Resnick a quick glance.

'There were rumours,' Resnick said, 'she might've been seeing someone else.'

'Jenny?'

'What I heard.'

'People say all sorts. Don't have to mean they're true.'

'It wasn't something you'd argued about, then?'

'Strike, that's all she were interested in. Soup kitchens. Makin' speeches. Shakin' her fist on picket line. More'n me. More'n her kids. I doubt she'd have time to give some other feller a second look.'

It was quiet. Somewhere, another room, the ticking of a clock.

'So at the time,' Catherine asked, 'where did you think she'd gone? When you thought that's what had happened.'

'Didn't know, did I? At first, I thought maybe gone off to see her folks, p'r'aps, over in Ingoldmells, both alive then. But, tell the truth, after a while I didn't much care. Last couple of months afore she left, like I say, almost never saw hide nor hair of her any road. An' when I did she were al'ays, you know, givin' me that look. Sounds wrong now, in light of what happened, but when it were clear she'd gone I were almost glad.'

He looked away.

Catherine gave it a moment. 'Is that why,' she said, 'it was the best part of a week before you reported her missing?'

'Maybe. Maybe so, aye. That and Christmas coming straight after.'

'Once it had been officially reported,' Resnick

said, 'Keith Haines, he was the one carried out the investigation.'

'If you can call it that.'

'How d'you mean?'

'Oh, he went round asking questions, right enough. Took – what d'you call 'em? – witness statements. Like that copper who were round here. Me, o'course. Jenny's sister, Jill, she were living in the village then. Few other folk, all local. Of course, nothing come of it. Not his fault, mind, Keith, one bloke on his own, whole bloody country up in arms – what was he supposed to do?' He shook his head. 'Nobody gave a bugger, not then, not really, that's the truth of it.' He laughed, no humour in it. 'An' here you are, thirty years too bloody late.'

Catherine opened her notebook, turned a page.

'We'll be talking to Haines, of course, hoping it might still be possible to look at his report. Statements that were taken at the time. But I wonder if there's anything you might like to add to your previous statement about the circumstances in which you realised your wife had gone missing? Just to give us, perhaps, a little more to go on.'

'Circumstances?' Hardwick nodded, wiped his hand across his face. 'Much like I said before. Friday, that's what it was. Friday, the twenty-first. I got back off shift half-expecting Jenny to be home, half not. She was off doin' stuff so much, round that time especially, you could never tell. Any road, instead of Jenny it were Mrs Jepson from a few doors along. Not one of the women as usually kept an eye on the kids at all, but Jenny had asked her as a favour, on account something had cropped up and she weren't sure when she'd be back. Might be late, might not. Nothing to say what she were up to, nothing like that.

'So, anyway, I get home and there's all three kids tuckin' into beans on toast. Mrs Jepson, she goes off and I think, well, she'll turn up, Jenny, sooner or later. Not overfussed, you know? But then when it gets towards end of evening, like, and there's still no sign, I leave Colin in charge and try the Welfare, but no one's seen hide nor hair of her, not since the day before. Peter Waites, he's off at some meeting somewhere so that's no help.

'I went round to her sister's, just in case, like, she had any idea where she were, but she'd not seen owt of her. Gave up after that, went back home, put the kids to bed. Thought whatever's happened, she'll be here tomorrow, either that or get in touch, that at least.'

He shrugged.

'There was nothing. Not a thing. Four days off bloody Christmas and, far as I could tell, she'd buggered off without a word. Not so much as a phone call, some kind of explanation, not even a bloody note. Kids all in a state. Brian, crying his eyes out. Course, I know

now. I know now why there was no sodding note, but then . . .'

The breath juddered out of him and his voice was quieter when he resumed.

'She'd wrapped presents for the kids already. Left them the same place as always, top drawer of the wardrobe, away from prying eyes. When I saw them, I thought then, she knew, you know, knew that she was going.'

For a moment, he closed his eyes.

Catherine slowly rose to her feet and Resnick followed suit.

'Thanks for your time, Mr Hardwick. And for talking to us about something that's clearly still painful. I dare say we'll be needing to speak with you again, but for now I think that's everything. And with regard to releasing your wife's body, it's for the coroner to issue a burial certificate after due consultation. The most usual thing, in cases like this, I'm afraid, is for the body to be kept so that the defence in any trial can order a post-mortem of their own. But in this instance the coroner might make an exception due to the passage of time. I'll try to make sure you're informed as soon as a decision's been taken.'

Just a few minutes later, they were back out on the street, the air damp and not without a chill.

'What do you think?' Catherine asked, once they were in the car.

'Hardwick? I don't know. He seemed genuinely upset. Whatever he thought of her, it must have been tough. And now, having to go through it all again . . . At the end there, he was close to tears.'

'You don't think that was an act? The tears?'

Resnick registered surprise. 'Did you?'

'It crossed my mind.'

Resnick grinned. 'So cynical, so early in your career.'

Catherine poked out a tongue, switched on the engine and slipped the car into gear.

11

'Drink, Duck?'

Jenny turns her head to where he's standing close behind her: donkey jacket, jeans, Doc Martens; smiling. She's seen him at the pithead these last few mornings, along with his mates. Not much more than lads, the lot of them. Laughing and fooling and lobbing stones. Down from Yorkshire and cocky with it.

'No, thanks.' In the fug and hubbub of the Welfare, she has to lean towards him to make herself heard.

'You sure?'

'Sure.'

The smile becomes a grin. 'Some other time, maybe.'

'Maybe.'

Edna Johnson takes hold of her arm and begins to steer her away. 'Cradle-snatching, are we?'

'That'll be the day.'

The older woman laughs. 'Peter Waites, he'd like a word.'

Waites is in the back room he uses as an office, empty canisters stacked against the wall behind him, crates of dandelion and burdock, boxes of salt-and-vinegar crisps. The trestle table he's using as a desk is busy with scraps of paper, empty cups and glasses, brown envelopes, ashtrays, a map of the local area marked roughly with coloured ink.

'Jenny. Come on in.'

'I'll leave you to it.' Edna closes the door behind her, shutting out most of the din.

'Knock them papers off the chair,' Waites says. 'Have yourself a seat.'

The sound of Duran Duran can still be heard, distorted, through the wall. Waites holds out a packet of Silk Cut towards her and, when she shakes her head, lights one for himself from the butt of the last.

'Edna says you've been lending a hand in kitchen, that and one or two other things.'

'I do what I can. Kids, you know, and . . .'

'Don't think it's not been noticed, that's all. Appreciated. Work cut out, Edna has, not just here, but being delegate to Central Group like she is. Meetings to attend. All takes time.'

Jenny crosses one leg over the other, tugs at the

hem of her skirt. She feels as if she's being interviewed for a job without knowing quite what it is.

'You mentioned the kids,' Waites says. 'Three, is it?'

'The kids are fine.'

'Your Barry, though . . .'

'Barry does as he sees fit. Always has.'

'No luck getting him to change his mind, then? Assuming you've tried.'

'He gets on with his life, I get on with mine.'

Waites taps ash into an empty pint glass.

Jenny recrosses her legs, trying to ignore the bra strap cutting into her shoulder.

'More you get involved,' Waites is saying, 'there'll be those'll not take to it kindly. Dirty looks thrown your way an' likely a sight more. And with Barry still working . . .' He smiles a lopsided smile. 'Not exactly stand by your man, is it?'

'What I'm doing, I thought you'd be pleased. Now it sounds as if you think I'm doin' wrong thing.'

'No, lass. Want to be sure you know what you're lettin' yourself in for, that's all.'

'Well, I am.'

'That's good. 'Cause the more you get involved, going out on women's-only picket, maybe, making the odd speech or two . . .'

'Do what?'

'There's lots of women angry, lass, you know that as well as me. Not afraid to shout and make themselves heard. On picket line, at least. But Edna, at the moment, she's one of few with bottle enough to stand up in front of a crowd and make 'em listen.'

'But I can't . . .'

'She reckons you can. With a bit of practice. No call to rush into it. Just when you feel you're ready.'

'Well, I don't know . . . I mean, will they listen to me, specially, like you say, with Barry still working?'

'Barry still scabbing, they'll likely listen all the more. But have a chat with Edna. Talk it through. If you do decide, she'll give you all help you'll need.'

'Right.' Jenny nods; gets to her feet.

'It's in a good cause,' Waites says, 'you know that.'

'I know.'

'Tell the lad behind the bar your next drink's on me.'

Jenny smiles. 'Another time. I'd best be getting back.'

If Edna reckons she can do it, she's thinking, then maybe she can. It was listening to Edna, after all, that got her started, made her want to get involved herself. And if now, in turn, she could do that for someone else . . .

As she nears the door, she sees the young Yorkshire miner watching her from across the room. Dark eyes, red hair. What had her mother told her about men with red hair?

12

Five-thirty, rush hour on the motorway, close to the end of another day. Resnick flicked his headlights at the Range Rover waiting impatiently to overtake and, in response to the driver's briskly signalled thanks, raised an acknowledging hand. Gentleman of the road.

No agreement yet on expenses, he was keeping a note of mileage, petrol. Nottingham–Worksop, Worksop–Nottingham. No car, either, not his own. The VW had been Lynn's and, after letting it idle in the garage for months on end, he'd taken it along to auction; too many memories, too many trips out to Bradgate Country Park or Rutland Water.

The car he was driving, a Vauxhall of uncertain vintage, he'd borrowed from a friend of a friend who owned a garage out past Mapperley Top.

'Won't let you down, Charlie. Mark my words.'

So far, so good. But making that journey day after day for what? Two weeks? Three? Only thirty-five miles, but in traffic it could take more than an hour, an hour twenty. As a prospect it was unappealing. Take a room up in Worksop, that's what he should do. B & B. Get that down on the expenses sheet, supposing there was one. Somewhere for the duration.

There was a Travelodge on the bypass west of the town, at the junction of the A57 and the A60. It was McBride who'd suggested it, shown him a picture on the computer. Set back off the road but not far enough, to Resnick it resembled an old people's home twinned with a hostel for young offenders. Due to the closure of the Little Chef restaurant that had formerly shared the location, the website had informed him, takeaway breakfast boxes were available for him to enjoy in his room or on the move.

Perhaps he'd stick with the drive.

Besides, who'd feed the cat?

'A favour, Charlie,' Catherine Njoroge had said as he was leaving. 'The family living in the house where Jenny's body was found – Peterson – Howard and . . . Howard and Megan. Cresswell and Sandford have spoken to them already, taken a statement, but it wouldn't hurt if you were to drop in, have another word. Giltbrook, that's where they live now, more or less on your way home I'd've thought. Unless you've got something else on, of course.'

Something on? That'd be the *News at Ten* and before that, with any luck, the next round of *MasterChef*.

As the sign for junction 26 approached, he lifted his foot off the accelerator and switched to the inside lane.

The house was a small semi-detached a short distance beyond the centre of what had once been a village; now, thanks to the vast retail park the flat-pack giant shared with the likes of Boots, Pets at Home and, of course, Starbucks and Nando's, it was better known as a suburb of Ikea. He and Lynn had driven out there one idle Sunday afternoon, Lynn thinking she might find something in Laura Ashley to wear to a colleague's wedding and finding what, to Resnick, for whom shopping for anything other than food or CDs was anathema, came close to a contemporary definition of hell. Several hours he was prepared to spend browsing through the racks in Eric Rose's Music Inn in the West End Arcade, but as much as fifteen minutes waiting while Lynn worked her way along a line of dresses was enough to bring him out in hives.

Howard Peterson answered the door a little self-consciously in an apron. Resnick introduced himself and showed identification.

'Best come in . . .' Stepping back to let Resnick enter. 'Megan's on lates this week, my turn in kitchen. No complaints, mind. Just as well one of us is, eh? In work, I mean.'

'Don't let me get in your way,' Resnick offered.

'Peelin' spuds, that's all. Come on through.'

They sat at a round table, Formica topped.

'I've not long mashed tea . . .'

Resnick shook his head, declined. Why was it, whenever a police officer called round, invariably the first thing the person they were calling on did was hustle off to the kitchen to make tea?

Learned behaviour, he supposed, all those cop shows on TV.

Peterson topped up his own cup, dribbled in milk. 'I told those two lads of yours all I could. Not sure if there's a great deal I can add.'

He made a face. 'Livin' there all that time an' not knowin'. Not knowin' what were there. Fair makes your skin crawl.'

'From what I understand,' Resnick said, 'the extension, it had been in place for some time?'

'Winter of eighty-one, two. Put it up myself with a mate . . .'

'A mate?'

'Geoff. Geoff Cartwright. We worked together down pit. Megan'd been on to me to do somethin' about the wind as used to get into back of house. Whipped round there somethin' dreadful. Regular whirlwind. She thought maybe somewhere for the washing machine an' all that gubbins – utility room, that what they call 'em? That'd keep it out.

And me, I'd always hankered after a bit of a conservatory. Plants, seedlings, you know. Ended up neither one thing nor the other. More trouble than it was worth, truth be known. An' that's without . . . well, without, you know . . .'

He shook his head.

'My fault, most like, mine and Geoff's. Foundations never set right. Slabs we'd used on surface, paving slabs you know, always uneven, kiddies trippin' over 'em, hurtin 'emselves. And then there was that performance with the drains. Went out there one morning afore work and the whole bloody lot was under half a foot of water. Not just water, neither.'

He paused to sup some tea.

'Coal Board sent somebody round eventually. Sorted drains, at least. Took their time, mind.'

'This was when?'

'November, would have been. November of eighty-four. Not a time I'll bloody forget, not ever.'

'And after the drains had been fixed, it was you and Geoff set the place to rights?'

'When we could. Still working, both of us, down the pit. No reason not. Been a ballot, we'd've been out, no two ways about that. But as it was . . . mortgage to pay, kiddies to clothe, Megan just with this bit of a job, mornings, pin money, nothin' more.'

He looked across at Resnick, as if wanting confirmation he'd done the right thing.

'At the end though, it was just Geoff more or less on his own. Plus whatever help he could get.'

'You'd had enough by then or what?'

'Away, weren't we? That Christmas. Strike, it were getting Megan down, affecting her health. Her folks, they had a caravan, North Wales. We went there. Time we got back, around New Year, everything was ship-shape out back. Bristol fashion. Geoff pleased as punch. Never have managed it all on his own, but, back then especially, no shortage of blokes grateful for a few days' graft, cash in hand. Did a good job, mind. Never give us a bit of trouble, not till the day we left.'

'And that was to come here?'

Peterson nodded. 'Not a lot of choice in the end. Joined the UDM, didn't I? Eighty-five. Oh, not just me, plenty of others. Union of Democratic Mineworkers. Thought to secure jobs, jobs for life. Load of bollocks that turned out to be. Government, Coal Board, used the UDM to screw the rest of the miners and then screwed us in turn.' A wry smile crossed his face. 'At least I got redundancy, more than most of those other poor bastards. Helped buy this.'

He glanced around. 'Can't say I've ever really got used to it, but staying where we were . . . long memories, some people. Resentments, buried deep. One minute folk'd be nodding at you in pub, asking after the missus, the kids, next they're lobbing a brick through front window, painting Scab in foot-high letters on your door.' He sighed. 'None of that here. Kingdom of bloody Ikea. Nor much else, either. Not that I should be complaining. Give Megan a job, right off. Part-time, mind, but work all the same. Kids off our hands long since, it's enough.'

He pushed back his chair. 'Leaves me time to go fishing. Peel spuds.'

'And Geoff?'

'Buggered off, didn't he? Canada.'

'Bit more extreme than Giltbrook.'

'That's for certain. Kept in touch at first, you know, sent the odd postcard or two. Christmas card one time.' He gave a shake of the head. 'Must be getting on twenty years since I heard. Could be anywhere by now. Could be dead.'

'And those cards . . .?'

'Long gone. I wrote back just the once, I remember. Always meant to keep in touch, but you know how it is.'

'A long time ago, I know, but you wouldn't still have the address? Written down somewhere? An old address book?'

'Unlikely. But if you think it's important, I could look around. See what I can find.'

'Thanks. I'd be obliged.'

'I will do then.'

He walked Resnick to the door. 'No disrespect, but

you must be near retiring age yourself, I'd've thought. Runnin' a pub somewhere, corner shop, that's what they do, coppers, isn't it, when they pack it in? Used to, any road.'

Resnick shook his hand. Turned the car around and headed back towards the motorway. *No shortage of blokes grateful for a few days' graft.* What chance was there of finding out who had worked with Geoff Cartwright at the rear of 20 Church Street, all that time ago? Cartwright and whoever else had been giving him a hand. Laying paving stones: safe, neat, secure. Those days between Christmas and New Year, 1984. Nights when the site would, in all probability, have been left unguarded and open.

So far they had no clear motive; if you disregarded the husband, which at the moment he was inclined to do, no clear suspect. As Catherine Njoroge had put it, they were no wiser about the reasons for Jenny Hardwick's murder than people were, centuries later, about the circumstances that lay behind Chesterfield's twisted tower.

13

He'd been thinking about her more than ever, these last few days. That was the way it seemed, though he could never be sure. Most times she was just there, somewhere close beneath the surface of his mind. His skin. As if, sometimes, he could reach out and touch . . .

It was the job, of course that's what it was. This job. Working with a woman, a major investigation; working with Catherine Njoroge, though it would be hard to find two women less alike than Catherine and Lynn. Save that they were good police officers both, good at their job.

He remembered the first murder case they had worked on together, Lynn and himself; Lynn new to the squad, keen, young. The body she'd almost stumbled over in the rear garden of an otherwise unexceptional inner-city house; a young woman wearing her wounds like ribbons in her hair. By the time Resnick had arrived, it had been covered from sight, a single high-heeled shoe close by, black, new.

Lynn had been inside, shaken, pale; when he stepped towards her, she had fainted into his arms, fingers of one hand caught fast against his mouth.

'There are those,' she said to him years later, 'who reckon I did it on purpose. Brazen hussy! Throwing myself at the boss's feet.'

'Think that, then they're fools.'

'Had to get you to notice me somehow, didn't I?'

'Likely've managed it of my own account.'

'Eventually.'

'Time enough.'

Something inside him locked tight. *Had we but world enough and time.* Where had that come from? Dredged up from school. Three years they'd lived together: twice those years now since she'd died.

He slowed at the roundabout, not wanting to continue home, back to the house they'd shared, but almost nowhere in the city was innocent of their lives, their time.

'What are you frightened of, Charlie?' she had asked him once.

The answer, of course, was everything. Scenes that played out in his head. Returning home one evening to find her standing in the hallway, suitcase packed and ready, keys in her hand. A note left on the mantelpiece, his name neatly written.

Dear Charlie . . .

A thousand scenes of leaving and never the one chosen.

From inside the house, the sound of a car backfiring.

But it had not been a car.

Not a car at all.

When he closed his eyes he could see her falling.

He had never seen her fall.

By the time he had reached the door and wrenched it open, Lynn's body lay crumpled on the path, legs buckled beneath her, arm outflung, her blood seeping, unstoppable, into the ground.

The first shot had struck her in the chest, close to the heart; the second had shredded part of her jaw, torn her face apart.

Resnick pulled slowly over towards the kerb, shut off the engine and, resting his head against the steering wheel, closed his eyes. Five, ten minutes before his breathing had steadied enough for him to resume his journey.

The cat was waiting for him on the low stone wall.

Inside, he shrugged off his coat, walked the house from room to room.

Made coffee and left it untouched.

Finally, in the living room, he burrowed through the shelves of albums and CDs, searching, not for something calming, consoling, nothing that might trigger a memory, happy or sad, but this: the Eric Dolphy/Booker Little Quintet *Live at the Five Spot*, New York, 16 July 1961. Track three. 'Aggression'. Sixteen minutes and forty seconds.

Resnick in the middle of the room, listening, slowly racking up the volume.

Louder, then louder.

Still listening.

By the time it reaches Dolphy's solo, the bass clarinet screaming, squawking, keening – the sound so fierce, so intense – he is no longer capable of thought, just feeling.

Fists clenched tight, absorbing the music's anger, he takes it for his own: this stuttering explosion of anger and pain.

Only when the music has stopped do the other sounds of the house slowly start to re-emerge: the central heating switching off and on, soft rattle of water in the pipes, the upstairs windows vibrating as a car goes past too fast; the cat brushing against his legs as it weaves in and out, impatient to be fed.

14

There'd been rumours for days. Weeks. The government had had enough. Time for a showdown. Stop the miners, the striking miners, in their tracks. Break the strike once and for all. Show them who was boss. Tales winding back on the grapevine from London of meetings between government officials, the Home Office and British Coal. Rumours of rumours plucked out of the air.

Less than thirty miles from where Resnick was stationed, the picketing of the coke works at Orgreave, just south of Sheffield, simmered on. Since the end of May, convoys of lorries, often with a police Range Rover at their head, and protected by police on the ground, had been passing into the works through lines of pickets, loading up, then carrying the coke away to the steelworks at Scunthorpe, some forty miles east.

Neither side was about to back down.

The numbers of pickets increased.

Tony Clement, the assistant chief constable in charge of operations in South Yorkshire, asked the NRC for more support.

What became increasingly obvious to Resnick and his team was that strike action around the pits in their immediate area had become less and less, as more and more pickets were diverted north to Orgreave: a strategy both the Notts and South Yorkshire police were happy to endorse. If there was going to be a showdown, that, Resnick thought, was where it would be.

At the end of May, mounted police at Orgreave had gone into action against the miners for the first time, a phalanx of eight horses charging into the midst of a large group of pickets which had a snatch squad of half a dozen officers surrounded. Predictably, reasonably, the pickets scattered and ran.

It was the precursor of what would happen, more spectacularly, more worryingly, later.

On Monday 18 June some ten thousand miners, their numbers augmented by men who had been bussed in from as far off as Scotland and South Wales, had gathered near the entrance to the coke works and in the fields to either side. Arranged against them were four thousand police officers on foot, all with batons, many with Perspex shields; twenty-four dog handlers and forty-two mounted police.

Watching the television news that evening, Resnick

was reminded of a scene from the film of *Henry V* they'd been shown when he was still at primary school: volley after volley of arrows soaring in a great arc through the sky, the sound of them like so many birds. Except here, instead of arrows, it was bottles, half-bricks, ball bearings, pieces of broken fence hurled like misshapen spears.

Horses charging headlong through a field of corn, their riders with reins held tight in one hand, a baton swinging from the other.

Men running as if for their lives.

Broken heads, blood-masked faces.

At the sight of a police officer standing over the crouched figure of a miner, striking him with his baton, again and again, Resnick had turned away, sickened, from the screen.

'No two ways about it, Charlie,' one of the Notts police who'd been present told Resnick later. 'There was some – both sides mind – got right carried away. Lost control. A wonder more weren't badly hurt than there was. Wonder nobody died.'

Surely that will end it, Resnick thought, said so to his team.

Surely now they'll get together round the table, come to terms.

Surely . . .

Months on, leaves turning towards autumn, winter not so far behind, there was still no sign.

15

So far, the search for Keith Haines' missing person's report had proved fruitless. Two boxes purporting to date back to a similar era had been found, waterlogged, in a basement storage space, their contents close to papier mâché, dandy for a project at the local junior school, but of neither use nor ornament to the investigation. Whether Haines' report was amongst them, they had no sure way to know.

Haines himself had proved easier to track down, living for some time now in fenland north of Cambridge, a two-hour drive from where they were based.

'Some kind of smallholding, that's what it sounds like,' McBride had said, favouring Catherine Njoroge with a jaundiced eye. 'Market garden, something of the sort. What with that and Hardwick's bloody allotment, case's turning into *Gardeners'* bloody *Question Time*.'

Sandford and Cresswell were busy locating as many of the Hardwicks' former neighbours in Bledwell Vale as possible, setting up interviews; contact had been made with members of the local miners' support group and a meeting arranged. The youngest of Barry and Jenny Hardwick's children, Brian, was still proving elusive, but the address of the oldest, Colin, had been confirmed and he was due to be interviewed shortly.

After consultation with Martin Picard and the CPS, the coroner had agreed there was no longer anything to be gained from Jenny Hardwick's skeletal remains and the Hardwick family had been told they could go ahead and set the funeral arrangements in place.

As for Geoff Cartwright, last heard of in Canada, the province of Saskatchewan – a vast area of prairie and forest, with most of its population living in the southern third, the remainder scattered far and wide – checks were still being made.

Needle, Resnick thought. Haystack.

Catherine had been distant but polite during the morning's briefing, tight-lipped ever since.

'You okay?' Resnick asked as they were leaving.

'Okay? Yes, why?'

'I don't know, I just thought . . . Maybe a bit under the weather.'

'I'm fine. Fine.'

He left it at that. Whatever was affecting her, if it was something to do with the investigation, sooner or later she would take him into her confidence, he felt sure. If it was something else, something private, then that's what it was, something else.

He leaned back in the passenger seat, happy to have Catherine drive, leaving him to his thoughts and the passing scenery, the land, beyond Peterborough, flattening out the closer they came.

At Downham Market they stopped for petrol, Catherine reparking the car at the far edge of the service station, stepping out on to the thin strip of grass for a cigarette.

According to the map, the road took them close by the path of the Little Ouse River, between Feltwell Anchor and Burnt Fen. All around was criss-crossed with drainage ditches, skimpy hedgerows that barely raised themselves above the ground, narrow lanes that seemed to lead nowhere, empty horizons, a paucity of trees.

'God, Charlie, look at it . . .'

Resnick nodded. He had known a police officer, a detective inspector, who had moved here, this region, with his family, looking for space, fresh air, room for the kids to grow; years later, he could still find himself turned around, completely lost, within a stone's throw of his home.

A quarter of a mile on, they realised they too had

missed their turning; backtracked to what had seemed no more than a broken gateway leading into a field.

A few hundred yards along, beyond the remains of what had once been some kind of dwelling, a barn perhaps, the path broadened out and led up to a flat-roofed bungalow, an area of cultivated land behind. Twin greenhouses, reflecting back the blue-grey pallor of the sky, the low watery sun.

'You know him, don't you, Charlie? Haines?'

'A little. Long time ago.'

'Get on?'

'After a fashion.'

Almost of necessity, he had met Keith Haines from time to time as the strike had progressed: local incidents that Haines, copper on the spot, had been called upon to deal with and whose reverberations had reached Resnick through one or other of his team and eventually brought the two men face to face. The seven-year-old child of a working miner who had spoken out strongly against the strike, and who had been pushed into a car on his way home from school, finally found twenty-four hours later, wandering, dazed and hungry, on the far side of the village. A fracas that had escalated beyond all control; a man, defending his property, left blind in one eye.

'Maybe you should do the talking? At first, anyway.'

'Better you, perhaps. Clean slate.'

As they got out of the car, a heron passed by low

overhead, the slow flap of its wings clear in the surrounding silence.

Then the opening of a door, the clicking of a gate.

Haines walked towards them, favouring his left side, hand raised in greeting, two dogs – black Labrador retrievers of differing ages – following close behind.

'Charlie, still in harness.'

'Not exactly.'

Explanations, introductions.

'Charlie for your bagman,' Haines said to Catherine, 'not go far wrong.'

They followed him inside, the dogs interested, pushing with their noses, busy with their tails.

The room was surprisingly large: stepping into it, the whole place seemed to expand. There were armchairs, wide, with well-stuffed arms, floral fabrics beginning to fade; tables, large and small, busy with seed catalogues, magazines. Half a dozen framed watercolours rose up, like a covey of ducks, along the far wall.

'The wife's,' Haines said, following Catherine's gaze. 'She's the artist round here. First prize five years running, local art show. Had to talk her into not entering in the end, give the others a decent chance.'

As if on cue, Haines' wife came through from the kitchen. About the same age as Haines himself, same decade, grey hair in a loose bun, wattle of freckled skin on her upper arms, she wore a flowery apron over an equally flowery house dress. If she sat in one of those chairs, Resnick thought, she'd disappear.

Something about her jolted his attention, made him look twice: a recognition he couldn't yet place.

'This is Jill,' Haines said proudly. 'Artist, horticulturalist, gardener – all that out there, fruit and veg enough to feed a small army through the year, all down to her. I just sit here and watch the racing on TV, once in a while get to swing a spade, dig the occasional trench, heft a sack or two of manure.'

'Keith, for heaven's sake! Don't pay him the least attention, please. A lot of nonsense. Showing off, that's all it is. He does as much as anyone else. Couple of lads from the village help out from time to time but most of the heavy work's down to him. Now, does everyone want tea? There's a few scones, fresh out the oven. Let me see to all that while you get settled, and then I'll be out of your way and you can talk.'

It was the eyes, Resnick realised, even as she turned away; small, bright, steely blue. She and her sister, they had the same eyes.

'Once the strike was finally over,' Haines was explaining to Catherine, 'first thing on my mind, I don't mind telling you, was to get away. Moving back into the village, Charlie'll tell you, eh, Charlie, so much ill feeling, not've been easy. Clearin' right away seemed best.' He smiled a lopsided smile. 'Never see another slag heap in my life, for all they're mostly grassed over, not be too soon. It was Jill's idea we ended up here, mind. She was the one with green fingers, like I say. Ambition. And with her sister gone, no sign of her coming back . . .'

'Jill and Jenny,' Catherine said, suddenly realising, surprised, 'they're sisters?'

'Yes, thought you'd have known.'

We should have done, Catherine thought; someone should.

'You must've known the family well, then?' she said, recovering.

'Not really. I mean, Jill and Jenny, they were close, of course. Sisters, after all. Somewhere like the Vale, fallin' over one another's feet all the time, or so you'd have thought. But Jill had a job down in Nottingham, not always full-time, but more or less, and there's Jenny with a husband and three kids – well, you can see, not living out one another's pockets, not at all.'

'You and Jill, you were together when her sister disappeared?'

'Not together together, if you get my meaning. Jill had been living with her mum and dad – hers and Jenny's – their house, really, I suppose. Then, spring of eighty-four, they got this little place just outside Mablethorpe. Ingoldmells. Her dad, he was having problems with his chest and they thought, you know, sea air . . . Wasn't till after that Jill and I started getting to know one another a bit better. So much flak going down I'd had to move out of village by then. Not always welcome back, either.'

He turned his head. Jill had just appeared in the doorway with cups of tea and warm scones on a tray, butter, home-made blackberry jam.

'Not easy, was it, love, eh? Seeing one another back then. Strike on. Not without a bit of sneaking round.'

'If you say so.' A faint blush on her cheeks, Jill passed around cups, plates. 'If there's anything else you need, just give me a shout.'

'Why don't you stay?' Catherine said. 'Join us.'

'Oh, you know how it is,' Jill said, straightening, backing away. 'A hundred and one things to do. Besides, police business . . .' She looked towards Resnick. 'He's been fair made up you were coming, you know. Chance to talk over old times.'

Resnick smiled appropriately. Jill turned and closed the door at her back.

'Jenny's husband,' Resnick said.

'Barry?'

'You got on?'

'Well enough, I suppose. Not that we spent a lot of time socialising. If at all.'

'Knowing the family, though,' Catherine said, 'even a little, when you were tasked with carrying out the inquiry into Jenny's disappearance, you didn't see that as putting you in an awkward position? A hindrance, maybe?'

Haines shook his head. 'I was there, wasn't I? Johnny on the spot. My job, had to be. As for knowing them, no, helped not hindered, I'd've thought.'

Carefully, Catherine split her scone and added butter, a lick of jam. 'Your report,' she said. 'So far we've had no luck tracking it down.'

'Landfill by now, most likely,' Haines said.

'Maybe you could give us the gist of what was in it? Any conclusions you might have come to.'

'You know all the basics, I suppose? Dates and the like?'

Catherine nodded to say that they did.

'Well, the gist, as you put it, the gist of it was – most likely scenario it seemed to me at the time – she'd done a runner. Gone off, had enough.'

'And you thought that because . . .?'

Haines shrugged. 'Attractive woman, still young, bright. Things between her and Barry – Jenny up on her hind legs, calling them as was working blacklegs and such while he was still pulling shifts – I doubt they had two civil words to say to each other. And that was without a few rumours flying round . . .'

'Rumours?'

'Word was she was having it off with one of the lads down from Yorkshire. Whether Barry got to hear of it, there's no way of knowing, bar his say-so, but it's difficult to believe he didn't.'

'He says not.'

'Case of not wanting to, maybe.'

'And was she?' Catherine asked. 'Having an affair? As far as you could tell?'

'Maybe, maybe not. There was this young bloke, set his cap for her, no denying that. Too many witnesses agreed. Ireland, that was his name, Danny Ireland. Doncaster lad. Or Rotherham, was it? Should know, but I can't be sure. Red hair, though, certain of that. Whether it all came to anything, anything more than wishfulness on his part, I couldn't say.'

'You heard his version of things?'

'Danny? Oh, yes. Fancied her rotten, that's what he said. Come right out with it. Barely get to sleep at nights for thinking 'bout getting into her knickers. Snatched a bit of a kiss once, but, that aside, reckoned she'd not give him the time of day.'

'And you believed him?' Catherine said.

'Lads like that, bit of a chancer, not like to admit they've not had their end away without it were true. More the other way round. Still, he could have had his reasons, I suppose.' He set down his cup. 'Ireland – you might have come across him, Charlie. Any bells?'

Resnick shook his head. 'Not right off.'

'No possibility she'd run off with him?' Catherine asked.

'Still around, wasn't he? Swore blind he never knew anything about where she'd gone or why and I believed him.'

'Foul play, Keith,' Resnick said. 'Before you decided she'd gone off of her own free will, you must have considered that?'

'Course. No note of any kind, nothing even for the kids, you'd have to. But then, what evidence was there? No body, no signs of violence, blood, clothing. Nothing.'

'And when you were thinking of that as a possibility, did you have anyone in mind?

Haines shook his head. 'Not really. Which was another problem. The husband, that was the obvious place to look, but again no evidence, and, arguments over the strike aside, little enough cause.'

'Those arguments,' Catherine said, 'they mightn't have got out of hand?'

'It's possible. But, like I say, bar a bit of shouting, there was little sign. Maybe raised his fist to her once or twice, but nothing more than that.'

'Nothing more? A woman's gone missing, no indication of where she might be, her husband's showed some signs of violence towards her and that didn't give you serious pause for thought . . .' Catherine could hear herself becoming strident and stopped. Reached for her tea instead.

'Start thinking murder on account of that,' Haines said, 'some scuttlebutt someone'd heard, bloke shows his wife a fist, maybe even gives her a slap, you'd have been arresting half the blokes in the village.'

'Except their wives hadn't suddenly disappeared.'

Haines leaned towards her. 'Look. I know what you're thinking. Domestic violence. Men lashing out in anger. Hear a lot 'bout that these days. But no. I don't think that's what happened. Didn't then and don't now. Even though the circumstances have changed.'

He sat back. From somewhere in the middle distance came the sound of a tractor, turning soil.

'Look, I was wrong. We know that now. Dead wrong, as it happens. Which is why that report of mine, if you could ever find it, isn't worth paper it's printed on.'

He looked from Catherine to Resnick and back again.

'Sticks in the craw, but there it is.'

Behind him, behind where he was sitting, his wife came out of the greenhouse, and with a quick glance back towards the house, walked away towards the garden end.

'I'm just going outside for a cigarette,' Catherine said, quick to her feet. 'I'll not be long. Then we can leave you in peace.'

'There's no need . . .' Haines began, halfway from his seat.

But Resnick was leaning towards him, catching his attention. 'One thing I've been meaning to ask, Keith, that poor bugger as lost an eye. Shotter, was it . . .?'

16

Jill Haines was standing by the far fence, head bent low, shoulders hunched. Catherine thought she could be crying, but when the older woman turned towards her, her cheeks were dry. There were tears there waiting, Catherine could see, stalled, banked up behind the eyes.

She took her cigarettes from her bag and offered one to Jill, who shook her head. Several fields away, a small flock of lapwings rose in wavering flight, turned through a slow, spiralling circle and tumbled back to earth.

Catherine held the first mouthful of smoke down in her lungs, then released it slowly into the air.

Jill leaned a little towards it, as if drawing it in.

'How long ago did you give up?' Catherine asked.

A smile. 'Five years ago now. Six.'

'Better for you.'

'Keith, he had a bit of a scare. All that stuff on the cigarette packets, the doctor told him, means what it says. Showed him an X-ray. Stopped there and then, not touched one since.'

'Expected you to do the same.'

'Only fair.' She reached for the cigarette in Catherine's hand. 'One puff, just the one.'

She took a long drag, handed it back. 'Why are you doing this?' she asked. 'After all this time? What good will it do now?'

'You want to know what happened to your sister, surely? Who was responsible?'

'I'm not sure I do.'

Catherine showed her surprise.

'Try to understand,' Jill said. 'As far as I was concerned, Jenny was living another life. With somebody else, on her own, I didn't know. After a while . . . I didn't really care. That sounds cruel, I know, unfeeling, but . . .'

She took another drag at Catherine's cigarette.

'All that was going on with the strike, for Jenny – getting up at meetings, making speeches, not just local, all over – it changed her. Made her dissatisfied. Someone I didn't really know.' She gave a wry smile. 'Knew even less. You could see it, see it in her face. What she had there, at the Vale, with Barry and the kids, it wasn't enough. Maybe it never was.'

'And you thought that's why she left? Because she was dissatisfied with the marriage?'

'Yes.'

'There was nothing more definite? More specific?'

'How d'you mean?'

'Barry, he wouldn't have given her cause?'

'Cause?'

'He wasn't ever violent, for instance?'

'Towards Jenny?' Jill shook her head. 'If he was, I never heard of it. Jenny never said.'

'And she would have done, d'you think?'

'It'd not've come easy, but if it were serious, yes, I think she might.'

'And if she'd been seeing somebody else? Would she have told you about that?'

'Confided in me, d'you mean?' Jill shook her head. 'Always had me down as a bit of a prude, Jenny did, right from when we were kids. So, no, if anything like that had been going on, I think she'd've kept it to herself.'

She looked off into the distance. A strand of hair had come loose and, reaching up, she pushed it back into place.

'You're still angry with her, aren't you?' Catherine said.

'Am I?'

'It must have been hard.'

'Hard for her kids. Barry tried looking after them

himself at first, but he couldn't really cope. How could he, working like he was? I did what I could, tried to lend a hand, but I was working, too. As for them, little Brian especially, they just didn't understand. Luckily, Mum and Dad were fixed up out at Ingoldmells by then.' She smiled. 'Grandkids, you know what some people are like. Glad to have them. Better off there, too. Sand. Sea air. Not be thinking each time someone's at the door it's their mum, come back home.'

'You weren't tempted to take the children yourself? You and Keith?'

A smile flickered across Jill's face. 'Children, his own or anyone else's, not big in Keith's plans. Never were.'

'And you didn't mind?'

Jill glanced back towards the house. 'Once Keith's mind's made up . . .' She let it rest, unsaid.

Keith Haines was already heading down the path, Resnick in his wake. 'Not leading my better half astray, I trust?'

Catherine stubbed out the cigarette with her shoe, scooped the butt up in her hand.

'There's a bin,' Haines said, 'by the gate on your way out.'

'Should we be needing to talk to you again . . .' Catherine began.

'Not a problem. Always here. Aren't we, duck?'

Jill smiled. They all shook hands.

'Good to see you again, Charlie,' Haines said.

'You, too.'

He walked them to their car. 'What really happened . . . I hope you can find out, put it all to rest.'

When Catherine looked back, Jill Haines was standing where they had left her, by the garden's edge, hands clasped behind her back.

They drove without speaking, field following field, barn after barn, the massed bulk of Ely Cathedral looming mistily to the west. After a mile or so, Catherine pulled over into a field entry, parked.

'I could have handled that better, Charlie.'

'You think so?'

'What did he tell us? Nothing we couldn't have guessed at, nothing that couldn't have been written on the back of a postcard.'

'Perhaps there wasn't much else to tell.'

'She was murdered, Charlie. Stuffed beneath tiles and concrete in someone's back yard.'

'And no one knew.'

'Someone knew. Someone killed her, for God's sake.' Sighing, she reached down to the floor for her bag, began to feel for her cigarettes. 'I'm sorry. I'm letting it get to me and I shouldn't. Not even sure why. And I do need a cigarette.'

They stood against the gate. Whatever was growing

in the field, neither of them could have named for certain.

The sun had slipped lower in the sky.

'What little I can remember,' Resnick said, 'the missing persons report – a copy would have come past me at the time – it was pretty much as he described. Interviews, of course, names of witnesses, people who'd been questioned. But nothing definite. Certainly nothing that would have pointed him towards what had really happened.'

'And that was it? Gone and goodbye.'

'Missing persons photographs were distributed, London, major cities. Agencies informed. There were sightings, as I recall, a few. None of them leading anywhere. And you've got to remember, the whole country was in an uproar, at least that's how it seemed.'

'One woman more or less gone missing – in the bigger scheme of things who cares?' Catherine stubbed out her cigarette, half-smoked.

Resnick was already looking at his watch.

'In danger of missing something, Charlie?'

'Jazz at the library, West Bridgford. Nottingham Youth Jazz Orchestra.'

'Thought it was books, more usually, libraries.'

'New strategy.'

'Downloads, Charlie, that's the new strategy. E-books. Read them on your Kindle, mobile phone.'

As if responding to the words, her own mobile

started to ring. Slipping it from her bag, back half-turned, she read the caller ID and declined the call.

'Little thanks for us, here, Charlie,' she said, moving towards the car. 'This investigation. However it turns out. Too many people getting on with their lives. Haines, Barry Hardwick, even Jill. What good will it do now, dredging all this up? That's what she thinks, what she said, more or less. Better, as far as they're all concerned, for Jenny's body to have stayed where it was buried, underground.'

Car in gear, she reversed back on to the road and away.

17

They gathered where the road forked, well shy of the first houses, the light just beginning to break. Men like Danny who were camping out in the fields, others who were billeted in the village; a dozen or more of them standing in twos and threes, heads down, stamping their feet against the cold; muffled conversation, bursts of occasional laughter, soft glow of cigarettes against the blackened hedgerow.

'Where the fuck are they?' says the man next to Danny. 'Should be fuckin' here by now.'

'Don't fret, they'll be here right enough.'

'Less'n they've been turned back already.'

'Look on't cheerful side of things, why don't you?'

Others are beginning to wonder aloud where they're going. Markham or Harworth? Bentinck, maybe. Ollerton.

'Silverhill,' says one with certainty. 'It's bloody Silverhill, I bet you.'

'Where the fuck's that then?'

'Fuck knows.'

They can see headlights now, faint, orange, approaching through the morning mist. Three cars and a Ford Transit. Windows wound down, a shouted greeting. Danny recognises Steve, Stevie, he's ridden with him before. And Woody, too. A laugh, Woody. Bit of a mad bastard, but all right.

Someone jumps from the lead car and hurries to the hedge to take a piss. It's not bloody Silverhill at all, it's Clipstone.

Danny and the bulk of the others clamber into the back of the van.

No seats, save at the front; someone's spread a length of old carpet on the floor in back but every bump and pothole in the road jars right through you. And it stinks of too many bodies clamped close together, stale farts and cigarette smoke.

'Who was that bird I saw you chattin' up at the Welfare?' someone asks Danny.

Danny grins and tells him to shut the fuck up.

They goad him a bit longer and he sits there laughing, lapping it up really, legs stretched out, back resting against the side of the van.

'Time you got married, youth. That'll take wind out your sails,' one of the older men observes.

'Not done that for you, has it?' one of the others says. 'Nobbin' around still wi' best of 'em.'

'Bollock off!'

Danny's thinking about the woman from the Welfare and not for the first time, either. Something about her, the way she looked back at him when he offered to buy her a drink. Defiant, yes, but something more. And when she left, later, doing her best not to look at him across the room, but looking just the same.

Where the Ollerton Road crosses with Netherfield Lane and the A616, the little convoy draws to a halt. Traffic cones warding them over to one side. Police in uniform. More than a few. Danny can see them over the driver's shoulder. Step out of the vehicle. Driving licence. Destination.

'Now turn this lot around and fuck off back where you come from.'

They're not local, Danny can tell. Tell from their accent. The driver of the first car is arguing and they're offering to arrest him.

'What charge? I've not done owt.'

'Whatever charge, sunshine, we bloody like.'

'You fucking would an' all, wouldn't you?'

As if to prove him right, two of them seize hold of him and bundle him back of their line, bending him sharply forward, arms tight behind his back.

There's more coppers now, coming close, either side of the van.

'Fuck this for a game of soldiers!' Danny shouts and, throwing open the rear doors, jumps out, evades a grasping hand and runs for the nearest gap in the hedge: vaults over a fence and away.

Glancing back over his shoulder as he runs, he sees several of the others have done likewise, spreading out in all directions, police chasing.

The two coppers who started after him have given up and are standing there cursing at the mud that's splashed up on to their uniform trousers.

Not really looking where he's going, Danny trips over a piece of uneven ground and goes sprawling, the upper half of his body landing in a cowpat of staggering proportions. Tears of laughter running down his face, he scrambles up and stumbles forward, desperate to find a brook or stream or maybe a farm-house with an outside pump, somewhere he can wash the worst of it away before getting back to the road and, with any luck, hitch a lift back to where he started.

18

Resnick woke, turned on his side, squinting at the clock in the semi-darkness of the room. 6.43. Fifteen minutes, a little more, to lie there and pretend it was just another day. Rolling back, he dislodged the cat from where it had been sleeping, curled into the V of his legs. Funerals, he'd had enough. More than enough for a lifetime. Graham Millington, his old sergeant, had been the most recent. A stroke. His wife putting on a brave face, taking Resnick by the arm, blue veins at the back of her hand. 'He loved you, Charlie, you know that, don't you? Not that he'd've ever said. Not in a million years.'

Over the protestations of the vicar and a few of Millington's near relations, she'd insisted on replacing 'Abide with Me' and 'Face to Face with God My Saviour' with a selection of Petula Clark's Greatest

Hits, Millington's coffin being carried towards its final resting place to the sound of 'The Other Man's Grass (Is Always Greener)'.

Worshipped Petula, Millington had.

Imagining him whistling along, Resnick had turned his head aside and wept.

He loved you, Charlie.

It didn't do to think about it, not overmuch.

No more than it did to think about Lynn. Except that he did.

On the day of her funeral, the traitorous bloody sun had shone practically from dawn till dusk, motes of dust dancing in front of the church windows, rose, silver and green. The ground inhospitable and hard. Tears drying on his face before they fell. And the youth who'd killed her – nineteen, not over-bright, desperate for respect – would be eligible, before too long, for parole. The possibility alive, for Resnick, of walking past him in the city, the opposite side of the street.

She had been in London, Lynn, a murder investigation, the last train from St Pancras home. When she'd phoned, Resnick had offered to meet her at the station.

No need. I'll get a cab.

Too easy to accept her at her word, settle back into the comfort of the armchair, Bob Brookmeyer on the stereo, glass of good Scotch close to hand.

No need.

At the sink, he splashed water in his face, stared at his reflection in the glass.

Wearing a black suit, calf-length skirt, hair tied back with purple ribbon, white flower in her lapel, Catherine met him outside the chapel. Behind them, small knots of people slowly gathered. Dour men in borrowed suits shaking hands.

Sandford and Cresswell were there, too, both slightly awkward, out of place. Names to be gathered, addresses; some already known and logged, others new; interviews arranged.

Barry Hardwick was talking to a younger version of himself, Colin, it had to be, the spitting image; a thin woman in a black hat, broad-brimmed, clinging on to Colin's hand. Close by, the daughter, Mary, was still recognisable from her wedding photograph, a blown-up version now of herself; her husband standing alongside her, one of those round Irish faces, broad foreheads, thick scrub of curly hair; their son, secondary school age or thereabouts, sullen, awkward, hands in his pockets, hands out; the daughter, a year or two younger, freckled face, barely ever lifting her eyes from the ground.

No sign yet of Barry Hardwick's other son, the younger brother, Brian.

A group of women of similar age, half a dozen of them so far and the number growing – miners' wives,

Resnick thought, wives and now widows both – stood talking earnestly, a little to one side, each new arrival greeted with exclamations, kisses and hugs. Edna Johnson, walking only slowly with the aid of two sticks, was the last to join them, each step an effort, her face creasing with pain and determination. Resnick had watched her getting out of the taxi, raised a hand in greeting; a half-smile of recognition in return. He'd thought to have seen her at Peter Waites' funeral, heard she'd been unwell, a hip replacement that had gone badly.

Catherine had seen Jill Haines earlier, talking to the vicar; her husband standing off to one side, in desultory conversation with someone she didn't recognise. Mary Hardwick she had already spoken to, agreed to meet before her flight back to Ireland in a few days' time.

Finding a moment to talk to Barry, she had filled him in on what little progress they had made so far; the son, Colin, who'd been listening, impatient for some sign of breakthrough now that the investigation had started, something more specific about his mother's death, someone to blame; Barry quieter, more resigned, weighed down, Catherine thought, by the occasion.

Soon enough would come the hearse, the coffin with its catalogue of bones, the sound of the organ calling them in.

*   *   *

Halfway through the service there was a commotion at the chapel door, raised voices, the door finally swinging open with a bang. The man who'd been arguing with one of the ushers fired off another curse and stepped unsteadily inside; almost immediately lost his footing, swore again loudly, and righted himself against the rear wall.

Heads turned; tutted, murmured, turned away.

Brian Hardwick – enough of a family resemblance to be sure it was him – suit unbuttoned, tie askew, shirt undone, made his way unevenly to an empty pew and lowered himself down.

The service continued.

From where Resnick was sitting, it seemed – and sounded – as if Hardwick had fallen asleep, but midway through the final hymn, he lurched awake and began to sing loudly, out of tune and off-key.

The chapel had barely emptied before Colin Hardwick had his brother by the lapels of his coat and was half-pushing, half-dragging him across the sward of neatly mown grass between the path and the first line of gravestones.

'You drunken feckless bastard, you should've fuckin' stayed away!'

'Fuck you!'

Colin punched him full in the face. Already stumbling backwards, Brian sank down on to one knee, shook his head, and pushing himself up awkwardly to his feet, charged forward, arms flailing. Stepping aside, Colin thrust out a leg, sending his brother sprawling.

'Bastard!' Colin said, and kicked him as he lay. 'Drunken piss-arse bastard!'

'Colin! Don't!' His sister, Mary, seized hold of his arm, tried to pull him away. 'Don't, please.'

'She's right, lad,' Barry Hardwick said, coming close. 'Let it be.'

Colin shook himself free of his sister's hand, cast one last glance towards where his brother lay, and strode off between the graves. Mary bent low and, taking a tissue from her bag, dabbed at the blood dribbling from the side of Brian's mouth.

'Come away now,' her husband said softly. 'Come on away.'

On the ground, Brian Hardwick groaned and was still.

The first of the cars was starting to leave, the first few mourners already heading off down the path that curved towards the main gate.

Resnick took hold of Brian Hardwick by both arms and hauled him to his feet. Led him to a bench between trees.

'You all right?'

'I look fuckin' all right?'

Resnick said nothing in reply.

'I said, do I look fuckin' all right? Do I?'

'You look like shit,' Resnick said.

'Fuck you!'

'You look like shit, you've a cut on your lower lip and you just came drunk to your mother's funeral.'

'Fuck her, too!'

It was all Resnick could do to stop himself from slapping him hard. Instead, he stood up quietly and walked to where a group of women, Edna Johnson amongst them, had surrounded Alex Sandford and were teasing him unmercifully.

'I was just telling your lad here,' Edna Johnson said, 'there was a time when all coppers in Notts were more'n six foot. Couldn't get in else.'

'Breed them for brains nowadays,' Resnick said, 'not brawn.'

'Which are you then?' one of the women asked.

'Charlie here,' Edna said, 'he's a bit of both.'

'First-name terms, then, Edna?' another woman said with a smile.

'Got to know one another during the strike, didn't we, Mr Resnick? After a manner of speaking.'

'Which manner were that, Edna?' someone else asked to much laughter.

The look she got in return suggested the joking had gone just about far enough.

Alex Sandford had taken the opportunity to back away. Over towards one of the cars, Catherine Njoroge was talking to Barry Hardwick and his daughter. Rob Cresswell was talking to a couple by one of the cars, notebook in hand.

'I was wondering, Edna,' Resnick said, 'if you had time for a chat?'

'Time? Aye, plenty of that.'

'Here, or . . .'

'Here'd be fine.'

They sat facing the chapel entrance, Resnick with a hand to her elbow as she lowered herself carefully down.

A little way off, Brian Hardwick lay curled along the bench where Resnick had left him, one arm trailing towards the ground.

'Poor lad,' Edna Johnson said.

'Brian?'

'Runt of the litter'd not be quite right, but he ran too much in his brother's shadow for all that. Barry, he always favoured Colin, you could tell. And Mary, of course. So then, when his mum . . . when Jenny . . .' She shook her head. 'I don't think he ever got over it, the thought that she just up and left them, left him. What'd he have been? Four at the time? Five, maybe. That at best. And then, learning his mum were killed, murdered. Maybe worse.'

'We don't know . . .'

'Not stop it goin' through his mind, all the same.'

Heading now to where her car was parked, Catherine Njoroge raised a hand towards them in greeting.

'Handsome woman that,' Edna Johnson remarked.

Resnick couldn't do anything but agree.

'How's it feel, I wonder?' Edna asked.

'How does what?'

'According to what lad talkin' to us said, no matter the years you've put in, she's the one in charge.'

'Too many years, Edna, that's the trouble. And besides, she's good at her job, getting better.'

'You to guide her.'

'Not the way I see it. Nor her, either, I don't suppose.'

'Then she's a fool.'

Despite himself, Resnick smiled. 'Mind if I ask you something?'

'Ask away.'

'When Jenny first disappeared, what did you think?'

'First? Thought she'd gone off, like most everyone else. Had enough. Flitted.'

'On her own, or . . .'

'I was never sure. She was a good-looking woman, Jenny, no getting away from that. And when she stood up to speak, meetings and the like, you could see the men in the audience, some of them – well, it weren't just what she were saying that were holding their attention.'

'And she was aware of that?'

'Ever known a woman who wasn't?'

'There's talk about a young miner down from Yorkshire . . .'

'Danny, Danny Ireland. Trailed round after her like a needy dog.'

'Red-headed lad?'

'Gingerish, yes. That's the one.'

'You ever think she could have gone off with him?'

'Copped off, maybe. Nice-enough-looking lad, all right.'

'But nothing more?'

'I never thought so. Not enough about him for Jenny to have upped and left a marriage. Home. Kids.'

'Then you thought it was someone else?'

'I thought it were possible, yes.'

'Did you know who? Have any idea?'

'Not really, no. But round about then, winter, that time of year, she'd been all over, making speeches, you know. South Wales once, I think it was. York. London. Union leaders, negotiators – brains and a pretty face, susceptible as anyone. And she had changed, Jenny, I could see that. As if all that had happened had made her restless, wanting more. Nor was she the only one, of course – changed a lot of women's lives, strike did.'

'For the better?'

'In the long run, yes, I think so.'

Briefly, she touched Resnick's hand with her own.

'P'raps I shouldn't say this, but when I heard – you know, when her body was found, where it was, I was almost glad. Not for what'd happened, of course, God no, not for that, but 'cause it meant she'd not walked out on her kids to go off with some smart-mouthed bloke in a suit and tie, lookin' for what she thought was a better life. Left her kids for that. That's what I mean by glad. Glad that wasn't the kind of person she'd become.'

Away on the other bench, Brian Hardwick roused himself, stretched, stood uncertainly up, took a few paces, turned and sat back down.

'I should be going,' Edna said. 'One of my old pals, offered me a lift.'

'Been good to see you again,' Resnick said.

'Funerals,' Edna said, 'about the only time these days you get to see your friends. Fewer and fewer each time, mind.'

He stood admiringly as, head up, she walked slowly away.

19

These last mornings, Jenny has been getting up while it is still dark, hurrying down to the kitchen, bowls out for the kids' breakfast, bread and jam for them to take to school, sandwiches for Barry's snap – she'd not deny him that and if she did he'd only scraight and moan all the more.

Out in the hallway, she pulls a comb through her hair, then reaches for her coat and shoes. Edna would be at the Welfare already, mashing tea, something hot for the lads before they set off for the day's picket: bacon cobs, if they were lucky – where the bacon came from, the money to pay for it, no questions asked.

There were collecting boxes on every street corner – not here, but in the bigger towns and cities, London even – miners standing beside buckets into which folk dropped coins, spare change, notes sometimes and not small. Stories of city bankers stuffing down ten-pound notes, twenties even. Drivers going past, sounding their horns in support. More donations, she'd been told, coming in from abroad. France, was it? That's what she'd heard. And Russia? Was that possible?

So many people acknowledging what they were doing was right.

Telling them to stand firm.

Stick together.

As long as they did that, then surely they'd win through . . .

Edna greets her with a smile and points towards half a dozen or more loaves, waiting for a scrape of margarine. On the table behind, one of the other women is peeling her way through a sack of onions for that day's soup, tears streaming down her face. From the far side of the room, the radio plays George Michael, 'Careless Whisper'.

As she stands there, Peter Waites comes breezing in, loud-voiced and cheerful, a quick word with Edna, barely a glance in Jenny's direction, and he's gone again. The first of the men drifting in now, that lad, the red-headed one, at the back there, jostling with one of his mates. Pushing and shoving like kids in the playground.

Laughing.

Jenny eases the hair back from her face and when

she glances up again, moments later, he's staring in her direction, bold as brass.

Pressing her lips together, she bends her head back down to the task in hand.

She's back in the Welfare at lunchtime, helping serve soup to those miners who are on strike, and then again that evening, the two youngest in bed. There are always jobs that want doing: trips to the cash and carry for weekly supplies; donations of food to be fetched from the central collection point at the Friends' Meeting House in Mansfield, then bagged up into family parcels; bags of second-hand clothes to be sorted through; fund-raising materials to be made for the stall by St Peter's Church in Nottingham. Never time enough, it seems, or hands.

There's talk amongst the women, some uncertainty, Jenny can tell, as to how long they can carry on as they are, and Edna Johnson listens for a while, just long enough for them to feel they've had their say, then quietly but firmly sets them to rights. As long as they're needed, one way or another, they'll find the means to carry on. End of discussion.

Not for the first time, Jenny finds herself admiring Edna for her clear-sightedness, the way she always seems able to say what's needed without fuss or bother; up on the platform at meetings, more often than not the only woman speaker amongst all those men, and the audience taking in her every word, listening. Not a little envious, Jenny wonders if, as Peter Waites had suggested, she will ever have the courage to do the same.

She's on her way home, the street next to her own, when he comes out of the shadows just ahead of her, making her gasp.

'Didn't mean to startle you.'

The street light close enough to show up the red in his hair.

'What the hell d'you think you're doin'?'

'Won't be seeing you again, not after tonight. Thought you'd like to know.'

'Seeing me? Is that what you've been doing?'

'Camping out, had a barrelful o' that. Back home, proper bed, sheets. Got mates'll drive me, wherever we've got to go.'

'Good for you.'

She makes to move around him, and he shifts his balance to block her path.

'Reckoned, before I went, you know, that drink you promised.'

'I promised nothing.'

'Maybe. Maybe not.'

He's standing close enough now for her to see the small scar on his cheek, close by his mouth.

'A goodbye kiss, then . . .'

When he lowers his head towards her, she swings an arm and slaps him hard across the face; pushes angrily past as, grinning, he steps aside.

'Another time then, duck, eh?'

Quickening her pace, she strides for home, the memory of his breath still warm on her face.

20

The band closed their first set with a tearaway version of 'Jumpin' at the Woodside', the young tenor player up from London taking advantage of the tempo to show off the speed of his fingering and romp up and down the scales with such speed as to leave the listeners practically seasick.

'Play that many notes, Charlie,' one of the regulars said, falling in step alongside Resnick as they headed for the bar, 'some of the bastards got to be the right ones, eh?'

Resnick nodded agreement, paid for his pint and, not feeling overly sociable, took it off to the side room, a seat in the far corner, fifteen, twenty minutes of his own company before the band regrouped.

Two days now since the funeral and for all the information they'd gathered, they were little closer to the truth of what happened. Catherine Njoroge was due to have a meeting with Martin Picard at headquarters later that week in order to outline their progress, a meeting she'd not been anticipating with any particular pleasure.

From the friends and neighbours of the Petersons that Sandford and Cresswell had so far been able to track down, it was clear a number of different people had been working with Geoff Cartwright on the Church Street extension, sometimes for as little as a morning, a day at most. Mixing cement, laying concrete. There was one period, close to Christmas itself, the nearest neighbour said, when no work seemed to be being done at all; but then, almost before you could turn around, everything seemed to have been sorted in double-quick time. When the Petersons got back from wherever – Wales, was it? Somewhere of that fashion – everything seemingly done and dusted.

From the women gathered at the funeral, there was ample testimony of the growing tension between Barry and Jenny Hardwick, arguments that had flared up in public, harsh words with Jenny most often giving as good as she got. Threats? The usual, nothing more. You wait till I get you home, that kind of nonsense. Hot air and blather. One time, all right, Jenny had been sporting a black eye, a real shiner, but when asked she'd said it had happened out on the picket line, run smack into someone's elbow.

'I'll be honest,' one of the women said, 'if he had

given her a backhander once or twice, it wouldn't have been 'cause she hadn't earned it. Goaded him sometimes, something rotten. Like she were saying, go on then, hit me if you dare. Felt right sorry for him, Barry, though I shouldna', scabbin' like he was.'

'Barry had let her have one, she'd've give him one back, an' all,' another said. 'Remember that lad? Ginger-haired bloke, set his cap at her. She walloped him once, by all accounts. Right proud of it, he were, too. Braggin' about it all over. Daft young bugger.'

Ginger-haired bloke – Danny Ireland – they knew his name, bits and pieces of past history, but not a great deal else. So far all attempts to track him down had failed. There'd been an address in Doncaster, a woman he'd lived with for a spell in Leeds, a child he might or might not have fathered in Goole. A spell working on the oil rigs, out of Aberdeen. Someone who might or might not have been him, applying for a job with P&O Ferries sailing from Hull to Rotterdam. Since which time, he didn't seem to have filed a tax return, applied for benefit, appeared on a voters' register: died.

The sound of the trumpet playing a few warning notes in the far room told Resnick it was time for the second set. He was just draining his glass, when the man slipped into the seat alongside him. Fifties, narrow face, spectacles, thinning hair combed sideways in a Bobby Charlton; raincoat that had seen better days.

'Detective Inspector Resnick?'

'Not any more.'

'The Jenny Hardwick murder, though, Bledwell Vale, you are involved?'

'Maybe.'

'Little bird told me I might find you here.' He held out his hand. 'Trevor Fleetwood. Let me get you a drink. I'll not keep you away from the music for long.'

'Just a half, then.'

Resnick watched him go. Fleetwood, Fleetwood, he knew the name from somewhere, but where? Over the hum of conversation, the burble of the fruit machine by the side wall, he could just make out the opening strains of 'Moten Swing'.

'We did meet once before,' Fleetwood said, back from the bar. 'Operation Enigma. The bodies in the canal. Ninety-six?'

'Seven.'

'Of course.'

'Got it now. You were writing a book . . .'

'*Death by Water*. I sent you a copy.'

'I remember.'

'What did you think?'

No answer.

'I know, coals to Newcastle. You probably only glanced at it anyway. But this time I thought I might help you.'

'Go on.'

'Michael Swann, ring any bells?'

'Not immediately.'

'The M6 Murderer?'

'Another book?'

'More of a sequel.'

Interest piqued, Resnick supped his bitter and waited for Fleetwood to continue.

'Nineteen eighty-nine, Kim Bucknall, sexually assaulted, murdered, body found in a derelict building close to junction forty-three of the M6, just outside Carlisle. Three years later, ninety-two, Patricia Albright, raped, murdered, her body left on waste ground near Fullwood, north of Preston, buried beneath old timber, tarpaulin, rubble. Then ninety-four, Lisa Plackett, raped, anally and vaginally, her body pushed down a storm drain near exit twenty-one on the edge of Warrington. Michael Swann was convicted of all three murders in nineteen ninety-seven. Five years later, he'd have been sent down for thirty years minimum. As it was, he was sentenced to life, given a tariff of twenty-five years. A possibility of parole after twenty. Just three years from now. Not that I'd rate his chances too high.'

'And you're suggesting, what? A connection?'

'Jenny Hardwick, how was she killed?'

Resnick held his gaze, made no answer.

Fleetwood essayed a smile. 'Unless I'm mistaken, blow or blows to the head with a heavy object. The same or similar to all three cases for which Swann was found guilty, and in each of which he took advantage of whatever the surroundings to conceal the body.'

'Timings aside,' Resnick said, 'and Jenny was killed a whole five years before the first of those murders, Swann's territory, the M6 like you say, it's a long way from North Notts. The other side of the country.'

Fleetwood took an envelope from his pocket.

'Take a look at this.'

It was a press photograph, in colour, fuzzy at the edges, the details clear enough to bring Resnick up short. Shoulder-length dark hair, just a few shades off black, sharp features, blue-grey eyes: it could have been Jenny Hardwick's younger sister.

'Donna Crowder,' Fleetwood said. 'Nineteen. Her body was discovered less than an hour's drive away from where Jenny Hardwick lay buried. Beaten about the head. Half-buried beneath bushes and brambles. Foxes found her before anyone else. No one's ever been charged with her murder.'

'And this was when?'

'Eighty-seven.'

'And you think it was Michael Swann that killed her?'

'I think he killed both of them, first Jenny, then Donna three years later. Then the others. I just need you to help me prove it.'

21

Resnick had made no promises to Trevor Fleetwood, other than a rather vague agreement to stay in touch. Before leaving the pub that evening, he had contacted Catherine Njoroge and arranged to meet her in Nottingham the following morning. Lee Rosy's in Hockley, opposite the Broadway Cinema.

Catherine listened without interrupting, sipped her tea.

'You think there's anything to it?'

'I think he'd like there to be.'

'So he can get another book out of it.'

'That and the publicity, yes.'

'I looked up his website last night, after you phoned me. All pretty unsavoury. Book jacket illustrations, mostly suggesting gore and mayhem. Knives, knotted rope, naked breasts, women screaming. Truly horrible.

I made a note of some of the titles, here . . .' She unlocked her mobile phone, tapped Notes. '*In the Ripper's Footsteps. Evil Intent. Death by Water. Famous Murder Trials of the Last Century.*'

'*Death by Water*,' Resnick said, 'about the canal murders. Operation Enigma. That's when I met him before. Getting on twenty years ago now.'

'What's it like?'

'The book?' Resnick shrugged. 'Sensationalist, of course. Pretty much what you'd expect. But otherwise . . . yes, it was accurate enough. He'd done his research, you could tell that.'

'There's a book here,' Catherine said, glancing back down at her mobile. '*Born to Kill*. Interviews with convicted murderers. One of them's Michael Swann. I downloaded it on to my Kindle. The chapter on Swann's one of the shortest. A rehash mostly of the murders. Some stuff about Swann's upbringing, childhood, but nothing out of the ordinary. Difficult to get any sense of what he's really like.'

'There's no suggestion he might have had other victims?'

'No. Fleetwood asks him, asks him outright, and, of course, Swann denies it.'

'Does he mention Donna Crowder? Fleetwood, I mean?'

'In the interview? No.'

A young couple came in, students, spoke quietly to

the man behind the counter and went to a table by the side wall, laptops out of their bags and open almost before they'd sat down.

'Nobody's made this suggestion before?' Catherine asked. 'In the Crowder case, for instance. Considered Swann as a likely suspect?'

'Not as far as I can know.'

Catherine arched her neck and smoothed her hair, worn loose today, away from her face with a brush of her hand. 'If this gets opened up, Charlie, it's a whole new territory. Two murders, possible links to a serial killer. There'll be no way of keeping that toned down. Not once the media get wind of it.'

Resnick nodded. 'What Fleetwood's banking on, I suppose. And certainly not what Picard and Hastings had in mind. Though as long as it drew attention away from the strike, they might even be pleased.'

'Something big, you could see Picard muscling in, wanting a bit of the limelight for himself.'

Resnick shrugged. 'Investigation that size, might not be such a bad thing.'

'Uh-uh. I want this, Charlie. It's my case, my investigation.'

'Fair enough.'

'So let's proceed, but gently, okay? Keep it close to home.'

'Okay.'

'Maybe you could take a look at the Donna Crowder

inquiry, see how closely Fleetwood's theories tie in to the facts.'

'And Swann?'

'Let's leave Swann for now. Talk to him later, if we have to.' She looked at her watch. 'Mary Connor, I promised I'd meet her. Let her know what's happening in the investigation as much as anything. She's been staying up at her father's place in Chesterfield since the rest of her family went back.'

She was on her feet, bag on her shoulder. 'You never know, it might give me the excuse for another word with Barry, too.'

Resnick nodded down towards his cup, the slice of apple and cinnamon cake alongside. 'I'll stay here, finish this.'

Catherine smiled, touched him briefly on the shoulder as she moved past.

The café was slowly getting busier. Another couple of students. A man in his late twenties, early thirties, sitting up to the window, roll-neck jumper, jeans, sipping espresso, scrolling through the news on his iPad. Near the back, a woman Resnick thought he recognised from his infrequent visits to the cinema opposite: fair hair, near shoulder length, face dimpling as whatever she was listening to through her headphones made her smile.

For Resnick, it had been across the street at Broadway that Operation Enigma had started. An evening when Milt Jackson, vibraphone player from the Modern Jazz

Quartet, had been making a rare one-off appearance: Resnick, sitting forward, eager with anticipation, the first notes of 'Bag's Groove' starting to roll out from the accompanying piano, when his pager had summoned him suddenly away. The body of a woman had just been discovered by the lock gates of the Nottingham Canal, close to where it joined the River Trent. A young woman, Eastern European it transpired, but otherwise difficult to identify; a silver ring on the little finger of her left hand, a gash deep into the bone above the right eye. One of three other bodies to have been discovered in canals in the preceding years. Operation Enigma. Like many things seen through water, the truth was often refracted, never quite what it seemed.

Trevor Fleetwood's book had topped the True Crime listings for a month or two before falling away; extracts had been published, Resnick remembered, in the *Post*. Another level of distortion, though, at root, the facts had been basically sound.

Pushing back his chair, Resnick lifted the last piece of cake with finger and thumb, shared a smile of half-recognition with the woman from Broadway, and stepped out on to the street. With any luck, the room he'd been allocated at Central Police Station would still be available, not too many questions as to the information he'd be searching for on the computer.

* * *

As chance would have it, Andy Duncan was just leaving the station as Resnick arrived.

'Student?' Resnick asked. 'Any change?'

Duncan shook his head. 'Goes on much longer, I can see 'em pulling the plug.'

Poor bastard, Resnick thought. Knight errant in a thankless world.

Ever since thinking of Milt Jackson and 'Bag's Groove', he hadn't been able to get the tune out of his mind. The original version, the first he himself knew, the first he'd heard. Miles Davis stating the theme on trumpet before playing several choruses with just bass and drums behind, Davis having told Thelonious Monk, the pianist on the date, to lay out whenever he was soloing. A request Monk didn't exactly take kindly. It was Christmas Eve and he'd wanted to be at home with his family, not working on somebody else's session for scale. And when it finally came to his turn to solo, Monk, even more idiosyncratic than usual, had jabbed out little phrases that seemed purposely to sing against the natural rhythm, the natural logic of Davis' own playing, his fingers often striking two keys at once, the space between.

Why does he play, Resnick's wife, Elaine, used to ask in the long long ago, as if he's got no arms?

Answer: because he can.

Why play the right notes when the wrong ones will do?

Resnick typed the name Donna Crowder into the computer and set the search engine chasing. The press photographs gave him the same jolt as before; she could have been Jenny Hardwick's younger sister, or Jenny herself just a few years younger. The same prettiness shot through with a strong hint of determination. Blue eyes staring directly back at the camera. A young woman, sure of herself and her place in the world.

Too sure, perhaps.

All too familiar a story.

Donna had been to a nightclub in Sheffield with friends, become separated, missed the last bus, and set out to hitch home to Rotherham along the Sheffield Road.

Less than ten miles.

At some point on her journey, the assumption was, she had accepted a lift. By the early hours of the following morning, having checked the local hospitals and contacted Donna's friends, her parents had alerted the police.

Donna's body was found three days later amongst the scrub and undergrowth alongside the River Don, where it runs more or less parallel to the road. Other than the fact that her clothing was torn, there were no apparent signs of sexual assault.

From reading the various news reports, it seemed that Donna's boyfriend at the time had come under suspicion, but, as far as Resnick could tell, neither he nor anyone else had ever been charged with Donna Crowder's murder.

It still lay open, unsolved.

The senior officer who'd been in charge of the investigation, Resnick saw, was Detective Chief Inspector Maurice Rawsthorne of the South Yorkshire Police. A photograph showed him in full uniform at a press conference the morning after the body was found. Seated to one side, Donna Crowder's mother; on the other, Detective Sergeant Paul Bryant, Rawsthorne's number two.

Rawsthorne, Resnick happened to know, had died some seven or eight years previously; but Bryant was not only still alive, but had only recently retired. A sometime colleague – Bryant had started out in the Nottinghamshire force and the two men had had occasion to meet up professionally over the years – Resnick thought it was time to look him up, take him, maybe, a little something to help him celebrate kicking off the shackles of the job.

22

Much of the past few days, confrontation either side of the picket line at a minimum, Resnick had spent kicking his heels, relatively little to report. A stalemate of sorts seemed to have been reached.

'You still alive up there, Charlie?' his operational commander had enquired. 'Still breathing?'

'Just about, sir.'

'Thought you might have gone AWOL. Gone native.'

It was like a storm waiting to break.

When it came the call was brief and to the point. At first he hadn't recognised the voice. Peter Waites. Since their first meeting in the early days of the strike they'd met again several times, developed a grudging respect. 'Might want to get yourself up here, Charlie. Bit of a to-do. Nasty. One of yours, as it turned out, on her way to hospital.'

Her?

Diane Conway?

'Which hospital?'

'Bassetlaw. Local.'

'How serious?'

'She'll live, if that's what you mean. Precautionary, I'd say, much as anything.'

Resnick was already reaching for his coat. 'I'll be there.'

He found Peter Waites standing close by three burned-out cars, one of which had been turned on to its side as a makeshift barricade. Circling the wagons, Resnick thought. The road was covered in splintered glass that crackled beneath his feet when he walked. Several of the nearby houses had had their windows broken; SCAB in jagged paint down one of the doors. Pieces of half-brick, smooth-edged stones.

Disappointment writ large on the union man's face.

'I know I said it'd not happen here, not on my watch. Cars set alight. All this. Pains me to say you were right, even though it's just the once.'

'What happened?' Resnick asked.

'Kicked off in the pub earlier, couple of the lads got into an argument. Usual argy-bargy. Result was, time comes for second shift, more on picket line than's been the case for good while. Well, you know. Police get wind up, whistle up reinforcements. Still shoutin' an' not a lot else until someone throws a stone. Catches one of coppers on side of head. And then they're away. Blue bloody murder. And I'll tell you what, Charlie, my life, him as threw that first stone, he was a copper, an' all. I've seen him, seen him front of police line afore now, an' there he was, civvy clothes, in amongst our lads, geein' 'em up, eggin' 'em on, hurlin' that bloody stone, could've taken eye out o' one of his own.'

'Police officer, you're sure?'

'Sure as I'm standing here.'

Resnick looked at the cars, the street. 'That was all up by the pit. What about all this here?'

'Some of the pickets got back down, found a bunch of lads from the village, bloody little tearaways, had torched their cars. Of course, they go looking for restitution. Next thing you know, coppers are down here, two Transits of 'em. Wading in left, right and centre. Which was when that lass of yours got hers. Back of the head. Flying bottle, some said, but I'm not so sure.'

'Meaning what?'

'Meaning I'm not so sure.'

'The officer you reckon you saw, threw the first stone, you'd recognise him again?'

'Maybe, aye.'

Resnick shook his head: a bloody mess.

'Keith Haines around?' he asked.

'He was. Little enough he could do, once it had all kicked off.'

'I'll get one of my lads to help him take statements. You'll talk to him, of course, tell him what you told me?'

'I will . . . not as it'll do a scrap of good.'

Diane Conway was looking better than Resnick might have feared, sitting up in bed with a pale face and bandaged head, riffling through an old copy of *Cosmopolitan*.

'Just had a word with the doctor,' Resnick said. 'No fracture. Miracle of miracles.'

'Get these bandages off, I should be home in a few days, so they reckon. Back at work in no time.'

'You'll do no such thing.'

'I can't just sit around.'

'Official letter saying you're fit to resume. Without that, I don't want to see hide nor hair, understood? Besides, as far as carrying on's concerned, after this, I'm afraid your cover's well and truly blown.'

'Yes, sir.'

He perched on the end of the bed. 'Your version of things, we'll need to have it in writing.'

A little apprehensively, she slid two pages of closely written A4 from between the pages of *Cosmo* and handed them over.

Resnick read them through once quickly, then a

second time more carefully, pausing several times with questions, wanting clarification.

'You're certain of this?'

'Yes, sir.'

'A uniformed officer?'

'Yes.'

'And . . .' He glanced back down at her report. 'At the time of the incident you were running away from the fighting?'

'Trying to.'

'And you were struck with the officer's baton how many times?'

'Three, sir. As far as I know. One as I stumbled and then twice more after I'd fallen. After that I must have lost consciousness.'

'This officer, you'd be able to identify him?'

'I'm not sure, sir. It was all so fast and until I fell my back was towards him. I'm sorry.'

'That's okay.'

Five days later, Resnick was standing before the operational commander.

'DC Conway, Charlie. Making a good recovery, by all accounts. No lasting injury?'

'No, sir.'

'Good. Capital. All part of life's rich pageant, eh? Going in undercover, always going to be a bit tricky. Own dangers. Nothing you won't have warned them of, I dare say. Nothing, in this case, to tell the officer concerned she was one of ours. Part of stone-throwing mob as far as he was concerned. Avoiding arrest.'

'He hit her three times, sir, with his baton, three times at least.'

'Heat of the battle, Charlie. You've been there. Heat of the chase.'

'A young woman, sir, unprotected, running away.'

'Equal rights, eh, Charlie. You're for all that, I'd have supposed. No special treatment asked for or given.'

'Use of force, above and beyond—'

'Charlie, Charlie. These things happen. Collateral damage. Write it off. Am I making myself clear?'

'Perfectly, sir.'

'Good. And there's no sense she's about to do something stupid like make an official complaint of assault?'

'No, sir.'

'Excellent. Keep it all in-house.'

Resnick took a breath. 'Will that be all, sir?'

'All for now.'

He was almost at the door when the commander called him back.

'This other business in your report, this allegation about an officer deliberately setting things in motion, acting as an agent provocateur – let's kick that out of touch here and now. Storybook stuff, Charlie. Someone with an overactive imagination. There might be a few wild cards from outside, but none of them are going to go that far, I'm sure. Why would they? Scargill's mob, out there flinging missiles enough of their own.'

23

Mary Connor's call reached Catherine Njoroge just as she was leaving the ring road and heading out towards the motorway. Instead of meeting in Chesterfield, as arranged, could they meet in Nottingham instead? She had come down the evening before to visit an old school friend and ended up staying over. She hoped she'd caught Catherine in time, wasn't putting her to any trouble.

Catherine assured her it would be fine. Where was she staying?

West Bridgford? Yes, she knew West Bridgford. The park off Central Avenue, by the new library? Of course. They could always nip in somewhere for coffee if it rained.

Mary was sitting on a bench by one of the municipal flower beds when Catherine arrived. Clouds of varying grey overhead, the sun yet to break through; the temperature, as usual lately, five degrees below the notional average. She was wearing a waterproof jacket, zipped up almost to the collar; blue jeans, faded and well worn; shoes that could have doubled for walking boots if need be. Her face was pale, dark lines around the eyes, shadow.

'You'll have to excuse me,' she said, once Catherine had joined her. 'I'm still a little hungover this morning. My friend and I, too much wine last night. Reminiscing.'

'You've known her a long time?'

'Since infant school, just about.'

'She's from Bledwell Vale, then?'

'Not really. Her mum was a teacher, at the school. Brought Nicky – that's her name – in with her every day. Retford, that's where they lived.'

'But you were close, even though her mum was the teacher, you and Nicky?'

'More so as we got older.' Mary smiled, remembering. 'I say older. Eight or nine, that's what I mean. Just kids, really. Nicky would come round mine after school to play. Her mum would pick her up later, after she'd finished all her marking, preparing lessons, whatever it was she had to do.'

'Eight or nine,' Catherine said. 'That's around the time your mum . . . around the time she disappeared.'

'Four days before Christmas.' Mary shook her head. 'That song, you know, "The Twelve Days of Christmas"?

On the twelfth day of Christmas my true love gave to me. For me, it's a little different. On the fourth day of Christmas my mother disappeared from the face of God's earth.'

Hands to her face, she lowered her head towards the ground.

Catherine could tell she was crying; rested a comforting hand on her shoulder; left it there, slowly moved it away. Gradually, the crying stopped.

'I didn't mean to upset you.'

'No? No, I suppose not. It's not possible, is it, any other way?'

'I'm sorry.'

'It's okay.'

'Would you rather go somewhere?' Catherine looked back towards Central Avenue. 'A cup of coffee?'

'No. No, thanks. I'd sooner stay out here. No one to see me if I start blubbing.'

Catherine's mobile started to ring and she slipped it from her pocket, checked the caller ID and declined the call.

'Go ahead and take it if you want,' Mary said.

'Not important.'

'They're a curse, aren't they? Mobile phones. Blessing and a curse. Out where we live there isn't any signal, of course. You have to drive the best part of a mile, get out on to this little hill and wave it around in the air.'

Catherine was reaching for her bag. 'D'you mind if I have a cigarette?'

'Not at all. I was a fearful smoker till Kevin was born. Even when I was carrying him, you know, I'd still have the odd one or two. His dad reckons it's why Kevin's such a bag of bones. Not a bit of flesh on him.'

'And you? You think that's why it is?'

'Not at all. He won't eat a decent meal, that's what it comes down to. Pushes his food around the plate and scarcely eats a thing. Fussy doesn't come into it. His sister scoffs down twice what he does and she's not but a slip of a thing herself. Maybe it's in the whatever . . . the genes . . . that's what it is.'

Catherine held the smoke down in her lungs, releasing it slowly into the air. A crocodile of small children was making its way along the path towards the library entrance, all, save the last few, holding hands.

'Sweet, aren't they?' Mary said.

Catherine nodded.

'You've not children of your own?'

'Is it that obvious?'

'No, not really.' Mary's face creased into a smile. 'Well, maybe just a little. Smart, professional. Dedicated, I dare say, to your job.'

Catherine's turn to smile. 'You left out strident, sexless, feminist, probably gay.'

'I didn't think you were that.'

'Which?'

'Gay.'

'People do. Even now. They assume. Career police officer, female. Lesbian, got to be.'

A mischievous smile came to Mary's face. 'I catch myself wishing sometimes I could've been a bit more that way inclined. Save an awful lot of trouble, wouldn't it now? Men, for one thing. Babies, breast-feeding, nappies.'

'Not so much the babies. Gay friends I know, they spend more time and energy trying to get pregnant than anything.'

'Instead of the old quick shag, you mean?'

Catherine laughed. 'Most cases, likely not an option.'

'Not even with their eyes closed.'

Catherine laughed again.

'I don't know why I'm talking like this,' Mary said. 'Must still be the effect of the wine.'

A woman shuffled past leading a small dog, its stomach almost brushing the ground.

'You know I have to ask you,' Catherine said. 'When Jenny – when your mother – disappeared, what did you think had happened?'

'Honestly?'

'Honestly.'

'I thought my father – I know I shouldn't say this, shouldn't even think it – but I thought, you know, that he'd . . . I don't know how to say it . . .'

'That he'd killed her?'

'Oh, Lord, no, not that. That somehow he'd driven her away.'

'You don't mean literally, literally driven . . .'

'No, of course not. I mean forced her, I suppose, forced her to go.'

'Can you explain?'

'It was tense, you know? Towards the end. Those last few months. At least, that's how it seemed. How I remember it now. Long periods of silence, nobody speaking, and then, once in a while, this awful shouting. The house suddenly full of shouting. And anger. He'd get so angry then, my dad. They both would. And it would get to the point where one of them would break something, just a cup or something, smash it, you know, on the table, throw it on the floor, and then one of them, my mum usually, would go slamming out the door.

'That's right, he'd say, shouting after her, go on, get out and don't come back. And he'd swear and I'd start crying and that would only make things worse. Brian and me – he was the youngest – we'd both be crying.'

'Not Colin?'

'Colin always took my dad's side against my mother. If ever there was an argument and we were there and afterwards she tried to say it would be okay, tried to say she was sorry, he just wouldn't listen. Wouldn't let her touch him or anything. Told her he hated her, more than the once. You don't mean that, Colin, she'd say. You don't mean that. But I think he did.'

Catherine stubbed out her cigarette. Angled above the trees, the sun was just beginning to leak through the grey.

'So you thought,' she said, 'that your dad had told her to go and not come back once too often?'

'Yes. Yes, I suppose so.'

'But you thought she would come back eventually?'

'Yes. Of course. I always, always thought that. Or that there'd be a letter, a phone call, something.'

She was crying again, not bothering to hide it this time, and when Catherine reached out for her hand she pulled it away.

'It's all right, I'm all right, I'm . . .' She pulled a tissue from her pocket and blew her nose, brushed the tears from her cheeks.

'I'm sorry to put you through this,' Catherine said, 'but there's just one more thing.'

'Go on.'

'When you thought your mum had taken your father at his word and gone, did you ever think she might have gone with somebody else?'

'Another man, you mean?'

'Yes.'

'Later, maybe. When, you know, I was older. But at the time, no, I don't think I ever did.'

'And when you thought, later on like you said, that perhaps it was a possibility, was there anyone in particular you thought it might have been?'

'No. Not at all.'

'That wasn't one of the things they argued about?'

'Mum seeing someone else? No. It was always the strike, the Welfare, the soup kitchen, all the time she was spending with all of that. Time he thought she should have been spending at home. With him. With us. Your kids, he'd say, my dad, your so-and-so kids, it's a wonder they still know who you so-and-so are.'

'And did you feel that? That your mum was perhaps ignoring you?'

Mary hesitated before answering. 'Yes. Yes, I suppose I did.'

Catherine walked with her to the edge of the park; brighter now – the sun had really broken through.

'What time's your flight?' Catherine asked.

'Not till this afternoon.'

'You'll be glad to be home.'

'Yes, I will. But you'll keep in touch? If you find out what . . . what happened, you'll let me know?'

'You and the rest of the family, as soon as ever we have something definite, yes, of course.'

'Thank you.'

Mary forced a smile and Catherine found herself

wanting to reach out and give her a parting hug but instead kept her hands by her sides.

'Just one more thing,' she said. 'Your friend, Nicky, if you could let me have an address? It's just possible we might want to talk to her – fill in some background, someone else who knew the family back then . . .'

'Why not?' Mary said. 'I'm sure Nicky wouldn't mind. And, after all, it can't do any harm.'

24

All Paul Bryant wanted to talk about, at first anyway, was the VW T25 camper van he'd picked up second-hand. 'Good as new, Charlie, no more than fifteen thousand miles on the clock. And a real beauty.'

Patient, Resnick allowed himself to be led through a litany of features that seemed to run from profession-ally lowered suspension and Porsche Fuchs aluminum wheels to an extra-long hook-up cable for campsite use and a twin gas hob and grill.

It had been late afternoon, shading into evening, when Resnick had arrived at the bungalow where Paul Bryant and his wife, Barbara, lived, some five miles outside Sheffield, not far from Hathersage and the Dark Peak. The van was parked ceremoniously out front, dwarfing the flower beds to either side.

'All you have to do, Charlie,' Barbara Bryant said, 'nod your head every so often and throw in the occasional grunt of appreciation. Sooner or later he'll wind down and you can talk about normal stuff like football or the price of a pint.'

One of the few police marriages Resnick knew that had survived; that it had was due in no small measure to Barbara's straight talking, sense of humour and innate good sense. A youngish PC when she and Paul had met, once she had realised things were going to become serious between them, she had left the force and retrained as a nurse. Just two months ago, she had retired from her post as senior sister in the neonatal unit at the Northern General Hospital in Sheffield. Resnick had met her no more than half a dozen times over the years and on each occasion found her more impressive than before.

'Not so long now, Charlie,' Paul Bryant said, settling into an armchair, 'and we're off down to Spain. Break the journey going down through France, bit of time in the Camargue, and then it's the foothills of the Sierra Nevada.'

Across the room, Barbara raised an eyebrow and kept her own counsel.

'What about you, Charlie?' Bryant asked. 'Got to kick it all into touch one day. What then?'

Resnick gestured with open hands. Who knows?

'Charlie,' Barbara said, sitting forward, 'what happened to Lynn, I've not seen you since then. I'm really sorry. It must have been awful, an awful thing.'

'Thanks.'

'And hard to move on.'

'Yes.'

'But we do. And you'll stay to supper, Charlie. Lamb. I can't imagine you've gone vegetarian. If Paul can prise himself up out of that chair, there's beer in the kitchen. Or tea, if you'd rather.'

He opted for beer. Oldershaw Great Expectations from Lincolnshire.

'Not entirely a social call,' Bryant said. 'That's what you said when you rang.'

Resnick nodded. 'Donna Crowder, eighty-seven. You were what, number two in that investigation?'

'Yes. Rawsthorne, the late lamented, was SIO.'

Succinctly as he could, Resnick filled him in on the details of Jenny Hardwick's murder; told him about Trevor Fleetwood and his assumptions, linking the two crimes together.

Bryant listened with interest, belatedly snapped the cap from his bottle of beer. 'Michael Swann, there's nothing to suggest – other than what Fleetwood says – that he might have been responsible?'

Resnick shook his head. 'Not so far.'

'Swann's victims, as I remember, they were all sexually assaulted prior to being killed?'

'Yes.'

'All attacked in the same way?'

'With escalating severity, yes.'

'Whereas in Donna Crowder's case there were no signs of sexual assault at all.'

'To which Fleetwood would doubtless say he was building up to it, becoming bolder, more excited, less in control.'

Bryant shook his head. 'I don't know, Charlie, it looks a pretty cockamamie theory to me.'

'Maybe. But he's been digging around this for a long time. Done his research, or so it seems.'

'Found what suits him.'

'Which doesn't necessarily mean it's wrong.'

Bryant poured his beer, taking care to tilt the glass.

'You believe him, then?'

'That's not what I'm saying.'

'You wouldn't have come all the way out here . . .'

'Hadn't seen you and Barbara in too long.'

'Bollocks!'

'Okay, Fleetwood's idea, I don't swallow it whole, no. But the way I see it, I've got to be interested. That, at least. Twenty-nine years – it's one hell of a long time and we're in danger of getting stuck.'

'Just as we were, back then.'

'Worse now. Too many people dead or moved away, difficult to find. Your investigation must have been up and running within days . . .'

'Didn't help us any.'

'You'll have had an idea, though, a serious suspect or two. We don't have that, not even close.'

'Oh, yes . . .' Bryant tasted his beer, made an appreciative face. 'For a good while, we thought it was the boyfriend. Seemed to be right in the frame. Early twenties, local, even had a little form – nothing major, but form just the same. Wayne, Wayne Cameron. Bit of a cowboy sort of name.'

'Wayne Fontana,' Barbara called from the kitchen.

'What about him?'

'Wayne Fontana and the Mindbenders,' she said from the doorway. 'I bet that's who he was named after. Sixties, for a lad, if it wasn't John, Paul or George it was some other pop group you got called after. Mind you, not a lot of Ringos. And, come to think of it, Fontana might have been later. "Game of Love"? Unless your Wayne's a bit older than you thought.'

'You know what?' Bryant said. 'Either way, I don't think it matters.'

'You mean, I should . . .?' She pointed back towards the kitchen.

Bryant laughed. 'I think that'd be a good idea, don't you?'

'Let you two get on. Men's talk.'

'Absolutely.'

'Okay, then.' An indulgent smile and she was gone.

'Bungalows, Charlie,' Bryant said. 'Not big on privacy. She'll be clocking every word we say.'

Resnick laughed. 'What's it going to be like in the van?'

Bryant rolled his eyes.

'Anyway,' Resnick said, 'this Wayne . . .'

'Yes, right. Him and Donna, they'd a humdinger of a row that evening, witnesses galore. He'd gone round to her place, early on, expecting her to go out with him, and there she was, dolled up to the nines, off into Sheffield with her mates. Right to-do. Effing and blinding. Would have clipped her one if others hadn't interfered. Walk out that door an' you'll live to fuckin' regret it. His very words. Course, poor lass, she never did.'

He paused, lifted his glass.

'We questioned him as soon as we knew she'd gone missing. After she was found, of course, brought him in again. Reckoned he'd been drinking, one or two pubs, town centre, which checked out, more or less. After that, drove round in his mate's car for a while, showed up in another pub later, the pair of them, not so far off closing time. After that, according to his story, he went back home to bed. Living with just his dad, mother had moved out long since.'

'And the father backs up his story?'

'Heard him come in, couldn't swear to the time. Not a lot of love lost between the pair of them, truth to tell.'

'You mentioned his mate's car – he didn't have a car of his own?'

'Borrowed his old man's from time to time. When they were speaking.'

'And that evening?'

'Father'd used it himself earlier. Wayne could've taken it later, gone off looking for Donna. Nothing we could ever prove.'

'She was killed how?'

'Blow or blows with a heavy object to the back of the head.'

Resnick nodded. 'Jenny Hardwick, the same.'

'Dragged the river searching for something the killer might have used and thrown away. From the nature of the wound, some kind of implement, hammer, maybe, iron bar. DNA testing was seriously starting just about then – a year later, you'll remember, Charlie, eighty-eight, those murders down in Leicestershire, first time it was used to secure a conviction – but in the end we came up with nothing. Nothing to say he saw her again after she left for Sheffield early that evening.'

'This Wayne, he's still around?'

Bryant shook his head. 'Less than three years later, motorway pile-up, six of them in a Ford Fiesta, two up front, four in back. Wayne had been sitting next to the driver, no seat belt – almost goes without saying – killed outright. One of the four in the back got a broken neck, serious injuries the rest of them. Driver walked away scot-free, barely a scratch.' Bryant shook his head. 'Makes you wonder.'

'Angel looking over him.' Barbara's voice from the kitchen.

'You still earwigging?'

'Turning these chops, that's what I'm doing. Eating in just about five minutes. Paul, you'd better get that table laid.'

'The driver,' Resnick said, 'just to round off the story . . .'

'Other vehicles involved, blame difficult to assign. First off, far as I know, they were going for manslaughter, but that was dropped down to dangerous driving. Eighteen months and disqualification from driving. Maybe got off easy.'

'Least he was alive.'

'Still is, far as I know.'

'Grub's up!' Barbara called. 'Charlie, you want another beer?'

'Best not.'

'Wise. And no more cop talk till we finish eating, okay?'

'What d'you want to do?' Bryant said. 'Talk about babies instead?'

Swivelling, she gave him a quick peck on the back of the neck. 'Left it a bit late for that, sweetheart. Not that I'd put it past you for trying.'

* * *

'What d'you reckon then, Charlie?' Paul Bryant asked. 'Michael Swann. Going to take it any further?'

They were outside, affording Bryant the opportunity for a runty little post-supper cigar. Clouds swivelled around the moon overhead; a scattering of stars, distant, indistinct.

'Might run with it a while longer.'

'Similarities aside, not a lot else linking him in with Donna, your lass neither. Distance, especially. Not his area at all. North-west, isn't that right?'

Resnick nodded. 'Fleetwood will have concocted some theory for that as well, I don't doubt.'

'He's not said?'

'Playing his cards close to his chest.'

'SIO in the Swann inquiry, you'll be talking to him next?'

'Can't do any harm.'

Bryant took a last pull at his cigar before stubbing it out. 'Now you've got me interested, keep me in the loop. Let me know how it pans out.'

'I'll send you a postcard to Spain.'

'I just hope, Charlie Resnick,' Barbara said, over their shoulders, 'you're not thinking of sneaking off without giving me a hug.'

'Wouldn't think of it.'

She held him close. 'Look after yourself, you big ox.'

'I'll do that.'

Before he'd gone as much as a mile down the road, there were tears nudging at the corners of his eyes, waiting to be blinked away. Other people's happiness, it could be a bastard at times.

25

Jenny's parents had been driving over to see them, just the second time since they'd moved out to Ingoldmells.

'Twelve we should be there by,' her mother had said, 'twelve or thereabouts. Lunchtime, I suppose. Don't you go bothering for us, though, just a nice cup of tea. I dare say we'll stop and have a sandwich on the way.'

Jenny had had to smile. What was it, eighty miles? A couple of hours' drive from the coast? Couldn't be much more, even in a clapped-out old car like theirs. But for her mother, ever since Jenny and her sister Jill were little, any and every journey, anything more than a quick visit to friends in the next village, or the weekly trip to the Co-op in Worksop, had to be planned like a major campaign. Sandwiches, a flask of tea, orange squash for the girls, a blanket in case it got cold or they wanted to sit on the grass by the side of the road; always some plasters and a little round tin of Germolene – her mum's favourite cure-all antiseptic – on the off chance anyone should cut themselves or fall and graze a knee; and, of course, a jerrycan full of petrol in the boot. If her mother had been in charge of Captain Scott's expedition to the Pole, Jenny sometimes thought, it might not have been the brave disaster it turned out to be.

By twelve o'clock, however, there was no sign.

Twelve-thirty.

One.

After dropping the kids off at school that morning, Jenny had popped in at the Welfare, explained to Edna she'd not be there in the middle of the day.

She was hanging out the washing – a decent wind, even though it was a shade overcast – when she heard the phone. Her mother's voice, strangely distant. They'd been stopped by police on the A57, just short of the county boundary. Stopped and turned back. Along with practically everyone else. Her dad had protested, told them straight out they didn't have the right. Police state, that was what he'd said, what it was coming to. If I hadn't pulled him away, her mum said, I think they'd have arrested him, there and then.

In the end they'd turned round and come back home – what else could they do? Next time, they'd come by bus, bus from Lincoln. Police wouldn't turn that back, surely? Not public transport.

Some words about the children – Brian's cold, Mary's funny tummy, Colin getting into trouble at school – and Jenny set down the phone, time to start thinking about what they were all having for tea. Something more substantial for Barry when he got back off shift.

'Not still making his meals for him, surely?' one of the women from the support group had said. 'Starve him out, that's what you want to do. Either that or let him make his own.'

'Likely be the same thing,' said someone else.

Jenny knew it wasn't that simple. It was only because Barry was still working, bringing home good wages, that there was food on the table. Ample compared to many that she knew.

'There!' Barry had said, just a few days before, slapping his wage packet down in front of her. 'Take it, go on, take it. Take your bloody housekeepin' and spend it putting food in our kids' bellies an' clothes on their backs, then fuck off down the Welfare and tell folk them as carry on working are no' but scabs and traitors. It's a wonder the words don't curdle in your mouth and make you sick.'

And that evening, when Peter Waites, half-jokingly she thought, had invited her to join them up on the platform, she had shaken her head and declined.

'Nowt amiss?' he'd asked later, last knockings and the crowd beginning to clear.

'No, no. Just a bit off colour, that's all.'

'Women's troubles, then, is it?'

'Fuck off, Peter,' she'd said and laughed.

Now, with the kids due back any moment, Colin and Mary between them with the task of picking up young Brian from the nursery class and shepherding him home, Jenny was caught wondering about the future – their future, hers and Barry's – what it might be like when finally the strike was over, as one day surely it must be, and some kind of normality returned.

How possible would it be for them to pick up where they'd left off, carry on as before?

And if it were, was that what she wanted?

What she wanted now?

She shook her head.

There was mince, there were onions, a carrot or two, potatoes; in an hour or so there would be cottage pie.

26

The spadework went on. Snippets of information filtered from the various interviews that had been carried out were recorded, cross-referenced, assessed for further action. A picture of life in Bledwell Vale three decades previously, in so far as it involved Jenny and Barry Hardwick, their colleagues, their adversaries and their family, began, bit by bit, to emerge. Names of people who were now well scattered, some deceased. Addresses to be searched for, phone calls to be made.

Just as gradually, perhaps more so, a timetable of the work carried out at the rear of the Peterson house, where Jenny's body had been found, was taking shape; what had proved impossible to compile so far was a list of names of those who'd worked with Geoff Cartwright on the job. One or two names only, and those at second-hand.

Cartwright himself, it had now been confirmed, had, indeed, emigrated to Canada in the late eighties and had been granted citizenship in 1996. From the records, he had married an Ingrid Marshall in 1993 and the couple had divorced in 2002. Having moved on from Alberta, Cartwright's last known address was in the province of Saskatchewan, but that was now three years old. Liaison with the Royal Canadian Mounted Police was continuing.

A Danny Ireland, meanwhile, had been placed at an address in Fort William, on the west coast of Scotland.

McBride found Alex Sandford at the drinks machine, about to give it a good kicking for ingesting his small change when he was seeking something warm and wet to help digest his energy bar and giving out nothing in return.

'Much as I'd like to be revisiting the land of the brave, it'll be your good fortune, yours and Cresswell's, to make that journey instead. Make sure to call the local force beforehand, let them know you're coming. Wouldn't like to see you arrested for trespassing in what, to all intents and purposes, is a sovereign country.'

When McBride arrived back at his desk, it was to find Catherine Njoroge waiting.

'Michael Swann, mean anything?'

McBride shook his head.

'Sentenced for three murders, nineteen ninety-seven. Warrington, Preston, Carlisle. Perhaps you could dig out some basic information. I imagine more than one force would have been involved, initially at least, but it would be good to know who was in charge of the overall investigation.'

'And this is needed, boss, because . . .?'

Catherine just stopped herself saying because I say so. 'Because it may be relevant to our inquiry,' she said.

'Prioritise this, should I, then or . . .?'

'End of the day would be good. Or sooner.'

'See what I can do, boss.'

'You do that, Sergeant.' She knew she probably shouldn't have said that either. Hated the way McBride, with just a look, a turn of phrase, could get under her skin. And knew it, too. Relished it, even.

Resnick had tried the mobile number Fleetwood had given him three times without success. It was mid-afternoon when Fleetwood called him.

'Now you've had time to mull it over, do some basic checks,' he said, before Resnick had the chance to speak, 'what do you think?'

'I'm not convinced.'

'Who've you spoken to so far?'

'What makes you think I've talked to anyone?'

'You rang me. I doubt you'd be doing that if you were kicking it out of court completely.'

'Maybe not.'

'Bryant, have you spoken to him?'

Resnick said that he had.

'A good copper. Solid, as far as that goes. But not, I suspect, with a great deal of imagination.'

'As a theory, Michael Swann – let's just say he wasn't over-impressed.'

'Now there's a surprise.'

'It's the location,' Resnick said. 'That's what it comes down to. It just feels wrong. Breaks the pattern. South Yorkshire, North Notts. Both a long way from the M6.'

There was a pause before Fleetwood spoke again.

'There is something. You'd find out for yourself, sooner or later. Always supposing you went ahead.'

'I'm listening.'

'For several periods between nineteen eighty-four and nineteen eighty-eight, Michael Swann worked as a minicab driver in Sheffield. Easy reach of where both Jenny Hardwick and Donna Crowder were killed.'

'Why didn't you tell me that before?'

'I thought, if you were taking me as seriously as you should, you'd have found out for yourself.'

Before Resnick could reply, he had broken the connection.

'He's playing games,' Catherine said. 'Wants to feel in control.'

They were sitting on open ground by the canal, a racket of crows rising and falling from the trees nearby. Catherine sucking an extra-strong mint in lieu of a cigarette, trying not to crack it too soon with her teeth; Resnick sat with a takeout cup of coffee, grown cold. Beyond the trees they could just see the old fire station tower and the blue-grey flour mills behind.

'He's messing us around, Charlie.'

'From his point of view, there's little use him laying out what he knows, step by step. Not without sufficient back-up, corroboration. What he wants is for us to find out for ourselves. Give it credibility. That's what he needs.'

'His problem, not ours.'

'Agreed. But as long as it might help . . .'

'You think we should push on further, then?'

'It's a line of inquiry. Legitimate, I'd say. And, right now, we're not exactly overwhelmed with other possibilities. Besides, if we ignore it, and it turns out he was right all along . . .'

Attracted by the silver on the wrapper from Catherine's mints, which had fallen to the ground and been blown a short way off by the wind, a large crow hopped warily towards it, picked it up in its beak and carried it away into the trees.

'See you tomorrow, then, Charlie,' Catherine said.

'Tomorrow.'

* * *

186

When Catherine got back to the police station in Potter Street, McBride had already gone, a red-and-yellow scarf – a football scarf, she supposed – dangling from the back of his chair.

A manila folder lay on the desk, the name Michael Swann printed in biro on the top right corner. Inside, a printout summarising the investigations into the murders for which he had been convicted. Catherine had been right – at various stages three forces had been involved: Cumbria, Lancashire and Cheshire. Once it had become clear the three murders were linked, overall control of the investigation had passed to Detective Chief Superintendent Arthur Hodgson from the Lancashire force, with a detective superintendent, Steven Walcott, from Cumbria as his deputy.

In total, some twelve thousand statements were taken over the entire period, from Kim Bucknall's murder in 1989 to Swann's arrest in January of 1997, a significant proportion of those owners of silver Ford Sierras, that make of vehicle having been identified in the proximity of two of the attacks.

Semen samples taken from the scene of the second murder were, at the time, too small to allow the extraction of a DNA profile that could be used in court.

Possible suspects – close to three hundred at one stage – were checked for criminal records, questioned and statemented, alibis verified, each item of information cross-indexed. There were still as many as forty people under serious consideration when Swann carried out an attack on a young woman in a lay-by on the A56, south of Altrincham. The woman fought back, injuring Swann quite badly in his left eye, and ran out to the road, signalling for help. Several vehicles stopped, in one of which was an off-duty policeman. When Swann attempted to drive away he was blocked in and held until being put under arrest.

After which, it all fell into place. As in so many instances, Catherine thought, a mixture of diligence and good fortune. And a young woman with the wit and courage to make use of the tweezers in her handbag.

Catherine put Arthur Hodgson's name into the computer.

He had retired, with his wife, to Portugal at the turn of the century and suffered a fatal heart attack on the golf course just a few days shy of his seventieth birthday.

Steven Walcott had also retired, comparatively recently, from the post of Deputy Chief Constable for Lincolnshire, and was living in a village in the Wolds, between Louth and Market Rasen.

Catherine switched off the computer, put the folder in her bag and switched off the overhead light. She'd call Resnick later, pass on the news, arrange to meet.

27

Resnick had made this journey before, in part anyway, the slow drift through the Wolds, eastwards towards the sea. A young girl had disappeared from the swings in the small park in Lenton, no more than a stone's throw from her home. Gloria Summers, six years old. She had lived, much of the time, with her grandmother, and it was to visit the grandmother that Resnick had been driving, a little over two months later, to tell her that Gloria had at last been found. A disused warehouse, close by the canal. The child's body, partly decomposed, wrapped in bin bags in the wasted dark.

The grandmother had crumpled in front of him when told, the air sucked out of her, blood running cold.

Resnick had offered the usual platitudes, the patted hand, the cup of sweet tea. Had stayed too long, forcing himself, anxious to be away. He could have sent somebody else, should have, perhaps, the coward's way.

'Thank you for coming. Telling me yourself . . .'

All the way back he had tried to erase it from his mind, the feeling of blame haunting her eyes.

'What happened,' Resnick had told her, 'it wasn't your fault.'

She would never believe him. Five minutes, she had looked away. A child in a busy park, the middle of the day.

'Charlie . . .' Catherine's voice jolted him back into the present. 'What is it?'

'Nothing.'

'Something's worrying you.'

'No, nothing. I'm fine.'

'You're such a liar.'

Embarrassed, even though the air conditioning was on he wound down his window far enough to feel the wind on his face. Trees either side of the narrow road. The land gently undulating. A patchwork of fields. Several miles since they'd seen another person, passed another car. Birds overhead, the only other things moving. Even the few beasts in the fields were still: recumbent, replete.

'You ever think about it, Charlie?'

'What's that?'

'The country. Retiring.'

'Not really.'

'Seems as if everyone else has. Sell up, move out. Certainly the thing to do where police are concerned. Keith Haines and now this. Walcott. I shall begin to feel like that woman if we do much more of this.'

'Woman?'

'You know, always on afternoon TV. Not that I ever watch afternoon TV, of course. Beeny? Sarah Beeny?'

'What I remember, you don't look much like Sarah Beeny.'

'Very funny. But you know what I mean. Senior police officer, good pension, wants to swap house in the city for quiet retirement property in the country. That sort of thing.'

'Maybe you've missed your calling?'

'Television?'

'Real estate.'

'God, Charlie, I hope not.'

So did Resnick, no great admirer of estate agents since his former wife had run off with one. A line from a book he'd started reading and never managed to finish came back to him. Something about it being the only job that gave you the licence to spend the afternoons making love in other people's beds.

'How much further?' he asked.

'According to satnav not far at all.'

The house was not that attractive, truth be told; but a charming little cottage, that's what it would doubtless have been called, the usual estate agent's tendency to see the best in everything. Brick built and square looking, red-tiled roof, small windows, green door; solid enough, but with a distinct lean to one side.

Its saving grace was the location: the edge of the village, some way back off the road, garden on three sides, two of them set to lawn. Generous shrubs, towards the rear a small stand of fruit trees, apple and pear. A state-of-the-art water butt decanting into a small pond.

The dog had started barking when they were still out of sight, back around the curve in the road.

Grace Walcott was up a ladder, renewing the creosote on the fence at the garden's edge. Beyond it, a ploughed field rose up towards a coppice of beech. Attractive enough, at that moment, to make Resnick think settling in the countryside might not be so bad after all. If the weather held, he might be able to stick it out for as much as a month, maybe even six weeks.

Seeing them arrive, Grace Walcott was nimbly down the ladder, a tall woman, trimly built, greying hair tied with a ribbon, dungarees, what looked like a man's collarless shirt, bare feet.

'You must be Catherine. Or should I say Detective Inspector Njoroge? Did I say that correctly?'

'Perfectly. And Catherine's fine.'

'Grace.' They shook hands.

'And it's Inspector Resnick?'

'Charlie.'

'Well, Charlie, you're welcome. My husband's out back, pursuing his new career. Or so he'd have us think. Come on, I'll take you round, then put some coffee on. You'd both like coffee, I suppose? And Frido, if you don't stop that stupid barking I'll take you off to the kennels and leave you there.'

Steven Walcott was sitting behind a small easel, a selection of watercolours on the stool alongside, painting the view above the hedge and along the sloping field to the trees at the top. Layers, overlapping, varying shades of brown overlaid with a tinge of lavender, a few lines of paler green higher up and then the brighter blue of the sky. Yesterday's, perhaps, not today's. Artist's licence. To Resnick it seemed competent, that at least.

'Not bad, eh?' Walcott grinned. 'From DCC down to Constable in no time at all.'

Quick to the reference, Catherine smiled.

'Not that this is anything like the real Constable, of course. *The Hay Wain* and all that. *Flatford Mill*. Can't do figures at all, not yet. End up looking like bloody Lowry. Stick men in bowler hats. Still, considering I'd never as much as picked up a brush till six months back, it's passable. Just about.'

Resnick was thinking of Keith Haines' wife, begged not to enter the local art show on account of being too good for the rest of the competition. Compared to that, Walcott had a way to go.

'Coffee out here, or d'you want to come inside?' his wife called.

'I think out here would be fine. Okay with you two?'

It was. A couple of extra chairs were found. Coffee in a cafetière, warm milk in a jug; almond biscuits, crisp at the edges; brown sugar.

'When we spoke on the phone,' Walcott said, addressing Catherine, 'you said – implied anyway – there might be a connection between Michael Swann and your current investigation. Jenny Hardwick, have I got that right? Presumed murdered as far back as nineteen eighty-four, the body only recently surfaced.'

'That's correct.'

'You think there's some chance Swann might have been responsible?'

'At this moment, we're just exploring the possibility . . .'

'Similarities?'

'Physical, certainly. The victim conforms to his preferred type. Plus the manner in which she was killed, the body disposed of.'

'Swann's other victims, they were all picked up on the road, taken somewhere quiet, sexually assaulted.'

'In this case, because of the length of time before the body was discovered, we've no way of knowing if sexual assault took place. Nor do we know very much, if anything, about the circumstances. She could have been picked up like the others and then taken to the house, either before or after she was killed. We know it was unoccupied at the time.'

'You don't mind me saying, that's one hell of a stretch. Awful lot of supposition. And that's without your crime scene being a good hundred miles at least from where Swann's known to have operated.'

'There is another possible connection,' Resnick said. 'Donna Crowder. Found murdered outside Rotherham three years later, eighty-seven. Link that to Jenny Hardwick and you've got two victims in the same area, same time span.'

At the mention of Donna Crowder, Walcott's expression had changed. 'This is that moron Fleetwood, isn't it?'

'Moron?'

'All right, too much of a pain in the behind to be that, too clever by half in fact, but that's who this is, right? Peddling his sorry-arsed stories for all he's worth.'

'You know him, then?'

'Know him? Drove me half bloody crazy once upon a time. Pestering me with letters, phone calls. Calling round where we used to live, unannounced. Did I think Swann had any other victims, prior to those he'd been convicted of killing? Surely Kim Bucknall couldn't have been the first? Practically stalking me at one time, couldn't go to the bloody supermarket without him turning up in the car park, just wanting to ask a few more questions, would I take the time to read this, that or the other.'

Walcott drew breath; broke a biscuit in half and dunked it in his coffee.

'This was all a while ago, mind. Thought he'd given up, found another poor dead bastard to carve a living from. But then, I suppose when your Jenny turned up, that was enough to get him excited all over again. Couldn't believe his luck. Not one but two unsolved murders. Attach those to a serial killer already behind bars and some publisher's got to be interested, slap another thousand or two on the advance.'

'And the first time he came to you,' Catherine asked, 'that was when?'

'At the trial.'

'You didn't think there was anything to it, the possibility that Swann had killed before?'

'Possibility, of course. But we already had Swann stone cold for three murders. The evidence of the Altrincham woman. Forensics – a blood sample with Lisa Plackett's DNA found in the silver Sierra he'd sold on. A confession of sorts, even though he tried to claw it back. Why muddy the waters? That would have been the CPS's verdict, you can be certain. Less wriggle room you give his brief the better.'

'According to Fleetwood,' Resnick said, 'Swann was based in Sheffield when the Crowder murder took place. Driving a minicab. Jenny Hardwick, too.'

'He tried that one on us, I remember. Went so far as to try checking it out. But by then, ninety-seven, we were a good ten years on. Short memories, insufficient records. Sometimes none. Nothing we found told us Swann was in Sheffield at all, let alone driving a cab.'

'Figment of Fleetwood's imagination, then?'

'He's a writer – why not?'

'Fact, not fiction.'

'So he'd have us believe.'

'You really think he pulled it out of clean air, just to help his story?'

'He might. Might well. I'd not put it past him. But if there was any provenance, it'd be Swann himself, I imagine.'

'They were in touch?' Catherine said. 'Fleetwood and Swann?'

'For a spell, yes, I believe so. I think Swan thought Fleetwood was going to write him up as some kind of folk hero, Jack the Ripper with a heart of gold. Either that or help him with his parole. When it turned out to be neither, he lost interest. As far as I know, refused to see Fleetwood again.'

The dog started barking. A car passing along the road.

'Anyone for a top-up?' Grace Walcott said, indicating the cafetière.

'Just a little,' Resnick said. 'Half a cup? Then we should probably get going.'

Catherine rested her hand, palm down, across the top of her cup and shook her head. 'No, thank you. Charlie's right, we've taken enough of your time.'

'Not exactly pressed,' Grace Walcott said with a smile. 'Neither of us. That's the beauty of it. Your own little bubble.'

'You don't miss the bright lights?' Catherine said. 'Shops? Restaurants? All the bustle?'

'If we do, there's always Louth.'

She laughed and Catherine joined in, without knowing exactly why.

Resnick kept silent. He'd been to Louth more than a few times and couldn't think of anything about it that was remotely funny.

'When he was caught,' Catherine said, 'Swann, would he have been high on your list of suspects?'

Walcott gave a quick self-conscious smile. 'Not even in the mix. We had interviewed him once, mind, some few years before, trawling through registered Sierra owners. Nothing to set anyone's antennae twitching.'

'The other suspects, though, they were serious? Serious possibilities?'

A shrug. 'Some, maybe. A dozen. Previous form

for GBH. Domestic violence. Accusations of rape. It's all there, somewhere, in the files. Before HOLMES 2, of course, so not all neatly indexed, analysed. But it's there, if you want it.'

Catherine smiled. 'Thanks for your time.'

'Not a problem.'

They shook hands, Resnick likewise. Walked around the building, back towards the road, she and Walcott side by side.

'Swann,' she said as they reached the gate. 'What's he like?'

'After all that time inside, who's to say?'

'But then?'

Walcott smiled. 'Quiet, unassuming. Bookish, even. Docile. Sort of bloke, if you were stuck somewhere, car broken down by the side of the road, Swann came by and offered you a lift, just to the nearest garage, anything to help, you might think, okay, why not? No real risk. No risk at all.'

28

Danny shins up the wall alongside the factory building and drops down into an alley on the other side. Old-fashioned cobbles, bins, a broken bicycle wheel. Backs of houses: two up, two down. One way seems to lead back in the direction from which he's come, the other narrowing down towards what might be an opening out into a patch of waste ground; from there it's hard to tell. Shouts ring out behind him, the sound of boots on hard paving, moving fast. Pickets, police, running in all directions. He'll take a chance.

Thirty, forty yards off he sees it's not an opening at all: at the end of the ginnel is a wire fence, some twelve feet high, blocking entry to the scrapyard beyond.

The sounds of pursuit are coming closer; over his

shoulder, two uniformed police, running fast. Poised on the wall behind them, a police Alsatian with its handler, about to leap down.

Danny puts on speed, hurls himself at the fence, jumping as he leaves the ground.

His fingers clasp the wire, feet seek purchase, slide away, swing back.

The wire is cutting into his hands.

'Get hold of the bastard!'

Danny starts to climb.

'Get down, you prick!'

A hand grabs at his ankle and he kicks it away.

Hauls himself higher.

The scrapyard crammed with rusting pieces of machinery, car tyres, the carcasses of old tractors, pallets stacked one above the other in uneven piles.

'Get back fuckin' down here or I'll set dog on you!'

Danny reaches for the top of the fence, catches hold and clings fast.

'Fuck you!' he shouts. 'And fuck your dog!'

The dog jumps.

As Danny tries to swing one leg over the top of the fence, two of the police take hold of the fencing lower down and start to shake it, in and out, hard as they can.

Danny nearly loses his grip; his trouserleg catches against a piece of wire sticking loose from the top of the fence and rips.

They're banging the fence with their batons now. Shouting at him to get down.

'Fuck you!' he shouts again, but one hand comes away and he swings wildly round. Just three fingers clinging on, taking all his weight, wire through skin. The dog jumps up and sinks its teeth into his leg above the ankle.

Pain sears through him, sharp, intense.

'Got you, you fucker!'

He falls with a crunch to his knees, can feel bone splintering, the dog still not letting go. Growling in the back of its throat until its handler makes the signal and it backs a short distance away. Hands on the cobbled surface, Danny pushes himself upwards but he can't move. Tries again and one of his legs gives way. Grabs sideways at the fence and misses. Falls.

One of the policemen laughs.

'Bloody spastic!' says another.

They haul him to his feet and hold him there.

'Good news, sunshine. You're under fucking arrest.'

The voice isn't local. London, maybe? Kent? He looks for the number on the officer's uniform like he's been told, but can't see one.

Groggy, he makes a sound in his throat as if he's going to spit, spit in the officer's face, and the officer knees him in the groin, grabs hold of him as he lurches forward and spins him round, thrusting him fast against the fencing so that the wire cuts into his face.

One of the others yanks his arms round behind him and cuffs his wrists.

'Result!' says the officer with a laugh.

Danny is put in a holding cell with nine others, taken out to be questioned – questions he largely refuses to answer.

'The advice from my union,' he says, 'is not to speak to police or make a written statement about any picket I may have been taking part in before seeing a strike committee official or a lawyer.'

The words don't sound right on his tongue.

'Never mind your union's advice,' says one of the two police officers sitting opposite. 'Do yourself a favour and stop being such a prat. Sooner you play along, sooner you'll be out of here and home.'

He says it with a smile on his face, friendly-like.

'I'm not saying owt,' Danny says.

'Suit yourself.'

He's taken back to the cell. Brought back. Questioned. Nothing. Fingerprinted and his photograph taken.

Next morning, taken before the magistrate.

One charge of using threatening words and behaviour, another of obstructing a police officer in the course of his duty, one of common assault.

Unconditional bail refused.

Almost before he knows what's happening, Danny is released on the conditions that he remains resident at his given address, doesn't cross the county border into Nottinghamshire and at no time ventures within half a mile of any property or properties belonging to or rented by the National Coal Board.

He hitches his way home, feeling sick.

29

'And you were going to tell me fucking when?'

'Sir, I—'

'When?'

'I didn't want to raise the possibility of another line of inquiry without first—'

'Didn't want to say, more like, you were getting your fancy knickers in a twist over some hare-brained idea spun out of some bastard journalist's head.'

'Sir, I—'

'Shut it! Just fucking shut it, okay?'

Okay. Catherine drew breath, chanced a sideways glance at Resnick, exhaled. The atmosphere in Picard's office smelt of air freshener, over-brewed coffee, spite.

They had been summoned to Radford first thing, the detective chief inspector's office; no pleasantries, no pack drill, just a straightforward bollocking, simple and pure.

Resnick shifted his balance from one foot to the other, mind running through the twenty or so places he'd rather be that moment than here.

'You'll remember,' Picard said, his eyes focused on Catherine, 'a conversation in this office. Keep in touch, anything you're concerned about, unsure of, run it by me.'

'Yes, sir.'

'You do remember?'

'Yes, sir.'

'So, what? Somewhere along the line you forgot? Selective amnesia? Or maybe you just thought, fuck it, he's never going to know, never going to care, I'll just go my merry fucking way regardless. Was that it?'

'No, sir.' Catherine looking at the ground, the carpet, industrial grey, able to hold his gaze no longer.

'And you,' Picard said, turning his attention to Resnick, 'crystal clear, or so I'd thought. Low-key, that was the way to pitch it. The way it was going to be. Low-key.

'Your experience, I expected you to keep things in check, under control. No call to go stirring up more than necessary, more than was needed. Instead of which you go haring off, the pair of you, on some wild fucking goose chase, till you're up to your armpits in serial bloody killers. Michael fucking Swann – how d'you think that's going to play once the media get hold of it? Well? Throw your low-key out the fucking window then. Eyes of the country, eyes of half the fucking world. Some bastard Japanese TV crew making a documentary, poking their mini-fucking cameras up your nose.'

Catherine broke the silence that followed. 'With respect, sir—'

'Respect? What fucking respect?' Picard furious, red faced, spittle on his lips. 'Any respect you'd have okay'd this with me from the start, let me know what you were thinking, instead of leaving me high and dry, having to find out for myself elsewhere.'

'How exactly did you do that, sir? Find out, I mean?'

'Never you fucking mind.'

McBride, Catherine thought – either that or a quick phone call from Walcott. Top brass to top brass, Walcott to Hastings, Hastings to Picard. Her money was on McBride.

'What I don't understand, how the basics here could have got so forgotten. And don't –' seeing Catherine was about to interrupt – 'give me any more of that respect bollocks. My take on the case, what happened to Jenny Hardwick – not that you've had the sense of protocol to furnish me with anything approaching a proper briefing – the two prime suspects, two you should be looking at, two in the frame, that twat from Yorkshire she was fooling around with and her old man.'

He looked from one to the other. 'Care to disagree?'

Neither did. Not there and then. Far too simplistic, Catherine thought, keeping it to herself.

'The husband – Barry, is it? Where are we with him?'

'Still accumulating evidence, sir. Hearsay, largely. Hostility between the pair of them, husband and wife, that's clear. Mainly over the strike – major difference of opinion there – possibly over any relationship she might or might not have been having with somebody else. Been interviewed on two occasions, due to be again.'

'That's all?'

'Apart from an informal conversation at the funeral, yes, sir.'

Picard raised his eyes towards the ceiling. 'Beyond fucking belief.'

Catherine chanced another glance towards Resnick, who was tactfully looking away.

'The bloke she was shagging?' Picard said. 'How about him?'

If she was shagging, Catherine qualified for her own intents and purposes.

'Scotland, sir, last we heard. Fort William. Sandford and Cresswell are up there now. Seems he's moved on.'

'On? On where?'

'Not the type to leave forwarding addresses, I'm afraid. Gave them another twenty-four hours. If nothing, report back. Start over.'

'So they're yomping all over the Highlands and you two are – where was it last?'

'Lincolnshire.'

Picard raised his eyes to the heavens, shot his cuffs, settled back behind his desk.

'Detective Inspector, perhaps you wouldn't mind waiting outside for a few moments, allow Mr Resnick and me time for a few words?'

Catherine bridled, seemed about to argue, thought better of it. 'Thank you, sir.'

Time, while the door was closing, for Resnick to feel embarrassed on her behalf.

Picard stared him down.

'What's the matter, Charlie? Standing there like someone's stuck a red-hot poker up your arse.'

'It doesn't feel right, undermining the SIO in this way.'

'Leave the way I manage to me, Charlie, okay? Hold her hand afterwards, if you like. Cuddle her tits. Whatever it takes.'

Resnick said nothing, waited.

'Straight question then, Charlie. Two, to be precise. This Swann business, now you've poked your toe in, anything to it? Worth the fuss?'

Resnick took his time answering. 'Swann himself, doubtful. Wouldn't rule it out completely, but, on balance, I'd say unlikely. But there were other suspects that investigation turned up, a dozen at least, maybe more. Some of those might fit our profile, such as it is. A few more bodies, civilian staff maybe, we could chase them up, re-interview where necessary.'

'All right, but more bodies, unlikely – you should know the staffing situation as well as me. What was it? Last spending review? Another nine thousand jobs going, nationwide? Go down that route, you'll have to find a way of doing it with what you've got. My advice, get round Johnny McBride's good side, for God's sake, instead of rubbing him up the wrong side of his bloody sporran. He can be creative when needs be.'

Resnick nodded. 'Do what I can.'

'Second question. And I want a straight answer.' Picard gestured towards the door. 'Is she up to this or not?'

'She's fine.' No hesitation, looking Picard square in the eye.

'I hope to Christ you're right.'

Catherine was waiting at the end of the corridor, the head of the stairs. They walked down side by side.

As they emerged on to the street, someone called Catherine's name.

A tall man, handsome, in an expensively tailored suit, dark hair brushed back, olive skin, liquid brown eyes, five-hundred-pound shoes.

'Catherine, you haven't been returning my calls.'

30

Time stopped. The man standing in the middle of the pavement, assured, smiling. Catherine with a hand to her lips, not quite touching. Resnick, off to one side, uncertain, waiting.

A photograph: not seen, untaken.

'Abbas, you shouldn't do this.'

The merest of shrugs. 'You didn't answer my calls.'

'My choice, Abbas.'

'You could have been sick, taken ill, I didn't know, anything could have happened.'

'And if I were . . .?'

'Then, of course, I should know.'

'Sick, ill, whatever . . . whatever happens to me, Abbas, it is no concern of yours.'

'You know that's not true.' He moved forward quickly as he spoke, his hand circling her wrist.

'Abbas, let go.'

For all that she is tall, he is taller still. Well-muscled beneath the fine lines of his suit. Sleek, the word that comes to Resnick's mind as he watches.

'Abbas . . .'

He tightens his grip instead.

'I think you should let go,' Resnick says. 'Move away.'

There are people watching now, a few. A woman with a buggy across the street; an elderly man with a shopping trolley; a pair of uniformed officers hesitating on the police station steps.

'Who's this?' the man called Abbas says.

'Never mind,' Catherine says. 'Just go.'

'You're taking a turn for older men, perhaps? A change from the real thing.'

'Abbas, you're making a scene. Please go.'

'We need to talk.'

'We have nothing to say.'

His fingers are still around Catherine's wrist. Resnick puts a hand on his elbow and he knocks it away. One of the two uniformed officers has started to walk cautiously towards them. Two small children and a teenager in a grey hoodie, who may be in charge of them and may not, make their way along the opposite pavement, oblivious. One of the children points at the old man's shopping trolley and laughs. The woman with the buggy is still where she was, rooted to the spot, agog.

Resnick takes hold of the man's arm again and this time he doesn't let go.

The man stares at him, their faces close. Something aromatic on his breath.

Nothing else is said.

The man lets go of Catherine's wrist and turns away.

Pale marks like bone against her skin.

Something has passed between the man and Resnick in the moment before he released his grasp. A moment of recognition? A warning?

He has turned on his heel and walked away, the old man with the shopping trolley pulling it aside to let him pass.

'Everything okay?' the police constable enquires.

'Are you all right?' Resnick asks.

In response to both she nods her head. Determined, even though he can no longer see, not to let her former lover have the satisfaction of somehow knowing she is rubbing her wrist to ease the pain.

They found a pub near the town centre, open early, breakfast still being served, the smell of toast and bacon, cooking oil that had been used too many times, unchanged; a table outside, wrought-iron painted white, the kind you find in a garden centre; not warm out, no sun, but this was so that Catherine could smoke. Which she did, two cigarettes almost down to the filter, one after the other, no conversation. She'd asked for, and was halfway down, a large glass of white wine, while Resnick had opted for coffee and almost immediately regretted it, returning for a bottle of pale ale, an approximation, he supposed, of the old Worthington White Shield that bar staff more often than not had asked you to pour yourself, leery of its volatility.

'Abbas,' she said suddenly. 'I met him when I was at university. I was in my final year and he was doing an MBA. Secondment of some kind from the City bank where he'd been working. His family, they're Iranian. Some of them came over to this country after the revolution; some stayed. Abbas and his two brothers, they were all educated here. His older brother, he's a doctor, he went back to Iran. The youngest, like Abbas, stayed here. He's some kind of lawyer, solicitor, barrister by now, I'm not sure.'

She reached for her cigarettes, reconsidered, drank some more wine instead.

'I'm not used to men hitting on me. Not, you know, out of the blue . . .' A quick smile. 'Apparently men find me intimidating. Some men. Anyway, Abbas just came up to me – I was with some friends drinking coffee – came up and asked me out. As if it never occurred to him I might refuse.'

'So you didn't?'

'I didn't. And it was like that. Suddenly we were in a relationship. From nowhere. He'd seen me – one of his friends told me this later – he'd seen me walking across the campus and asked who I was. Decided he was going to have me. Marry me, that's what his friend said. He was going to marry me.'

'And did he?'

Catherine shook her head. 'No, but it all moved along so fast, there was a time when it just might have happened. One minute we were dating, spending practically every minute when he wasn't studying for his precious exams in one another's company. The next we were flying out to Tehran to meet that side of his family. My exams, my finals – looking back, it was as if they didn't matter. That I got the good result I did was up to all the work I'd done previously as much as anything.'

'So what went wrong?' Resnick asked.

A single-decker bus slowed to a standstill a stone's throw from where they were sitting, cloaking them in a fug of diesel.

'I saw the light – or, rather, I had some friends who saw it for me – realised I'd hardly made a decision of my own in months. Where to go, what to think, what to wear.'

'Doesn't sound like you.'

'It wasn't. That's the point. I broke it off. Tried to. He wasn't having it, of course. At first, he simply refused to believe me. Then did everything he could to change my mind. Maybe he thought he could buy me, I don't know. When it finally clicked that I was serious, he told me I was making the biggest mistake of my life and I'd regret it for ever.'

'And did you?'

'Sometimes. Yes, if I'm honest, there were things about him I missed. But now I had my degree and, of course, I didn't know exactly what I wanted to do with it. Made the usual half-hearted journey around the capitals of Europe, my gap year I suppose. Came back and joined the police. Shock horror from my parents. Why are you throwing away a good education, the usual sort of thing.'

'Abbas, what had they felt about him?'

'Well, of course, they thought he was marvellous. Well-to-do, beautifully mannered, rich and likely to get richer. A good family. A family of doctors and lawyers and bankers. They must have thought it was a perfect fit. Although, when we stopped seeing one another, I think – although they've never said it – I think secretly they were pleased. No, relieved.'

'Something about him they didn't like? Didn't trust?'

'Perhaps. I think, also, in some way they feared I was a little out of my depth.'

Resnick drank some more of his beer; asked Catherine if she wanted any more wine but she shook her head.

'All of that,' Resnick said, 'seems to have been quite a long time ago.'

'It was.'

'And now, suddenly, he's started calling, wanting to see you?'

Another smile, grudging this time. 'Not exactly. Abbas can be persuasive, as you can imagine. All he needs to do is catch you at a weaker moment and . . .' She gestured with her hands. 'I've seen him – I mean, we've been together, a couple, on several occasions since. Once for as little as three weeks, once, the last time, almost a year. It was not long after . . . not long after the investigation into Lynn's murder. I was feeling, I don't know, a bit low, I suppose, and Abbas did his usual thing of sweeping you into his orbit. You go along, and why not? It's fun, exciting. For a time you stop asking questions, and then, gradually, you do.'

She looked at Resnick, drank the last of her wine, looked away. Traffic sidled past. A young man of no more than twenty, face the parchment pale of the perpetually poor, came, hand out towards their table, mumbling something about needing his fare to Derby. Resnick gave him a handful of change and sent him on his way.

'This time he was nasty, threatening. Accused me of using him, telling lies. What was it? Spreading my legs for money like any other high-class tart. The last time I saw him, before today, he made one more effort to get me to change my mind, and when I wouldn't he called me a black whore and punched me here.'

She indicated a spot at the centre of her chest, a few inches below her breasts.

Resnick recalled the look that had passed between them, Abbas and himself.

'What will he do now?'

'I don't know. Try phoning again. Try to intercept me. Maybe nothing at all.'

'Does he know where you live?'

'Now? I don't think so. Otherwise he would have been unlikely to have come here.'

'He found that out somehow.'

'I imagine, if he gave a good enough reason, they'd tell him at HQ where I was stationed. But they'd never let him have my home address.' She looked at her watch. 'We should be getting going. Don't want to give Picard any more ammunition than we have to.'

A couple of sooty, ragged-tailed pigeons waddled towards their table as they left and went away disappointed.

31

The meeting had been called for Monday 8 October, speakers from the Kent coalfield, from Scotland and from Wales. Jenny had travelled down to Mansfield with Peter Waites, Edna Johnson and others. Five hundred striking miners in the hall, standing round the edges of the room some of them with all seats taken. Following the Labour Party's annual conference the previous week, at which Arthur Scargill had asked for and been given an overwhelming vote of support, morale was high.

'I condemn the violence of the stone throwers and the battering ram carriers,' Neil Kinnock, the Party leader, had said from the platform, 'and I condemn the violence of the cavalry charges, the truncheon groups and the shield bangers.'

Those who wanted heard the last part of what he

had said, ignored the first; fed on the rumours that NACODS, the union of pit overseers, was on the verge of joining the strike. If that happened – as the speaker from Scotland told the meeting – then without overseers to ensure that proper safety procedures were in place and being followed, by law no pit could remain open. So what would the NCB do then?

'The people of this country,' the Welsh speaker said, rising to his feet, 'the ordinary people of this country are on our side. No matter what the government says . . .' Cheers. 'No matter what MacGregor says . . .' Cheers. 'No matter what Maggie says . . .' Louder cheers. 'We have the popular support and we will win.

'And not only have we got the people on our side,' he continued, truly hitting his stride, 'we have God, too. God's spokesman, no less, the Bishop of Durham, you heard him, last week at his enthronement, calling for MacGregor – what did he call him? that elderly imported American – calling for him to go. Calling this Tory government to task for embarking on a war at the other end of the world rather than spending that money on the poor and the elderly in their own country. Calling them to task for spending more and more money on the police at a time when they are being used as a blunt instrument of government policy, in an attempt to force this movement, this union, into submission.'

Near uproar; he waited for it to subside.

'You will have heard,' he continued, 'the NUM's false promises, heard MacGregor, this unwanted old man from the other side of the ocean, who has already decimated the steel industry in this country, claim there will be new jobs within the industry for any miner whose colliery is closed, which we all know is a lie.'

'Yes!'

'Claim there will be no compulsory redundancies, which I know and you all know is another lie.'

'Yes!'

'Promise that for those who do voluntarily accept redundancy, their increased payments will be full and fair.'

'No! No!'

'Because we know, to echo the words of the Bishop one more time, that while redundancy payments may be all very well, what redundancy means is no more jobs for those who have been made redundant and no more jobs for their children.'

Loud and prolonged acclaim. Jenny and Edna exchanged excited glances. The palms of Jenny's hands were damp with sweat.

While the applause was still ringing round the hall, the Kentish speaker rose to his feet.

'Comrades, I may not have always agreed with everything Arthur Scargill has done during the course of this strike . . .' Murmurs of disapproval, scraping of chairs. 'I may not have agreed with everything he's said . . .' Scattered shouts of protest, calls for him to sit down. 'But I wholeheartedly endorse, and call upon all of you gathered here to do so too, Arthur's words from the month just gone.

'"Our members," he said, "will not submit to the butchery of their livelihoods and their communities. There was only one course of action: to fight.'"

Cheers of agreement, raised fists, banging of chairs.

'And . . .' the speaker continued, shouting above the crowd, '"That fight has been an inspiration to working people around the world.'"

Anything else was lost in a tumult of sound.

In the car, heading home, Peter Waites leaned across to Jenny in the back seat.

'Don't you wish that'd been you up there? All that acclamation. All that applause.'

'Me? In front of all those people – you must be joking.'

He patted her hand. 'Can't keep putting it off, you know. No need to start with hundreds, not at first. Thirty or so will do.'

The headlights cut through the gathering mist, lighting the road ahead.

32

A bottle of single malt aside, and that destined for McBride's bottom drawer, Sandford and Cresswell came back from north of the border empty-handed. The address in Fort William turned out to be a one-room flat above a pizza restaurant close to the station. Single bed, sink, two-ring cooker, one easy chair, pint-sized television, shared bathroom one floor down. Danny Ireland had been there a little over three months, firstly doing manual work at the Lochaber Smelter north of the town, after that picking up odd jobs here and there, including a spell in the restaurant kitchen, washing pots.

Those few who had met him described him as distant, not exactly unfriendly, but the kind who liked to keep himself to himself; reliable, though, a good worker, not afraid to roll up his sleeves, muck in. Ask him to come for a drink after work and the answer was always a shake of the head.

One of the men Cresswell spoke to, someone who'd worked with Ireland at the aluminium smelter, said he'd come across him once, quite high on the hills to the west of Glen Nevis.

'What on earth are you doing here?' the man, who was out walking the West Highland Way, had asked, surprised.

'Keeping the fuck away from the likes of you,' had been the reply.

The restaurant proprietor, who also owned the lease on the flat, told them Ireland had just disappeared, no warning. One evening he was there, the next morning gone.

'Sneaked off in the night, then?'

'You could say that.'

'Any rent owing?'

'Gonna pay it, are you?'

'What do you think?'

'Anyway, only kidding. Left what he owed, tucked under the corner of the TV. Correct to the penny.'

'Any idea where he was headed?'

'Not a one. But aside from what he stood up in, everything he owned fitted into a duffel bag he could sling over his shoulder. Could have gone anywhere. Tell you one odd thing about him. Even though he had a bed in his room, far as I could make out he chose to sleep on the floor. Like he was camping out. Some people, eh?'

When they asked at the station, the clerk thought he remembered a man answering Ireland's description buying a ticket for Mallaig. But then, someone they got into conversation with in Cobbs Bar reckoned to have seen a man with some kind of big rucksack hitching a lift on the A82 north towards Invergarry and Fort Augustus on Loch Ness, this the day that Ireland had disappeared.

Catherine Njoroge was quite adamant when they phoned in for instructions. 'Check back in with the local force, whoever you spoke to before, then get yourselves back down here as soon as possible.'

'No passing Go then, boss,' Cresswell asked, 'not even if it means picking up two hundred pounds.'

Catherine broke the connection without answering. Monopoly, a game that brought out the worst in everyone.

She'd confronted John McBride first thing, the morning after her uncomfortable interview at Serious Organised Crime Unit headquarters.

'Detective Chief Inspector Picard – you've been passing on information to him about the investigation.' More a statement than a question.

'No more than he asked me.'

'Which was what?'

'He wanted to know how things were going. Simple as that. I told him.'

'It didn't occur to you to ask yourself why he was making enquiries through you and not me?'

'I thought he must've had his reasons.'

'And what did you tell him exactly?'

McBride lifted his shoulders in a lazy shrug. 'What's been happening with the inquiry. Just a summary. Interviews carried out, information received, actions allocated.'

'And that was all?'

'Yes, boss.'

'He didn't ask you to express an opinion on how things were progressing?'

'Not in so many words.'

'How many words, I wonder?'

'I'm not sure I understand.'

'Don't you? I think you do. I think you saw an opportunity to stick a knife in my back and you took it.'

'Not true, boss.'

Catherine steadied herself, straightened, making use of all the height she had.

'Nobody else here, Sergeant, just you and me. So listen. In future no detailed information about this investigation is to be passed on without my explicit say-so. Is that clear?'

'Yes, boss.'

'We're understood?'

'Understood.'

'And is that the beginnings of a smirk on your face?'

'No, boss.'

'All right. Now listen. Names that have come down to us from the Swann investigation, the file you showed me, how far have we got with winnowing down that list of names?'

'Only so many hours in the day, boss.'

'Okay, but let's speed things up as much as we can.'

'Will do.'

'And Cartwright? Where was it, Saskatchewan somewhere?'

'Another call in today, RCMP.'

'Good.' Still focused on McBride's face, she took a step away. 'We're going to nail this, right?'

'Yes, boss.'

'God, Charlie, you'd have handled it better.'

'You've got to stop thinking that.'

'Believe me, you would.'

They were in the Half Moon on the Chesterfield Road, a barn of a place with low ceilings, fake wooden beams and a range of two-for-ten-pounds Square Deal meals. But it was out of the town centre and, at that time of the evening, quiet enough to talk without being overheard.

'Other things aside,' Catherine said, 'McBride would have responded better to you. Man to bloody man.'

'He's got issues with you being a woman, that what you mean?'

Catherine smiled. 'Not just a woman. I'm black, Charlie, in case you hadn't noticed. And not Beyoncé black. Very black. The kind you can't miss. And promoted above him. Giving him orders. How do you think he feels about that?'

'He may not be as prejudiced as you think.'

Catherine shook her head. 'How many years do you think he's got in, McBride?'

'Twenty? Twenty-five?'

'And I've less than half that. Which leaves him sitting there asking why is she a DI while I'm still a DS? And the answer comes, positive discrimination.'

'I don't think so.'

'Come on, Charlie. So many points for being female, so many more for being black, a few more still for a halfway decent degree. And McBride's what? White, Scottish, most likely not a graduate. What's that expression my father used to use? Pulled himself up by his boot straps? And how far? I might be pretty angry if I were him.'

Resnick reached for his glass. 'I had a DS at Canning Circus. Graham Millington. Practically all the time I was there. Good copper. DS when I arrived, DS when I left. Wouldn't have wanted it any other way. A little responsibility but not too much. Go home nights and forget about the job.'

'Married?'

'Yes.'

'You think McBride's married?'

'Between divorces, far as I know.'

'Children?'

'I don't think so.'

'What's he got, then, Charlie, aside from the job?'

'Partick Thistle?'

'What's that?'

Resnick grinned. 'The Notts County of Glasgow?'

It was growing dark when they left. Catherine taking the opportunity for a cigarette before the drive south. Lorries heading off towards the motorway. Years ago, Resnick thought, they would have been carrying coal, coke, steel. Lord knows what they were carrying now. Logistics – what the hell was that?

'Swann,' Catherine said. 'We'll go and see him?'

'We probably should.'

She dropped her cigarette to the ground in a small shower of sparks before stubbing it forcefully out.

'Night, Charlie.'

'Goodnight.'

They climbed into their respective cars and eased out into the traffic.

Resnick was still driving up and back in his borrowed car, neither relishing the time he spent alone in the house at the end of each day, nor feeling strongly enough that he wanted company, wanted a change.

For all it held memories that as well as being pleasant, happy even, could be disturbing – the sound of a door opening and then closing above, a footstep on the stair, reminders of a presence no longer there – there was something about that house where he had lived for many years now that was reassuring. Comforting. His own things for one, things that had accumulated over time; pieces of furniture moulded to his shape and size. Records, far too many of those, CDs. A shelf or so of books, including, with the train ticket still marking her place, the book Lynn had been reading the day she died. The way the cat would circle round his chair, push its nose against his leg, then wait, poised, before jumping into his lap, circling and then settling down, head between its paws.

Catherine drove with the radio on, items of news spooling out largely unregarded: youth employment reaching a new high, a car bombing in the centre of Beirut. There'd been a large bouquet of flowers waiting for her at the station in Potter Street that morning, a note of apology written in Abbas' practised cursive hand.

'Admirer, ma'am?' the officer on the desk had said.

She had torn the note in half and half again, asked

the duty sergeant to make sure the flowers got to the local hospital before they wilted and hoped that would be the end of it.

Indicating clearly, she accelerated into the outside lane.

33

There had to be, Catherine thought, a more appropriate address for HM Prison Wakefield than Love Lane. A high-security prison, with four units housing somewhere in excess of seven hundred prisoners, one hundred or more of them Category A, it specialised in high-risk sex offenders and those found guilty of violent crimes against women and children.

Catherine had dressed carefully: a dark loose-fitting trouser suit, flat shoes, hair tied back, no jewellery, little or no make-up. Nothing that would emphasise her femininity. Alongside her, Resnick, nevertheless, looked drab, ordinary: a middle-aged man in an ill-fitting suit with creases in his shirt and fading food stains on his tie. Over the past fifteen to twenty years not so much about his overall appearance had changed; he had just got older.

They would be seeing Michael Swann in one of several small rooms separate from the main visiting centre. A low table with four chairs, in one corner a small play area for children, against one wall a machine dispensing drinks and snacks.

With apologies, it was explained there would be a short wait.

Resnick thought about getting a Mars Bar from the machine; thought better of it.

'You've been here before, Charlie?' Catherine asked.

'This particular unit, no. But Wakefield, yes. More than a few times, unfortunately.'

'Bad place? Bad memories?'

'All prisons are bad places, pretty much all, just a matter of degree. Ones like this – Long Lartin, Full Sutton, Manchester – lifers, prisoners on lockdown, there's a sort of hopelessness – I don't know – malignancy. You want to shake it off, wash it away . . .'

Footsteps approached the door, stopped, went off in another direction.

'Last time I was here,' Resnick said, 'Wakefield, it was to see a man who'd systematically abused most of the children in his family, boys as well as girls, children as well as grandchildren, over a period of thirty years.'

'And nobody knew?'

'Of course people knew,' Resnick said, suddenly angry. 'They knew, somewhere inside they knew, but to say anything would have been to admit those things had really happened. Not that, in that respect, he was any different. Didn't matter how much therapy, how much talk, multidisciplinary intervention, whatever they call it, he remained in denial. Which meant, of course, when he went before the parole board they turned him down.'

'He's still here?'

Resnick shook his head. 'After he failed to get parole a second time, he started self-harming, talked about taking his own life. For the next two months he was on suicide watch, round the clock. The day after the psychiatrist pronounced him safe and the watch was withdrawn, he was found dead in his cell. Hanged himself.'

Catherine hesitated. 'How did that make you feel?'

'Not good. Not necessarily. But then I thought about the children, the harm he'd done to them and I didn't feel so bad.'

The door opened and Swann was escorted in.

Late sixties, he looked older. Below medium height, he walked slowly and with a slight stoop, the beginnings of a hunched back. His face was round, its shape accentuated by his glasses; cheeks that sagged a little, a surprisingly small mouth. Grey trousers, grey shirt, black socks, brown slip-on shoes, no laces.

Several paces into the room he stopped, looking at Catherine with evident surprise.

Catherine promptly introduced herself and Resnick and, as if playing host, Swann gestured towards the chairs, bidding them sit.

'I'll be just outside,' the prison officer said, and closed the door behind him.

'There,' Swann said, 'trusted, you see. Some inmates, the dangerous ones – challenging, that's what they're supposed to call them nowadays – they stay in here, two of them sometimes, just in case.' His voice had traces of a Northern accent, north-west, a suggestion of a lisp. 'Me, I'm a pussycat compared to some. I mean, just look at me.' He smiled. 'Not hurt a fly.'

Just three young women, Catherine thought, three we know about for certain.

'But I'm sorry to have kept you waiting,' Swann said. 'I was in the braille shop. Turning books into braille so the blind can read. It's lovely work. Restful.' Placing the fingers of his right hand on the skin of the other, and stroking it up and down, he closed his eyes. 'You grow sensitive to it, after a while.'

Angling his head towards Catherine, he slowly opened his eyes. Still fingering his arm, he held her gaze.

'We think you might be able to help us,' she said, unfazed. 'I'm leading an investigation into the murder of Jenny Hardwick. She was killed in the village of Bledwell Vale a little under thirty years ago. Late nineteen eighty-four.'

'Cold case, is it then? I know about those from the telly.'

'Killed in a manner you'd be familiar with.'

Something stirred in Swann's eyes.

'You don't know the victim's name? Hardwick? Jenny? it's not familiar at all?'

'I'm afraid not.'

'Or the place? Bledwell Vale?'

'Wales, is it? Sounds Welsh to me.'

'Nottinghamshire. North. Between Worksop and Chesterfield.'

'The crooked spire.'

'That's right. You know the area, then?'

'Everyone knows the crooked spire.'

'But you are familiar with the area?'

'Not really, no.'

'I thought you were.'

'Pretty, was she, Jenny? I don't suppose you've got a photograph? If I could see a photograph, then I might know . . .'

A look of anticipation came to his face as Resnick reached inside his coat; faded as all that emerged was a small black notebook that was flicked open to a particular page.

'Nineteen eighty-four,' Resnick said, glancing down, looking at what was, in reality, a blank page. 'Sheffield. That was the first time you drove a minicab?'

'Lorries, that was my thing. Vans, too. Always liked

vans. Short haul.' Bending his head towards Catherine, he smiled again. 'You know, man with a van. No job too small.'

Catherine's stomach lurched and it was more than she could do to stop her eyes from blinking.

Behind his owlish glasses, Swann's own eyes grew large.

'Eighty-six to eighty-eight,' Resnick said. 'Sheffield again. Close on two years. All for the same firm, was it? Or more in the way of moonlighting? We weren't too sure.'

'I don't know why you want to know all this. The woman you're talking about, Jenny, nineteen eighty-four you said.'

'How about Donna Crowder,' Resnick said. 'Ring any bells?'

Swann shifted a little in his seat.

'Found murdered close to the A6178, the Rotherham–Sheffield road. Nineteen eighty-seven.'

Shifted a little more.

'Someone, we think, picked her up on her way home. Offered her a lift. Minicab, possibly. Likely not a booking. Off the clock. Or maybe someone in a van.'

Swann blinked. 'Look, I thought this was supposed to be helping me towards my next parole hearing. That's what I was told. That's the only reason I agreed . . .'

'So it could,' Catherine said. 'Full acknowledgement

of what you've done wrong. That's what they'll want to hear. Clear the decks. Show remorse.'

'What I've done? I've paid for what I've done. And what you're doing is throwing every unsolved murder in the book at me in the hope one of them'll stick. Well, it's not going to happen.'

Unsteadily to his feet, Swann shuffled back towards the door, signalling through the glass.

'We might come and see you again,' Catherine said, standing. 'When you've had time to think. Or if you want to speak to us, it's easily arranged.'

But Swann was no longer listening.

'Visit over?' the prison officer said from the doorway.

'Visit over,' Resnick said.

34

Jenny was elated, exhausted, unable to tell exactly which way she was going, what exactly she was feeling, which way was up. Tonight had been the night of her first speech from the platform – Peter Waites had finally persuaded her – only there in the Vale, admittedly, people for the most part she knew, men and women who would never have been there, listened, had they not been fully in support of what she was saying. But even so, once she had got over the frozen moment when Peter had introduced her, the yawning gulf between where she was sitting and the microphone at the front of the stage, seemingly impossible, too vast, too daunting to cross; once the first words had broken, startled, from her mouth, thoughts racing ahead, worrying, worrying would she remember, would she remember what she'd been rehearsing incessantly these last few days since Peter had told her, invited her to join him on the platform; realising, even as the exact words of the prepared speech slipped away from her and she struck out on her own – what she felt, what she really felt important, what mattered – realising then, all the faces turned towards her, listening, listening, knowing she had them, had them in the palm of her hand. Her own bloody hand!

Sweat running down her back, her top sticking to her, near transparent, sweat between her legs, itching, clinging; her hair damp with it, eyes bright. The applause, a few people on their feet, loud, continuing.

'Where's your old man?' someone shouted. 'Back home, hiding?'

Peter Waites shook her hand heartily and when, finally, she stepped offstage, Edna Johnson enveloped her in a hug.

'I knew you could do it. Fair made me proud.'

Walking home, two brandies later, sounds of congratulation still ringing in her ears, she found herself scanning again through the rows that had been spread out in front of the stage, searching through the faces. For one moment, earlier, she thought she'd seen him, there amongst the group of men standing by the side wall, but when he turned again, the hair was different – not red but reddish brown – the face rounder, the eyes not seeking out her own.

*　　*　　*

Barry scarcely glanced up when she came into the room.

'The kids—' she began.

'In bed long since.'

She waited for him to look up from the paper, ask, even, how it had gone.

'I'll be getting off to bed myself then . . .'

'You do that.'

The flap of the paper like a slap across her cheek.

35

Catherine had put down a deposit on the flat less than three days after first seeing it. Someone will snap it up before the week's out, the estate agent had said, and, for once, Catherine had thought that was probably right. Borrowing the capital she lacked from her parents had been the only difficult part; having to go cap in hand when she was well into her thirties.

'Don't they pay you in the police force?' her father had asked. 'Promotion and all, I thought you'd have been coining it by now. It's not as if you're living down here in the south-east, after all. That I could understand.'

'Your father and I,' her mother had said, smiling, 'had been looking forward to you supporting us in our old age.'

'Ah, well,' Catherine had said, returning her smile,

'there's always the state pension, the winter fuel allowance. That's without all those investments Daddy's been cleverly making over the years.'

'Economic downturn, haven't you heard?' her father said. 'Not worth the paper they're printed on.'

'I don't know,' Catherine said, looking pointedly round. 'You don't seem to be doing too badly.'

'How much exactly,' her father had finally asked, 'is it you want?'

She told him.

'I thought property in Nottingham was cheap?'

'Some is.'

'Let me have your account details. Email them, that's best. I'll have the money transferred.'

So there she was, a top-floor flat on the Ropewalk, tastefully converted. No throwing out all the old with the new. Oak floors and sash windows: open-plan living room, kitchen in steel and chrome, en-suite bedroom. Views out across the city to the front; from the rear she could look high over Park Valley towards the Trent and beyond that to hills and open fields.

Long enough living there now to feel comfortable, comfortably at home. Looking forward to it at the end of the day. Close the door; close out the world. The world she dealt with as part of her job.

Somehow Michael Swann kept sneaking back.

The way he had stared at her. Wasn't she used to being stared at enough? But this had been different.

Knowing what he had done, this apparently mild-mannered man, what he had done to three young women, women who, for some reason, had put their trust in him.

A pussycat compared to some . . . just look at me . . . Not hurt a fly.

When he had rested the tips of his fingers against his own softly wrinkled skin and moved them gently along, she had felt his touch on her arm.

Man with a van. No job too small.

Could she imagine him, the early hours of the morning, driving along the Sheffield Road? Perhaps he'd just dropped off a fare in Rotherham and was on his way back when he'd seen her, Donna, thumbing a lift on the opposite side of the road. Driven a short distance further before executing a three-point turn.

'Need a ride, love?'

'No, you're all right,' Donna might have said. 'I'm spent up.'

'No worries. Just hop in. No skin off my nose.'

Is that how it had been?

The scene played out in her mind. Easier with Donna – they knew more, easier to fill in the spaces, connect the dots.

But Jenny . . .

With Jenny they still knew next to nothing of the circumstances leading up to her death. A little rumour. A little insinuation.

Donna Crowder, though – almost as soon as she was mentioned, Swann had called the interview to an end. Perhaps they should go back, interview him further, under caution. Resnick could talk to Paul Bryant again, ransack his memory . . .

But Donna Crowder's case, she told herself, was somebody else's – or would be if the investigation were reopened – and not her own.

Through the window, the lights of the city were like something from a movie, something more glamorous than the place she knew to be real. Six months she'd patrolled the streets: drunks, junkies, homeless teenagers with nowhere to go; men in raucous groups shouting lewd suggestions across the road; women with skirts that barely covered their buttocks, holding on to each other so as not to go – what was that charming English expression? – arse over tit.

Cold, Catherine turned up the heating a notch, fetched a glass from the kitchen; a bottle of red wine – Barolo – on the table waiting to be opened.

Why not?

The CD she'd been listening to recently was still in the player and she flicked it to life with the remote. Bach Cello Suites, Pablo Casals. She had bought it after seeing a film about a string quartet. Rather wonderful, really. Christopher Walken, suffering from Parkinson's. Catherine Keener, whom she'd seen several times before without realising they shared a name.

There was a scene in which Walken is talking to a group of young music students he's teaching: telling them of meeting the famous Pablo Casals. Then playing, unaccompanied, as Casals had, a passage from the Cello Suite No. 4.

Catherine didn't think she'd heard anything more striking, more beautiful.

On the disc it was the same. Casals recorded in Paris in 1939. The year before the German army invaded the city. So many years before she was born.

Her mobile rang and she picked it up.

Abbas.

She declined the call.

Leaning back, she closed her eyes.

It rang again. Different tone. A text this time.

I'm at your door.

It was as though she had pins and needles in her arms, her fingers, her toes.

The message, staring at her.

Why should she believe him? How could he have got her address? As soon as she asked herself the question, she knew the reply: her parents, of course. She could see him, smart, smiling, winding her mother around his little finger, shaking brisk hands with her father, man to man.

'I thought, since I was going to be in Nottingham – not for long, just passing through – it would be a nice gesture to call on Catherine. Nothing heavy, just to wish her well, see how she is. Make it something of a surprise.'

Oh, yes, they would like that. A shame, they'd always thought, the two of them hadn't been able to work it out. Catherine, really, she'd been the problem. Perhaps this time . . .

She sipped a little more wine, set down the glass.

Walked, barefoot, towards the door.

Leaned her head against it, listening.

Listening for what?

His breathing?

All of a sudden he kicked, kicked against the base of the door and her head jerked back.

'Catherine! I know you're there.'

Another kick; the sound of fists, hammering.

'Catherine!'

If he carried on like that, he'd raise the neighbours; one of them would phone the police. She imagined two uniformed officers arriving, dragging the protesting Abbas away, asking her to open the door . . . perhaps they would recognise her straight away, perhaps not.

'Catherine!'

She unlocked the door, stepped aside, waited for him to enter. Closed the door behind him.

Watched as he walked through into the living room as if nothing untoward had happened. The same Abbas: smart, handsome, strong; more self-confident, Catherine thought, than anyone she had ever met.

'It's nice,' he said, looking round, appraising. 'A little impersonal, maybe. Like a budget hotel room, I suppose. No, that's unfair.' Smiling. 'Three stars at least.'

His eyes focused on the Barolo.

'Aren't you going to offer me a glass?'

'Abbas, what do you want?'

'I said, a glass of wine. A glass of wine and a little civilised conversation. Is that too much to ask?'

'And after that you'll go?'

'Of course.'

She was half-afraid he might follow her into the kitchen, but when she returned with an empty glass, he was lounging back on the settee, legs outstretched, one expensive shoe hooked over the other.

'Tortelier?' he asked, with a nod towards the stereo, where the Bach was still playing.

'Casals.'

'Tortelier's better. The eighty-three recordings, not the later ones.'

Seeing her expression, he laughed. 'All right. Absolute bullshit, I know. Eighty-three, ninety-three, who knows, who cares?'

Catherine poured wine into his glass, not too much; refreshed her own. Sat in the Eames-style chair between the settee and the door.

'What brings you back to the East Midlands?' she asked. 'Or have you been here all along?'

'I could say it's to see you, but that would just be more—'

'More of your bullshit.'

'Exactly.'

Abbas smiled a practised smile. Good teeth – mostly, if Catherine remembered correctly, his own.

'So are you going to tell me?' Catherine said.

'What?'

'Why you're here?'

He uncrossed his legs, swivelling round until he was facing her across the table. 'Even in this benighted part of the country, there are still people one can do business with. Though, all too often, it's buying up their sorry little failing companies before they go under completely.'

'Not out of charity, I imagine.'

'Hardly.' Another smile. 'Helps put them out of their misery.'

The CD came to end. Abbas was on his feet, moving towards the window overlooking the Park Estate.

'Those big houses down there – the Park Estate – mansions some of them. I was reading about it the other day. You know who they were built for? Those Victorian Gothic monstrosities? People with ideas, ambition. Captains of industry. Coal barons. Lace. Where would they be today? China? India? The Gulf?'

'You could always join them.'

'You'd like that, wouldn't you?'

'Abbas, I don't care where you are. Just as long as—'

'As long as I stay away from you.'

'Exactly.'

Sitting easily back down on the settee, he lifted his glass, raised it towards her as if in a toast, and drank. Looked at her over the rim.

'You know, you're a very silly girl sometimes.'

'I'm not a girl.'

'Semantics. Woman, then. What does it matter? You know what I mean.'

'I don't think I do.'

'You realise the life we could have—'

'Yes, Abbas.'

'And yet you choose this. This anonymous little flat. Your grubby little job.'

'Abbas, I think you should go.'

'I'm just trying—'

'Please . . .' Rising to her feet. 'Just go.'

'Very well.' He looked at the glass. 'Shame to leave this all the same.'

Setting down the glass, he stepped around the table; stood beside her. She could smell his cologne, the oil in his hair.

'Goodbye kiss . . .?'

As he leaned his head towards her, she twisted hers away.

'Abbas . . .'

He caught hold of her wrist. Her arm. Pressed his face against hers.

'You remember how we used to make love . . .'

She struggled to free herself and he pushed her back against the wall.

'Abbas!'

'The way you used to scream.' He was fast up against her, forcing his leg between hers. Whispering in her ear. 'Nobody else can make you come like that. You know it. Nobody.'

His mouth moved over hers, his tongue between her lips.

Catherine allowed her own mouth to open further, then bit down hard. Bit into the edge of his tongue, his lower lip, tasting blood.

'You bitch!'

His elbow swung and caught her in the face and sent her stumbling back. He made a grab for her and, avoiding him, she swivelled away, seized the bottle from the table and lifted it above her head.

When he made another lunge towards her, she brought it down on his arm at the elbow, hard as she could.

When he cried out, blood spluttered from his mouth.

'Get out! Get out!' Stepping further back, she threw the bottle at his head. Missing, it smashed against the wall, the remaining wine splashing across the chair, the kitchen door.

Backing away, blood still dribbling from his mouth, he stared at her in disbelief.

'You stupid cunt.'

'Just go.'

As soon as he was outside, she slammed the door shut, double-locked it, turned and leaned her back against it; sinking slowly then, sobbing, to the floor.

36

In the local paper, the *Nottingham Post*, it was front-page news, with an editorial and a double-page spread inside. Police question convicted serial killer about the violent deaths of two more women: best-selling true-crime author Trevor Fleetwood tells how his years of research into these terrible crimes finally led to the cases being reopened. A photograph of a serious yet smiling Fleetwood showed him holding a copy of *Born to Kill* – the book which first told the truth about Michael Swann.

The same photograph was liberally used throughout the national press.

The *Telegraph*, *Metro* and the *Mail* featured the story strongly; as did *The Times* and the *Express*, the *Independent* and the *Star*. Blurry photographs of Michael Swann's three acknowledged victims were printed in the *Sun* alongside pictures of Donna Crowder and Jenny Hardwick, with a head-and-shoulder shot of Swann himself at the centre and the 36-point headline, *How Many More Did This Man Kill?* The *Guardian* had an article on violence against women on its Comment page and a news paragraph on page 9.

The Internet was having a field day.

Trevor Fleetwood's website had in excess of a thousand extra hits, his Twitter account was going crazy, and, by mid-morning, *Born to Kill* had risen eight hundred and fifty places on Amazon, with *Death by Water* and *In the Ripper's Footsteps* close behind.

Resnick had picked up two double espressos from the café on Bridge Street and handed one to Catherine as soon as she arrived.

'Thought you might be needing this.'

'Thanks. Three messages on my phone from Picard already.'

Resnick followed her into the building.

'Plus,' over her shoulder, 'someone from Corporate Communication at Force Headquarters wants to see me as a matter of urgency. And several messages from Barry Hardwick – and his oldest son – demanding to know what's going on.'

'Meanwhile Fleetwood's sitting back laughing.'

'You think he's played us for fools?'

'Let's hope not entirely.'

At the top of the stairs, overhead lights bright and unforgiving, Resnick stopped, touched her arm. 'Your face, what happened?'

There was a swelling, slight but noticeable, over Catherine's left eye; bruising showing through the natural darkness of her skin.

'It's nothing.'

'Catherine . . .'

'I fell, that's all.'

'You fell?'

'Yes, slipped. At home of all places. The kitchen. Some oil that had got spilt on the floor.'

'But you're okay?'

'Yes, of course. Fine. Nothing a couple of ibuprofen couldn't cure.'

'You've been to hospital, though, had an X-ray?'

'Charlie, come on. It's just a little bump, don't make a fuss.' Brushing past him, she pushed into the office.

'Good picture of you online, boss,' McBride said, swinging round from behind his screen. "Black detective leads investigation into double murder. Serial killer interviewed."'

Catherine swore beneath her breath.

Almost immediately, her phone rang. Picard. Raising an eyebrow in Resnick's direction she winced; went out of the room to take the call. She was likely to be some time.

'Now all this has blown up,' McBride said, 'those

M62 suspects we've been looking at, carry on with that or not?'

'Much of interest so far?'

'Still early to say.'

'Then whatever Fleetwood's motives, let's stick with it a bit longer.'

'I took a look at him, Fleetwood, just out of interest.'

'Anything?'

McBride shrugged. 'Married twice, twice divorced, two grown-up sons. Lives in Leeds, or he did. Last-known address. Started out as a reporter in the north-west: *Rochdale Observer*, *Northwich Chronicle*, *Manchester Evening News*. Crime, courts, you know the kind of thing. Bit of success with the books and went freelance. But look at this . . .'

He opened another page onscreen.

'Sued for libel, twice. One case settled out of court. The other, after a retrial, found in his favour.'

'What grounds?'

McBride read it off the screen. '"On the grounds that statements he had made in print had been without malice and in good faith, from a reasonable belief to have been true." So yes, let's not be taking everything he said without more than a good pinch of salt.'

By lunchtime a spokesperson for the force had issued an official statement. The ongoing investigation into the death of Jenny Hardwick had not been extended to include any other crime. Officers had visited HM Prison Wakefield and spoken to a man currently serving a life sentence, but there was no direct link with the investigation in question and the man had not been interviewed under caution.

Resnick had tried calling Trevor Fleetwood several times to give him a piece of his mind, but, as before, Fleetwood wasn't answering.

He went back to McBride. 'Fleetwood – you said he was living in Leeds.'

'Far as I know.'

'And we've got an address?'

'Planning on making a call?'

'Could be.'

'Need company? I could do with getting my sorry arse out from behind this desk.'

Meanwhile, the e-book edition of *Born to Kill* was sitting at number forty-seven in the top one hundred. And rising.

37

The last of the washing pegged out, Jenny looks at the clock as she comes back into the kitchen, gives a little shake of her head in disbelief. Some mornings she doesn't know where the time goes. Between putting in a stint at the Welfare, ferrying the kids to school, doing jobs around the house, it can be lunchtime before she knows it and time to collect Brian from nursery. Not a minute even to sit down with a cup of tea. Not a minute to herself. At least today, Linda from across the road has said she'll pick Brian up with hers, drop him back.

A right pain he'd been this morning. Colin, too. Hanging on to her at the school gates when they'd arrived and carrying on something dreadful when she tried to get him to let go. 'Mummy, Mummy, Mummy!'

Clinging to her legs and screaming. Embarrassing in front of everyone else.

It had taken one of the teachers – Nicky's mum – to calm him down, entice him away. Nicky and Mary already skipping off across the playground, laughing, giggling, holding hands.

Barry hadn't exactly helped, either. Like a bear with a sore head ever since he'd hefted himself out of bed. Barely spoken when he left for the early shift. No more than a token picket out today, Jenny knew, most of the recent effort further south in the county, Clipstone, Annesley.

Truth of it was, he'd been in a right mood since last night in bed. Sliding one heavy leg over hers a few minutes after Jenny had switched off her bedside light, pushing up against her behind, a hand reaching for her breast. She'd felt herself go tight, muscles clenching. 'Barry, no. No, Barry, not tonight, not now. I'm tired.' Hating herself for saying it, what it made her sound like. Knowing the last time they'd made love was an age ago, way back before her last period, a hasty grab and go that had left her unsatisfied and sore.

When he'd tried again, not so many minutes later, she'd rolled out of the bed, taken one of the blankets and spent the rest of the night on the sofa, waking every so often to the sound of his snoring.

Pulling his boots on that morning, he'd seized hold of her as she went past. 'I am still your husband, you know.'

'I know.' And stood there till she'd stared him down and he let her go.

She'd been upstairs, brushing Mary's hair, when she'd heard the slamming of the door.

'What's the matter with Daddy?'

'Oh, nothing. Nothing really.'

'Then why is he so angry?'

The radio is playing in the other room, voices talking – *Woman's Hour*, is it? – but then it's pips and the news. She stops what she's doing to listen. Increased violence in Beirut, she hears, without being certain exactly where Beirut is or what they are fighting about. Funeral processions in South African townships. Talks between the National Coal Board and the National Union of Mineworkers have been adjourned. We believe, a spokesman from the National Coal Board is quoted as saying, that considerable progress has been made and that an agreement is close.

Is it, buggery, Jenny thinks.

She swivels her head. A sound at the back door? Someone knocking? She clicks the radio off.

A shadowy shape through the frosted glass.

Cautiously, she opens the door; not all the way. 'What the hell are you doing here?'

'Come to see you, didn't I?'

'What d'you mean, come to see me?'

'What d'you think?' A quick look back over his shoulder. 'Now for fuck's sake, let me in.'

'I'll do no such thing.'

'I'm breaking me bail conditions bein' here. Anyone sees me, they'll have 'em revoked, have me back up in court.'

Grudgingly, she opens the door wide enough for him to step through; closes it fast behind him and, after a moment's thought, slides the bolt across. They stand looking at one another, little more than an arm's length apart.

Danny is wearing the same old donkey jacket, boots, jeans. Looks as if he might have been sleeping rough; a couple of days, at least, since he's had a shave.

Jenny realises she's staring, feels the colour flush to her cheeks.

'How did you know where I lived?'

'Not a secret, is it?'

'Anyone could have been here, Barry, anyone.'

He smiles. 'Kids at school. Old man still scabbin', on shift.'

She shakes her head. How does he know all that? 'You've got to go.'

'In a while, eh?'

'No, now.' Her throat is dry, the words come out

awkward, uncertain. She can't stop looking at his mouth.

'I don't think so,' he says. 'Eh, duck?' And smiles.

And then he's kissing her and it's like one of those stupid films because she's kissing him back and one minute they're standing there and the next they're stumbling sideways, his jacket shucked off to the floor.

Tongue sliding into her mouth, he pulls her to him, leans her back.

The sink is hard against her spine; breakfast things stacked up, plates slipping, one over the other on the draining board, as she flings back an arm. His hands are on her, all over her, his leg pressing between hers, and she does nothing to push him away.

Pulling up her thin cotton sweater, he reaches beneath and frees her breasts.

Jenny gasps as, lowering his head, he takes her nipple, hard, in his mouth, biting gently down, and they start to slide, meshed against one another, towards the floor.

She frees an arm, tugs at his hair, lifting his face back up towards her own. When his hand starts to move up inside her skirt she arches backwards, positioning herself to meet him, wetter than she can remember being, so wet, wanting him.

Wanting him inside her.

* * *

At the last moment, he's pulled out and orgasmed, bucking, against her belly and now she lies there, still shaking, still a little bit in shock but happy, enjoying the rich slithery feel of his semen against her skin.

Danny is stretched out next to her, eyes closed, smoking a cigarette.

A while since either of them has spoken.

'Well,' he says eventually, 'that was a long time coming.'

She looks at him to see if he is joking.

'That first time I clapped eyes on you, up the Welfare.'

'And what now? Tick me off in your little black book? Had her, soft cow, knew I would.'

'Don't talk like that.'

'No?'

'No, that's not what it's like.'

She props herself on one elbow. 'What is it like?'

'Fancy you, don't I? Can't take me eyes off you. Mates ribbin' me about it, somethin' fierce.'

Now she sees them up close, really close, his eyes are dark brown, flecked with green. 'Well, now you can tell them,' she says.

Danny shakes his head. 'I'll not do that.'

She looks at him questioningly, raised eyebrow. Disbelieving. It's what blokes do, young blokes like Danny especially. By tomorrow it'll be all over the

South Yorkshire coalfield. How I shagged mother of three in her own kitchen.

He leans towards her and kisses her with surprising gentleness on the mouth. She can taste the tobacco on his breath, feel the warmth of his face close to hers. Over his shoulder she's doing her best to catch a glimpse of the kitchen clock. Linda could be back with Brian any time. Expecting to come in, cup of tea and a chat.

Danny's starting to stroke her shoulder and she pushes him away.

'Don't.'

She can feel his semen starting to dry on her belly, small contractions on the surface of her skin.

'You've got to leave.'

'Ah, come on . . .'

'No. Go, now. Please.'

One quick movement and she's up on her feet, pushing her skirt back down from where it's been bunched up around her waist. As soon as she's got shot of him, everything she's been wearing, straight into the wash. What the hell was she thinking?

'Hurry, please, you've got to go.'

Bustling around him now, while he slowly tucks himself in, zips himself up.

'Okay, okay . . .'

She shepherds him towards the back door, slips back the bolt.

'See you again, then . . .'

'No.'

'What?'

'No, you won't. Don't think it because it's not going to happen.'

'Didn't enjoy it much, then?' he says, grinning. 'All that carrying on.'

'Out. Now. Go.'

Pushing him, she shuts the door more or less in his face. Hurries to the bathroom and strips off her clothes; runs warm water over a flannel and wipes her belly, wipes between her legs. Smell him, she can smell him, smell the pair of them. Jesus Christ, if she can, so will Linda when she brings back Brian. So will Barry. So will the kids.

'Please, Mum, what's that funny smell in the kitchen?'

It's not funny.

She laughs, despite herself. Applies deodorant, a quick spray of the perfume Jill gave her the Christmas before, quickly dresses. Takes the air freshener from the toilet and uses it liberally above and around where they've been. Where they've been making love – no, fucking, for Christ's sake, that's what it was – where they've been fucking on the kitchen floor.

She's taking the freshener back when the doorbell rings.

Linda with Brian and her own four-year-old; Brian

hurling himself at her, arms reaching up; Linda's lad hiding behind her legs, too shy to show his face.

'Fancy a cup of tea?' Jenny says.

'Ooh, yes,' says Linda, 'that'd be lovely.'

38

Trevor Fleetwood lived on Moorland Road, midway between the university campus and the Grand Mosque, an upper-floor flat in a tall terraced house overlooking Woodhouse Moor. His name beside a bell which didn't appear to work. In the absence of a knocker, McBride shouted upwards and was rewarded, after his third attempt, by Fleetwood's head and shoulders appearing through an opened window.

Recognising Resnick, he signalled that he would be down.

The linoleum that covered the centre of the stairs had worn almost translucent with use. Dust huddled in the corners of each step. The bannister rail smooth as marble to the touch.

'About all the press,' Fleetwood said, when they reached the landing. 'I meant to warn you.'

'Did you fuck!' McBride growled.

Resnick said nothing.

They followed Fleetwood into a broad, high-ceilinged hall. It could have been a display from a small municipal museum in need of funds. On a walnut table at the centre, next to what Resnick thought was probably an aspidistra, a stuffed animal with a pointed face, sharp teeth and a patchy white coat – some kind of weasel – reared up inside a glass dome. Extravagantly framed Victorian oils crowded the heavily papered walls, portraits and sombre landscapes, small children walking away into the sunset down an avenue over-hung with trees, holding hands.

'I got lumbered with a lot of my mother's stuff after she died,' Fleetwood explained. 'Keep meaning to do something with it, sell it, stick it on eBay – one thing and another never get around to it.'

The main room was bay-windowed, wide, almost every conceivable surface – oak table, a pair of leather settees, sideboard, an old green filing cabinet, two armchairs – piled high with papers: newspapers, pages of manuscript, magazines. Only a second table, positioned in the bay, survived relatively paper free: two computers, one a desktop, one laptop, a printer, a cordless phone in its base.

Bookshelves covered one wall.

'I mean what I said. My understanding was they were going to hold off another few days at least. The

Post wanted a jump on them, I suppose. Then, once it was out there . . .' He made a gesture of helplessness. 'The rest followed.'

'And your books,' McBride said, 'went flying up the bloody charts.'

'Not of my doing. Out of my hands.'

'That's why you've been all over the Web this last twenty-four hours – Facebook, Tumblr, Twitter and the rest – lordin' yourself to the fuckin' nines.'

'It's called earning a living.'

'It's called takin' the fuckin' piss.'

'Why don't we,' Resnick suggested, giving McBride a warning look, 'all take a breath, sit down and talk?'

'Aye,' grumbled McBride, 'if we can find somewhere to fuckin' sit.'

'First things first,' Resnick said, once they were all three settled. 'All that stuff you were feeding me, the photograph of Donna and so on, was that all just bait to get us interested or what?'

'No. Not at all. Anything I told you, I told you in good faith.'

McBride made a sound of deep disbelief.

'It's still all conjecture, though, isn't it?' Resnick said. 'For all your efforts, you've not come up with one piece of solid evidence that ties Swann in to either crime.'

'Not surprising, surely. There's a limit to what I can do on my own. You're the ones with the resources, after all.'

'Meantime,' McBride said, 'this side of libel, you can say the first thing that comes into your head.'

Fleetwood allowed himself the beginnings of a smile.

Resnick let the silence hold a moment longer. 'Just how long was it after we left,' he said, 'that Swann made the call?'

'What call?'

Resnick glanced towards the phone in the bay. 'You needed his confirmation we were there. Some idea of what we'd asked, what had been said. Without that, whatever story you were spinning to the press, it was never going to fly.'

Fleetwood looked a little less than comfortable; looked away.

'You want me to check with the prison?' Resnick offered. 'There'll be a record of outgoing calls.'

Fleetwood was already shaking his head. 'No, no need.'

'What I can't help wondering, why he'd be so keen to do that, when you're busy setting him up for two more murders?'

'He doesn't know.'

'What d'you mean,' McBride exclaimed, 'he doesna know?'

'As far as he's concerned, any interest the police have got in linking him to further crimes, that's come from them, not me. If I'm asking him questions, he thinks it's to refute whatever the police might be claiming, not the other way about.'

'Leaving you cleaner than a pig shitting in church.'

'He thinks I'll help him towards his appeal for parole.'

'At the same time as putting him in the frame,' McBride said with a grudging hint of admiration. 'You're a tricky wee bastard, right enough. But once he clocks all this ballyhoo about how you're going to write a book accusing him of two more murders, how're you fixin' to wriggle out of that?'

'I'll find a way.'

'I bet you will.'

'But unless,' Resnick said, 'we come up with something tangible linking Swann to those crimes, that book's not going to get written.'

'Not necessarily,' Fleetwood said with a smile. 'I just write a different book. About a killer and sex offender who paid his debts to society, served his time and got paroled back into the world, despite police attempts to link him to further crimes.'

'You think you've got your bread buttered both sides, don't you?' McBride sneered.

'Using my wits,' Fleetwood said. 'Manoeuvring things to my best advantage, no law against that.'

'No?' Anger flashed in McBride's eyes. 'How about wasting police time, under section five, sub-section two of the Criminal Law Act? You want to suck on that for starters?'

'You think? The CPS won't give it the time of day and you know it.'

'Right,' Resnick said, rising. 'That's us done. Come on, John, I think we've said what we had to say.'

As Fleetwood got to his feet, Resnick took a pace towards him, pointed a finger.

'Word of advice – tread carefully. Any further communication between yourself and Michael Swann, anything germane to any ongoing investigation, come straight to us with it. Otherwise you could see yourself looking at a charge of perverting the course of justice.'

'It's always been my policy,' Fleetwood said, po-faced, 'to liaise closely with the police wherever possible. And whatever the circumstances.'

'We'll see ourselves out,' McBride said dismissively. 'No call to get off your fuckin' high horse to open the door. Besides, I'd not like to see you slip down all them stairs.'

McBride lit up the moment they were on the pavement. 'What'd you reckon to that?'

'I can see why they keep you chained to the desk most of the time. Letting a Rottweiler out without its muzzle.'

'That was nothing. You should see me when I've a drink or two inside me.'

Resnick laughed.

'What?'

'Just amusing, seeing you steering so close to the stereotype.'

'Wait till tomorrow, I'll come in wearing ma kilt an' a fuckin' sporran.' He winked. 'That'll give yon Kenyan lassie something to think on.'

Resnick walked around the car. 'The Kenyan lassie, John, as you call her. Cut her some slack, okay? The job's difficult enough without you making it more so.'

39

After yet another session in the DCI's office at Central Station, Catherine doing whatever she could to deflect blame for the recent flare-up of publicity on to Fleetwood's devious machinations and away from Resnick and herself, there was agreement on the way forward. The information, such as it was, linking Swann with the Sheffield area would be handed over to the South Yorkshire Force, where a cold case team was preparing to review the investigation into Donna Crowder's murder. They would take evidence, Catherine assumed, from Trevor Fleetwood and interview Swann under caution. Anything with possible implications for their own investigation, they would continue to pursue.

She had spoken to Barry Hardwick, taking care to stress that reports in the media of a link between his wife's death and a convicted serial killer were little more than media rumour and conjecture. They would, as a matter of course, take the possibility of any link seriously, but, as things stood, there was little if any evidence to suggest that Michael Swann was involved in any way in Jenny's murder.

Bledwell Vale, the Christmas of 1984.

So long ago.

Now Catherine was having tea with the woman who had been Jenny's daughter's best friend, only too happy to be sitting there in the relative quiet of a suburban garden.

In a good light, Nicky Parker could pass for a lot less than her actual age, which had to be thirty-seven, thirty-eight, within touching distance of forty. This was a good light. Clear air. The afternoon sun carrying a little warmth for a change and the temperature higher than it had been for days. Weeks, it seemed. The two of them sitting in deckchairs in Nicky's garden, only the second or third time they would have tried that this year. Nicky wearing a striped Breton top and nicely fitting blue jeans, her hair cut in a neat bob, not a hint of grey, and, unlike her friend Mary, for whom age had done no real favours, looking all of late twenties, not a scrap older.

The house was in an area of West Bridgford called Lady Bay; midway along a street of houses which looked out over the meadows leading down towards the Trent.

Nicky had met her at the door and ushered her through a small, tiled hall – wellington boots, buggies, waterproofs, a scattering of toys – and on through the kitchen into a neat but busy garden: flower beds, shrubs, herbs growing in an old decommissioned sink. A wooden table and chairs.

'It's lovely,' Catherine said.

'It's affordable,' Nicky replied with a quick smile. 'Just about. And since they built a defence wall along the Trent a few years back, there's no call to pump out the cellar every time there's a flood warning. So, yes, you're right, it's lovely. A day like this especially.' The smile broadened. 'If you're foolish enough to buy somewhere sitting on a flood plain, you get what you deserve.'

She left Catherine to her own devices and re-emerged a short time later with a fully laden tray.

'I've brought an extra cup for Richard, in case he gets back from the university and wants to join us. I hope that would be all right? He said something about finishing early.'

'That's where he works, the university?

Nicky nodded.

'Nottingham Trent or the other?'

'The other. Carved out of Portland stone. Some of it, anyway. Associate professor of culture, film and media.' She smiled. 'Sounds grander than it is.'

'And you?'

'I work at a local nursery in the mornings. With the really little ones. Our Lottie goes there, which makes everything a lot easier. William's at primary.'

'Following in your mother's footsteps, then?'

'In a way. Though with me it's more changing nappies, reading *Brown Bear, Brown Bear, What Do You See?* until I can recite it in my sleep. And do.'

She poured the tea, held out a plate of scones.

'Yours?' Catherine said, slipping one on to her plate.

'I wish. Birds Confectioners, on the Avenue.' She smiled. 'More of a proper West Bridgford mum, I'd have baked them myself.'

'Your mum, is she still teaching?'

'Joyfully retired.' Nicky glanced at her watch. 'Just settling down to a hand of bridge round about now.'

'It was through her you met Mary, I suppose? If she hadn't been teaching there, in the Vale, you wouldn't have gone to the same school at all.'

'That's right.'

'And, from what Mary said, you used to spend a lot of time there, at the house?'

'Almost every day.'

'So you must have seen quite a bit of her parents, too?'

'Her mother, yes. Jenny. I was really upset when I heard what had happened. It was horrible.' She took the butter knife, split a scone. 'I didn't see nearly as much of her father. Most of the time he was off at work – at least, I imagine that's where he was – and when he wasn't, well, I think he kept well out of our way. Two giggly girls, who can blame him?'

'You were a handful, then?'

Nicky smiled. 'I'm sure we were. Racing around, shrieking. Singing. What was that song? "Girls Just Wanna . . ."'

'"Just Wanna Have Fun."'

'That's right. Singing it at the tops of our voices, bouncing up and down on the settee. Sooner or later, Jenny would come in and ask us to calm down. Mary's dad's sleeping, that's what she'd usually say. And then we'd tiptoe round, hush, hush, hush, you know, all exaggerated, creeping past the bedroom. Pretending there was some kind of monster the other side of the door.'

Nicky's eyes were bright, remembering.

'He came out once, suddenly. Out of the bedroom. Just, you know, in his pyjamas. Pyjama trousers. Almost fell over us. We'd been crawling along the floor, right outside the door. He picked Mary up – she was the nearest – grabbed her, really. Lifted her off the floor as if she weighed nothing, as if she were a doll or something. Really angry. Shouting and swearing. I'd never seen anyone so angry.'

Her expression had changed. The brightness disappeared; replaced, Catherine thought, by something akin to fear. Real remembered fear.

'What happened?'

'Nothing. I thought – at the time I thought, I don't know, that he was going to swing her round, round his head, throw her against the wall. The way he was holding her. I really did. But he didn't. Didn't do anything of the sort. After a few moments, he put her down. Just, you know, gently. Went wherever he was going without saying a word. Off to the bathroom, I suppose.'

Catherine waited, drank some tea, giving Nicky time to recover.

'Did you talk about it afterwards?' she asked then. 'You and Mary?'

'No. Never. Stopped playing monsters, that was all.'

'And that was the only time you saw him lose his temper?'

Nicky nodded emphatically.

'You're sure?'

'Yes.'

'Never with Jenny, Mary's mum?'

'No.'

Catherine leaned away. 'It's okay,' she said. 'I'm sorry.'

'What for?'

'All those leading questions. As if I'm giving you the third degree.' She gave a wry smile. 'Back to interviewing class for me.'

'Are there such things?'

'More or less.'

'Passed yours with flying colours?'

'Scraped a C.' Catherine laughed, took a bite out of her scone. 'It's just, Mary and her brothers aside, you're the only person we've found who was in that house over an extended period – one of the few people who can give us a sense of what it was like.'

'Apart from Linda.'

'Linda?'

'Yes. She lived opposite.'

'And she and Jenny, they were what, friends?'

'I suppose so. I mean, I don't really know. But she was in and out of the house a lot, I know that. Her little boy – I should be able to remember his name – David? He must have been the same age as Brian, Mary's younger brother. They went to nursery together.' She pushed a hand up through her hair. 'They could've taken it in turns, I suppose, her and Jenny, you know, collecting the little ones, taking them in. It happens all the time.' She smiled. 'What mums do.'

'And this Linda, you can't remember her other name? Surname?'

'No, I'm sorry. But then I probably never knew it in the first place. Just Linda.'

'Don't worry,' Catherine said, 'someone will know.'

'You'll talk to her?'

'If we can.'

Nicky added jam to half a scone. 'Can I ask you something?'

'Go ahead.'

'That bump, there on your forehead . . .'

Catherine's hand started to move towards it instinctively. 'Oh, it's nothing. I slipped, that's all.'

'What? On the pavement? They're treacherous, sometimes.'

'No, indoors. My own kitchen.'

'Too much wine?'

'I wish.' She dipped her head. 'Olive oil. On the floor.'

The rear door opened and a tall man in tweed jacket and jeans stepped out and raised a hand in greeting. Older than Nicky, Catherine guessed, by a good few years.

'You want some tea, Richard? There's some in the pot.'

'No, thanks. You carry on. I thought I'd go and collect Lottie.'

'Okay.'

'William comes home on his own,' Nicky said, somehow feeling the need to explain. 'It's not far. Just the one big road to cross. But you have to let them, don't you? At least that's what I think. Be independent. How else are they going to learn? Mums driving round in great four-by-fours, picking their kids up at the school gate, shepherding them everywhere. Frightened to let them out of their sight, almost. As if there's some bogeyman out there.'

Looking at Catherine, she slowly shook her head.

'But that's not where it happens, is it? You must know that better than anyone. Children, anything bad that happens – abuse, whatever – most times it happens in the home.'

40

Ever since it happened she's tried to wipe it from her mind. Scrub it clean away, just as she washed every trace of him from her body, hot water, washcloth and sponge. But still she feels his hand on her shoulder when she turns; in bed, when she edges away from Barry, it is his – Danny's – mouth on her breast, so real, this, that it aches, the nipple erect.

Sometimes, when she goes into the kitchen, gone to get more squash for the children, or to check if the potatoes are boiling, she sees the pair of them, Danny and herself, wrapped around each other on the kitchen floor.

No one to talk to about it, it's driving her crazy.

She's thought about telling Edna, but fears her disapproval. Hears Edna telling her to get a grip, cast it out of her mind and think about the real issues instead. Time enough for slippin' around when this lot's over. Not that I'm sayin' you should.

She thinks about telling Linda, but that's a nonstarter. Nice enough, but a bit strait-laced where some things are concerned; too embarrassed, almost, to knock and ask if she had any spare tampons when she'd run out herself and the shop was closed. Talk for England, could Linda, as long as it didn't mean talking about her bits.

She thinks about asking Jill . . . and realises she hasn't the least idea how her sister would react.

Close when they were little, aside from the usual covetous spat over this or that comic or doll, after going up to the big school they had drifted apart.

Chalk and cheese, their mother had said.

Jill the more studious, the one who'd invariably be found stuck in the corner with a book, while Jenny was outside playing hopscotch, taking turns with one end of the washing line she and the other girls used as a giant skipping rope; Jenny teasing the boys.

Yet it was Jill who had a boyfriend first: a quiet lad with National Health spectacles who trailed Jill everywhere, waited for her after school and then walked home five paces behind. One Sunday evening, she had shocked them all by asking if Gordon – Gordon, that was his name – could come to tea the next weekend.

Their mum had got out the best tablecloth, best chinaware, bought a nice piece of boiling bacon from the butcher, made a trifle. Poor Gordon had scarcely eaten a thing, hardly said a word.

'Well,' their dad had said when it was over, 'he's a poor thing and no mistake.'

Jill had fled the room in tears.

Gordon never came to tea again and when Jenny asked, somewhat maliciously, it's true, if they were still going out together, Jill had told her not to be so stupid, she had more important things to do, like passing her O levels. Unlike you.

Jill had transferred up to the grammar school, a forty-five-minute journey each way on the bus.

Jenny had stayed at the secondary modern.

Net result: Jill went on and took her A levels, thought seriously about applying for university, but settled instead for a junior position in the administrative department of Nottingham University, which was where she still worked. Jenny stayed put, got married, had kids.

End of story.

Not quite.

Jill kept her private life, in so far as she had one, very much to herself. She was still living at home with her parents, after all.

Once in a while – Sunday lunch, say, all the family round the table, Jenny and Barry's kids in their best clothes, best behaviour – someone would ask, politely, if Jill were seeing anyone, and Jill, just as politely, would say no, not right now, and move the subject along.

There was somebody Jenny saw her with once, a tallish man who'd smiled out from behind rimless glasses and looked for all the world, Jenny thought, like a Gordon grown up – except that Gordon would never have smiled. They'd met, Jill told her later, at the art class she went to Wednesday evenings and occasional weekends. She never told her his name.

Since the summer, since their parents had moved away, she knew Jill had only been working part-time, first four days a week and then three. Not only the coal industry was feeling the pinch.

Today, Jenny knows, is one of Jill's days off. She thinks about ringing first, to make sure she's in, but wonders what she'll say, not wanting to start explaining over the phone. And if Jill has gone out, she's likely not gone far.

Besides all of which, it's not exactly far to walk. The other end of the village, the place their parents had moved into when their father first got a job down the pit. Not much more than a two up, two down, with a kitchen extension at the back, bathroom above that.

A chill in the air, Jenny tucks a scarf down into the

collar of her winter coat. She sees one of the women from the support group on the opposite side of the street and waves, rather than stopping to chat.

She feels a slight tug seeing the house she grew up in; though, in truth, if she has crossed its threshold more than a few times since her parents moved, she'd be surprised.

Different courses: different lives.

Though it's mid-morning a light still burns in one of the upstairs windows. Left on, Jenny thinks, by mistake.

She knocks and waits.

Maybe Jill has gone out after all.

Oh, well . . . she knocks again, less in hope than expectation. Turns away. She's halfway across the road when the door opens.

'Jenny?'

Jill is standing on the front step, tucking her blouse down into the waistband of her skirt.

'I thought you were out,' Jenny says. 'Given up.'

'Did you knock before?'

'Twice.'

'I didn't hear you.'

The two sisters look at one another.

'You'd best come in,' Jill says.

There's a man seated in one of a pair of easy chairs in the front room. He half-rises as Jenny follows Jill in.

'You know Keith,' Jill says.

Yes, she knows Keith. Keith Haines. He's the village bobby, has been these past several years. Had a house in the village, a police house, but moved out a good month back when his windows were smashed for the third time in as many weeks, paint thrown over the front door.

'Just dropped in for a cup of tea,' Keith says.

'You'll have one,' says Jill. 'There's plenty in the pot.'

Still not quite able to take it all in, Jenny shakes her head. 'No, it's okay. I only popped in on the off chance. You've got company, I'll go.'

'No call on my account,' Keith says, though she can tell he doesn't mean it.

'What on earth's going on?' Jenny manages to whisper at the door.

'I'll tell you later,' Jill says.

There is no later.

Jill neither phones nor calls round. Jenny feels awkward about making the next move herself. When she bumps into Keith Haines a few days later – almost literally, turning a corner – he gives her a cheesy grin and carries on walking past.

41

It nagged at Catherine for the remainder of the afternoon and on into the evening: the picture that Nicky had created. Two little girls playing monsters and the monster had suddenly, terrifyingly, become real. Even after all that time, the fear had been tangible in her voice, her eyes. Little girls exaggerate, of course, tease themselves with made-up tales of evil witches, wizards, wicked stepmothers; talk themselves into nightmares that leave them shaken in their beds, hair damp and skin slick with sweat. Tales of Snow White and Little Red Riding Hood coming home to roost.

Catherine's parents had read those stories to her in Mombasa when she was little; but they had read her Kenyan stories too, like the one about the hare who escapes from the farmer's cooking pot by outwitting the chicken into taking his place. Catherine had felt sorry for the chicken, but admired the hare for his cleverness and cunning. And, unlike Little Red Riding Hood, there'd been no need for a woodsman to come to the rescue swinging an axe.

Back at her flat, she sliced a banana into a bowl of yoghurt, added a cocktail of seeds she'd bought at the health-food shop and stirred in a teaspoon of honey.

Before sitting down, she changed the Bach CD that was still in the stereo for the new KT Tunstall. Scottish, wasn't she, Tunstall? Perhaps she should try dropping her name into the conversation in the office, impress John McBride. Except McBride wouldn't know KT Tunstall from Mary, Queen of Scots.

And anyway, McBride hadn't been quite such a pain lately. That morning he'd even smiled in her direction, showing off a motley collection of misshapen teeth.

Opening her laptop she pulled down the files from the inquiry, statements Sandford and Cresswell had taken from people in Bledwell Vale. Friends of the Hardwicks, neighbours; members of the Women's Support Group. No mention of a Linda that she could see.

Linda?

Linda what?

It should be easy enough, first thing tomorrow, for one of the team to check the local census, voting records, whatever. Maybe the older Hardwick boy would be able to remember a name. Mary, even; she could phone Mary. After which would come the rigmarole of tracking the person down. Something a little more straightforward this time, she hoped, not another Geoff Cartwright, off in the wilds of Saskatchewan; another Danny Ireland, astray somewhere in the Scottish Highlands.

Didn't anybody stay at home any more?

Not that she could talk.

With all that extra chasing, she would have to speak again to the divisional commander at Potter Street, see if she couldn't get another body seconded to her team, even if just temporarily; someone to work the Internet, make calls. If the DC was still being sticky, she supposed she could always approach Picard, ask him to intervene, but only as a last resort.

Pouring herself a glass of wine, white from the fridge, she scrolled down from statement to statement, searching for something she might have missed in response to questions about the Hardwicks' relationship.

Tension between them, there had to be, the way they'd been straddling both sides during the strike. Not too many families can go on like that, riven down the middle, without coming to blows. And the rumours Jenny might have set her cap elsewhere, that'd not have helped. Nor was there any doubt that Hardwick had something of a temper. It was not solely Nicky Parker's vivid memory that gave testimony to that. Reading through the interviews again, the signs were there. Harsh words, a fist raised in anger, but over almost as soon as it had begun. Meant nothing, people said. Letting off steam, that's all it was. Better out than in.

Search as she might, Catherine could find nothing that suggested those threats, those raised fists had become blows, nothing that testified to any actual violence being meted out. Perhaps, if it had happened at all, it had remained unseen?

What was that corny old song her uncle used to sing at parties? Her uncle, the only known Kenyan country-and-western singer in captivity. There was even a clip of him on YouTube, stetson hat, waistcoat with silver buttons, bootlace tie, black face shining.

'Behind Closed Doors', that was the song.

She reached for her phone and speed-dialled Resnick's number. 'Charlie, probably the last thing you want at this moment is company . . .'

He had bought a jar of marinated herrings with onions and dill from the Polish deli, a large jar of pickled gherkins and a loaf of black rye bread. As a treat, a bottle of Cornelius unfiltered wheat beer.

He'd thought he might sit and read a little, listen to some music – a toss-up between Monk with Sonny Rollins or Cannonball Adderley's *Somethin' Else!* – watch the *News at Ten* and then have an early night.

'I'm sure I'm disturbing you,' Catherine said, as she followed him into the house.

'Not at all.'

Evidence suggested otherwise. There was a plate still balanced on the side of his favourite chair, half a slice of bread, herring, a piece of half-eaten gherkin; a glass of beer on the table next to an old copy of *The Jazz Scene* he'd found in a charity shop; Cannonball, slinky and sensuous, playing 'Dancing in the Dark'.

'You've eaten?' Resnick asked.

'Yes. Sort of.'

'You like herring?'

'I suppose so. I'm really not sure.'

In the kitchen, he buttered bread, forked pieces of herring from the jar.

'Gherkin?'

'Pass.'

'I'm afraid I've almost finished the beer . . .'

'I should have brought some wine . . .'

'There's whisky. Springbank. Only ten years old . . .'

'Only?'

He grinned. 'Someone gave me a bottle of eighteen years once.'

'Good?'

'Worth every penny of the sixty-odd pounds it would have cost. Likely more than that now.'

'You should treat yourself.'

'Maybe.'

'Anyway, I'm sure this will be fine.'

'Water?'

'Just a little.'

'You can brag to McBride you've been enjoying a good single malt.'

Catherine looked at him questioningly. 'Have you said anything to him lately?'

'Said?'

'About me?'

'No, why?'

'He's been close to what probably passes for McBride as charming.'

Resnick nodded, pleased. 'Let's take these next door.'

The CD had come to an end.

'More music?'

'I don't really mind.'

'What would you do at home? If you were sitting around on your own. Would you play music then?'

'Yes, probably.'

Resnick went across to the stereo. 'This okay?'

'I liked it. What I heard.'

He pressed play. 'Autumn Leaves'. Sat down, careful not to dislodge his plate from its precarious position. 'Could be, when you phoned, you were bored and desperate for company, but somehow I doubt it.'

Catherine smiled. 'There is something. It's been

bugging me. Since I saw Nicky Parker – Mary Connor's friend – this afternoon.'

'All ears.'

She told him about Linda, the missing neighbour, and, what had been preying on her mind most, the incident Nicky had so vividly described.

'Aside from anything else, it's difficult to match it with the man we talked to in Chesterfield. Happily pedalling back from his allotment; helping out the old lady next door.'

'People change. Mellow. And besides, she could be exaggerating. Nicky. Not meaning to. But things can get magnified with time. Something like this especially. Something that made that much of an impression on her when she was just a kid . . .'

'Which it clearly did.'

'That could account for it looming so large now.'

Catherine took a sip of whisky, decided she liked it, had another. The herring was another matter.

'You think we should pay it no heed then, no special attention, log it and let it be?'

'Not at all. And I certainly don't think another chat with Barry Hardwick would be a waste of time. But let's see first if we can't track this Linda down, the neighbour, see what she has to say. If she was in and about as much as Nicky says, she should be able to tell us something.'

'Let's hope so.'

Resnick polished off the last of the contents of his plate, took a last swallow of beer.

'The way I see it, all this Michael Swann business, we allowed ourselves to get sidetracked. It happens. Fight against tunnel vision and sometimes, without noticing, you go too far the other way. Everything becomes possible. And with a team the size of ours – yours – that's got its own problems.'

'I know. I just wish we had something more definite, something to hone in on. Instead of just Nicky's story and whatever it is that's nagging away at my insides.'

'You don't suppose that could be the herring?'

Catherine laughed. It was a good sound, easy and free.

Resnick relaxed back into his chair. This was the first time, he realised, that another woman had been in the house – let alone sitting there in the living room, a glass in her hand – since Lynn had been killed.

It felt strange; strange, yet strangely good.

The cat wandered in, sniffed around Catherine's ankles, and wandered back out. The music slipped, almost without a pause, from one tune to another.

'The other day,' Resnick said, 'when I asked you about the bruise on your forehead . . .'

'I said I'd slipped.'

'And if I asked you again now . . .'

'The same answer. I slipped on some oil.'

'That man in Worksop . . .'

'Abbas.'

'Abbas. It was nothing to do with him?'

'No, nothing at all.'

The mood broken, it wasn't so very much longer before Catherine decided it was time to be on her way.

'See you tomorrow, Charlie. And thanks for letting me disturb your evening,' she said at the door.

'Any time.'

He watched her go, the tail lights of her car. Looked out across the garden, the low wall separating it from the pavement, the road. Remembered. Fought against remembering. Went back inside. Another whisky, warm against the back of his throat. It helped, but not a great deal.

All the way home, driving across the city, Catherine worried at it like a cat with an injured bird. Couldn't leave it alone. Something she had read in the statements taken after the funeral: something about Jenny sporting a black eye, an injury, she'd claimed, sustained on the picket line.

The truth or a lie?

Perhaps, like Catherine herself, Jenny had thought it was nobody's business but her own.

On the stairs going up to the flat, the thought of Abbas flooded her mind, the fear he might be there, waiting to spring out of the dark.

Monsters?

No.

Abbas would never be hanging around, she knew that, not after what had happened. Too proud by half.

She turned the key in the lock, stepped inside and locked and bolted the door behind her. Not too late for a bath before bed.

42

The following morning, as she was just stepping out on to the Ropewalk, Catherine's phone rang: the cold case team looking again at Donna Crowder's murder. Could she possibly spare them an hour or so? The sooner the better, all things considered. Catherine tried Resnick's number, caught him just as he was leaving. Michael Swann, that's what they were going to want to talk about, Fleetwood also.

'Best drive up together, Charlie. Sheffield. Meet me here. We'll go in mine.'

An hour or so became two. The cold case team comprised a detective inspector nearing retirement and two former detective sergeants brought back into service. By the time Catherine and Resnick arrived at the Worksop office, further delayed by a four-car pile-up on the motorway, it was well into the afternoon and things had changed.

Conscious of the coming extra workload – by the end of the day, names from the Donna Crowder inquiry would, doubtless, be added to the load – John McBride had smuggled in a couple of extra computers, two extra desks, and, more importantly, had called in sufficient favours to have acquired the temporary services of two of the station's civilian staff.

Vanessa and Gloria. Mother and daughter.

Identical outfits, identical hairstyles, save that Gloria's was darker at the roots. One was busy inputting, the other checking employment records, chasing addresses.

Without wanting to disturb them unduly, Catherine made herself known, thanked them for their help.

'Not a problem,' Vanessa said. 'Is it, Gloria?'

Gloria shook her head. 'Makes a nice change.'

'This Linda you're after,' Vanessa said. 'Gets around.'

'You've got a name, then?'

'Several. Beckett, that's the name she had when she was living in Bledwell Vale.'

'Her husband's name,' Gloria explained.

'Got divorced in eighty-nine, went back to using Stoneman, that's her maiden name. Then, when she remarried in ninety-three, she became Price, Linda Price. Moved to Taunton.'

'A nightmare,' Gloria said, 'keeping track.'

'Matthew Price, died from a brain tumour in two

thousand and five. Linda went off the rails a bit, by the look of things. Reading, you know, between the lines. Quite a bit of time in hospital.'

'Medical records,' Gloria explained. 'Difficult to get hold of. Details, at least. Confidentiality.'

'From her credit records,' Vanessa said, 'it looks as though she started using her maiden name again round about two thousand and nine. Stoneman. There's an address in Melton Mowbray. She's got family there, or she did. Worked for a short time at Dickinson and Morris. You know, the pies.'

'She's still there now, the same address?' Catherine asked.

Vanessa shook her head.

'I spoke to an aunt,' Gloria said, 'as close to gaga as makes no difference. Difficult to get much sense out of her at all. But from what I did gather, Linda's not lived there now, Melton, for a good couple of years.'

'We'll keep at it,' Vanessa said.

'Well,' Catherine said, 'it seems to me you've done brilliantly so far.'

Both women beamed.

Seeing Resnick in conversation with McBride and Cresswell, Catherine went over. Four names in eighteen-point on the screen of McBride's computer: Eric Somerset, Derek Harmer, James Laing, Joe Willis. All now in their fifties. Each had been interviewed more than once in connection with the crimes for which Michael Swann had later been convicted; each had recently been checked against the Police National Computer, their files requested from General Registry.

'Might want to take a closer look at these two,' McBride said. 'Willis and Harmer.'

Catherine read through the files.

A long-distance lorry driver for most of his working life, Derek Harmer had been the subject of a restraining order after his then wife made a complaint to the police that he had assaulted her just four days after she'd returned home from hospital with their third child. After that, a succession of relatively minor misdemeanours, mixed with more serious incidents of indecent exposure, gross indecency and indecent assault; short prison terms and periods on probation. His work frequently took him north and south between Carlisle and London, west and east along the M62, Merseyside to Yorkshire, Liverpool to Hull, with detours to Sheffield, Derby, Nottingham, Leeds.

According to their information, Harmer's current address was in Kingston upon Hull.

'I've got a pal,' McBride said. 'DS. Humberside Police Headquarters on Priory Road. Could always ask him to call round, check dates and places, rattle Harmer's cage.'

'Do that. Get him to report back to us.'

Joe Willis's file, augmented by some basic Googling, was, as McBride explained, a sight more complicated.

Something of a soccer player, he had been on the books of Mansfield Town, his local club, for a time; a young full-back showing promise, one or two of the bigger clubs sniffing round. After a couple of seasons, a poor disciplinary record led to a transfer to non-league Altrincham. Willis remained with them for three seasons, before drifting out of the game. It was while working as a bouncer in Manchester that he first came to the notice of the police, a number of incidents involving violence, warnings as to his future behaviour, charges that never made it into court. An eighteen-month sentence, suspended, after a complaint for assault was brought against him by his then partner; two years later, on a visit home to Mansfield, he was arrested on a charge of rape by a woman who claimed he'd attacked her in a pub car park after closing, a charge that was later dropped when the woman declined to give evidence in court. Then, just a year before Jenny Hardwick was murdered, he picked up a woman at a slip road leading off the M1 at junction 32 and heading towards Doncaster. According to the testimony she gave later, Willis assaulted her in a lay-by, insisting she perform oral sex on him by way of payment for the lift and striking her when she refused. He was arrested, charged and a short while before the case came to court, the CPS withdrew the charge and he walked free.

A nasty but charmed life.

He was currently living back near Mansfield, Kirkby-in-Ashfield, unemployed and claiming benefit.

'Sandford and Cresswell?' McBride suggested.

'You think they're up to it? You know them better than me.'

McBride's face slanted into a grin. 'Gotta get bloodied some time.'

'All right. But not without back-up. Make a call to Mansfield, will you, John? Don't want them walking into something nasty.'

'Right, boss.'

'But before you do that, more names, I'm afraid. Suspects questioned back in eighty-seven over Donna Crowder's murder.'

She set the printout before him.

'I've marked the ones Charlie and I consider most likely, but you'll want to check them yourself. Sheffield are sending the files over today.'

Any further conversation was halted by a triumphant shout from Vanessa at the other side of the room.

'Linda Stoneman, gotcha!'

'Where?' Catherine asked.

'Lands' End.'

'Fuck that for a game of soldiers!' growled McBride. 'All the way to the arse end of fucking Cornwall!'

'No,' said Vanessa, 'not that Land's End. The clothing company. You know, mail order, online. Their headquarters, it's in Oakham. About an hour's drive.'

43

Much of the euphoria Jenny felt earlier – the big rally in Mansfield, her own first time on the platform – was beginning, just gradually, to fade. She'd spoken again on several occasions – to a group of firemen in north London, some schoolteachers in Stoke-on-Trent, and at a meeting of the National Union of Railwaymen in York – and it had felt good, the sense of people listening, going along with her arguments, but more and more there was a sense of preaching to the converted.

Read the papers, listen to the news and you'd think the strike was on its last legs, the Coal Board and the government victorious, but then the papers, the media were all in the government's pocket – just about all – and what you got from them was a jaundiced version of the truth at best.

What happened at Orgreave, for instance – the Battle

of Orgreave, as people were calling it – the way it had been reported on the *Nine O'Clock News*. Edited to make it seem as if the police action – mounted officers charging downhill into groups of fleeing miners, batons swinging – had been in response to miners hurling bricks and stones, whereas, in reality, it had been the other way round. The police had charged, the stones been thrown in self-defence.

Of course, the BBC denied it. What else would you expect, as Peter Waites had said. Government have got them in their pocket, haven't they? Toe the party line, or next spending round find your licence money trimmed by half.

And the trouble was, with so many people, it worked. In Notts, where the strike had never been as strong, especially.

The drip, drip, drip of misinformation.

Wives asking her in whispers after meetings, how much longer were they going to have to hold out? The most militant areas aside, the slow drift back to work continued. The temptation of increased redundancy money too great for some near-starving families to resist.

Christmas was coming, as Peter Waites had said, and MacGregor and his mates the only bastards growing fat.

Edna had called a meeting of the wives' support group to make plans for a big communal get-together, ensure presents for each and every family with children. A toy and a turkey for each striking household, that was what was wanted. Hard to promise, difficult to deliver. But a lorryload of toys was already reported to be on the way from the Ruhr Valley in Germany, and, before the deadline, there would be others.

'I don't know,' one of the women at the meeting said. 'It don't feel right, somehow. Accepting charity that way. It makes me feel like I'm a step off the poorhouse or something.'

'That's because you are, duck,' said another. 'We all are.'

'Look at it this way,' Edna said. 'If it was foreign miners out on strike – French, German, Russian, whatever – fighting for their rights, their livelihoods, wouldn't we be the ones helping them out any way we could?'

'Put it that way . . .' said the doubter.

Jenny liked to think that would be so. One for all and all for one. She'd scarce had a political thought in her head before all this had blown up and now it was full of them. Wriggling round like little sperm cells, mostly, looking for something to fertilise.

She hadn't thought so much about that till recently, either.

Unbidden images of her one-off encounter with Danny coming to her a little less frequently now, maybe, but not fading away.

Sometimes, despite her best intentions, she deliberately encouraged them not to.

She's sitting gossiping with Linda one afternoon, the two youngsters playing cheerfully enough with bits and pieces of Lego, pushing them together and then pulling them apart again, when there's a knock at the back door.

Jenny's immediate thought, it's Danny, and how's she going to explain that to Linda. Blood rushing to her cheeks she's hoping hasn't been noticed.

'Hang on a minute!'

Fumbling the door open, her heart's going nineteen to the dozen, but it's Jill, standing there solemn, expression just this side of apologetic.

'Come in,' Jenny says, stepping back. 'Come on in.'

Jill looks round as if she's hardly been there before, which is not so far from true.

'Linda, this is Jill, my big sister. Jill, Linda. Linda's lad goes to nursery with Brian.'

Linda smiles, starts collecting her things. 'All right now,' she calls into the other room, 'time we were going.'

Five minutes later, give or take, the sisters are sitting either side of the kitchen table. Jenny's made a fresh pot of tea, scrabbled together enough biscuits to cover the surface of a small plate, though neither of them has shown much interest in eating.

'That day . . .' Jill starts.

'You don't have to explain.'

'That day, when you called round . . .'

'I said, there's no need to explain.'

'I don't want you to think . . .'

Jenny looks at her sharply, a smile forming. 'Think what?'

'You know.'

'That you were having a quick shag in the middle of the morning.'

'Don't say that.'

'That's not what you were doing?'

'That's not what I mean.'

'What then?'

'Don't call it that.'

Jenny laughs. 'Shag?

'It makes it sound . . .' She's not sure what it makes it sound.

'Cheap?' Jenny suggests.

'Yes.'

'Furtive? Sudden? Keith, the local bobby, calls round waving his truncheon and the next minute you're all over him, ripping off his uniform . . .'

'Stop!'

'Dragging him upstairs to the bedroom . . .'

'Stop it! Just . . . stop it.' There are tears at the corners of her eyes and her face is white with anger. 'You never did, you never could take anything seriously. Everything a big joke. School. Everything.

Unless it was about you and then, of course, everyone else better realise just how serious it was. Your marriage. Your kids. And now, your bloody strike.'

The tears have gone, disappeared.

Across the table, Jenny is shaking, literally shaking.

She hasn't seen her sister like this since they were teenagers, one evening when Jill had suddenly erupted over seemingly nothing, a borrowed pair of shoes, a cardigan, a lipstick.

But this is different.

'I'm sorry,' Jenny says. 'I didn't mean to . . .' But realises that she did. Changes tack. 'How long . . . Keith, how long have you been seeing him?'

'A month. A month or so.'

'And what? It's serious?'

'Yes. Yes, I think so.'

Jenny leans back, picks up her cup but doesn't drink. 'You never said.'

'Now you can see why.'

'Jill, I'm sorry.'

She reaches out a hand, but Jill doesn't take it.

'It was just, you know, a bit of a joke.'

'But it's not that.'

'I know. I know that now.'

'And I didn't want you going round gossiping . . .'

'I haven't. Jill, I wouldn't . . .'

'While all this is going on – the strike – we thought it best to keep it quiet, between ourselves. Otherwise it all gets mixed up with everything that's going on, and Keith . . . one way and another, he's had a lot to contend with.'

Jenny nods, though she thinks Keith Haines has got pretty much what he's deserved. Bit of a nasty side to him, or so she's heard. The kind who'll take advantage, given the chance.

'Have you said anything to Mum and Dad?' she asks.

'We're going over next weekend.'

'You and Keith?'

Jill looks at her as if to say, who else?

Jenny is thinking, faced with a police officer as a son-in-law – which she supposes all this will mean – her dad will have a right conniption.

Jill is drinking her tea, glancing round, making ready to go. Out of sight, Brian starts to cry and, with a sigh, Jenny goes to see what's wrong. When she comes back, Brian in her arms, sucking a thumb, Jill is over by the door, anxious to go.

'When you see Mum and Dad,' Jenny says, 'give them my love. Tell them I'll bring the kids over soon.'

There was a time when they would have shared a quick hug, a kiss on the cheek; now Jill quickly nods and turns busily on her way. Despite his best efforts, Jenny sets Brian back down and starts to clear away. Jill and Keith Haines, it's fair taken her by surprise.

44

Linda Stoneman's house was on a new estate, close by the ring road, no more than a stone's throw, as she liked to say, from the old rugby ground. 'Sold to developers,' she'd said, chatting away to Catherine as if they'd known one another for ages. 'Nine hundred new homes they're building. Nine hundred. How the town'll cope, I can't imagine. Doctors' surgery's moved into bigger premises already.'

Following Catherine's call to check directions, the GPS persisting in ordering them the wrong way round a new roundabout, Linda had met them at the gate. An ample woman in a floral dress, cardigan over otherwise bare arms, she had greeted them cheerily, apologising for living somewhere that wasn't yet on Google Maps, and invited them inside.

After Catherine had properly introduced Resnick

and herself, the pair of them followed Linda along a paved drive and into a house that positively shone, the lingering smell of citrus air freshener mingling with that of pine disinfectant.

'How long have you been living here?' Catherine asked.

'Six weeks tomorrow. Though sometimes it seems like six months. Others, the day before yesterday. But please, sit yourselves down. I put the kettle on when you phoned. You would both like a cup of tea?'

Both nodded.

Interviewing people in their own homes, Resnick was thinking and not for the first time, you ended up drinking as much tea as one of those chimpanzees from Twycross Zoo who did the PG Tips ads on TV.

'I was living in Melton,' Linda explained when she came back through. 'Then, when Mum passed away, I thought to move here. I'd got the job at Lands' End by then and it saved a good half-hour or so's journey either way. Besides, the smell from Pedigree Pet Foods when the wind's in the wrong direction . . .'

She wafted a hand front of her nose.

'I had a nice little flat here at first, but when Gerry and I got together, I mean, really thought we might make a go of it, we needed somewhere bigger – he's got grandchildren, has Gerry – so we took the plunge. Not easy that either, neither one of us spring chickens and both married before, twice in my case, baggage by the vanload, if you know what I mean. But anyway, Gerry brought me out to take a look at it, did the sums, said as how, if we didn't go crazy – go crazy, us, at our age – we could manage the payments, so I thought, why not? In for a penny, in for a pound. Gerry had got this little nest egg when he retired. Mind you, he's back working part-time. Lands' End, same as me. One thing, though, however much he asked me, I said I'd not change my name. Not again. Stoneman I was and Stoneman I'd stay. And so here we are.'

All that with scarcely a pause for breath,

'What do you do?' Resnick asked. 'At Lands' End?' Enquiring out of politeness as much as anything.

'Me? Front End Quality Tester. Make sure all your buttons are in place. Your zip's not been sewn in upside down or back to front. You'd be surprised.'

She poured the tea.

'Enough of me,' she said. 'It's not my life story you've come to hear.' She shook her head. 'Poor Jenny. I always thought – liked to think, anyway – she was off somewhere, somewhere nice, a new family maybe, a new life. Thought she'd met the man of her dreams, down London somewhere . . .'

'London? Why London?'

'Oh, down there quite a bit, Jenny was. That winter. Union business of some kind. At least, that's what I think. Something to do with the strike, anyway.'

'Making speeches, you mean?' Resnick asked. 'Rallies and so on?'

'I'm really not sure. All I know is, she'd ask me, last minute usually, could I come over and babysit. That'd be when Barry was on nights. So I'd take mine over and we'd all camp out in their living room. Kids loved it, you can imagine.'

'And how often did this happen?'

'Ooh, two or three times. November, December. Maybe more. Late, an' all, she'd be sometimes, getting back.'

'And Jenny never said anything about meeting somebody down there? A man, I mean?'

Linda smiled. 'Tall dark stranger? Love's young dream? No, that was me. Imagination working over-time. Too much Mills and Boon.'

'Her husband,' Catherine said. 'How did he feel about it, do you think? These trips to London?'

Linda ran it through in her mind before answering. 'What you have to realise, by then at least, there were a lot of things they weren't talking about at all. Living under the same roof, it was the only thing they could do. Anything of Jenny's to do with the strike, I never heard him say a word. She just got on with it and so did he.'

'They didn't argue, then? That's what you're saying?'

Linda set down her cup in its saucer. 'What I'm saying is, they didn't argue about that.'

'What then?'

'Oh, usual things. Bickering, really. Stuff to do with the kids. Jobs he still expected her to do around the house. Iron his shirts, have a dinner in the oven when he came off shift. So, you know, iron your own bloody shirts, get your own bloody dinner, there'd be a lot of that. And the occasional plate'd go flying.'

'He had a temper, then?'

'They both did. Barry worst of all. Not often, maybe. Not, you know, truly lost it. But when he did . . .'

'Can you remember any . . .'

'One. One time especially. November, it would have been. Somewhere towards the end of November. I don't know what caused it, mind. But I'd just popped in to see if Jenny wanted me to take Brian in next day and it was like, I don't know, walking into some kind of thunderstorm. Both of them shouting and screaming in one another's faces. I was fair frightened, I don't mind saying. And then Barry, he shouts, "I'll kill you! I'll f-ing kill you!" And he's got his fist, raised, like this, and I'm standing there thinking, he will, he will. And then he turns away from her and puts his fist right through the wall, the partition wall. And I realise I'm shouting, too. No idea what, just words. And Jenny, she's standing there, just staring at him. Defiant, you know. You dare. You just dare. Barry, he walked away. Wrapped his hand in a tea towel and walked away. And, after a minute, Jenny, she starts talking to me as if nothing out of the way had happened. And I remember thinking, I couldn't live like this, I just couldn't.'

For a moment Catherine looked down at the ground.

'Next time I went round,' Linda said, 'wall'd been repaired. Painted up like new. He was good like that, though, Barry. DIY, you know? Proper handyman, if he put his mind to it. One time when we were having problems with the toilet, for instance, blocked up, not draining away, I was all for getting on to the Coal Board, asking them to come round and fix it, but Barry said not to bother, he'd see to it and he did. Good with his hands, that's what it is. Comes maybe from working down the pit.'

Driving back towards the A1, Catherine flicked on the radio: more bad news about the economy in Spain, or was it Portugal; some dreadful tragedy somewhere, people trapped in a factory. China? India? She knew she should care and in a distant way she did. She used to care more. Sent money, signed petitions. What had happened?

'You listening to this?' she asked.

'Not really.'

She switched to another station, local radio, lowered the volume.

'Proper handyman,' she said. 'Hardwick. Good with his hands.'

Resnick nodded. 'Good enough to knock a hole in the wall, then set it to rights so no one would notice.'

'What d'you think? You think there's enough to bring him in?'

'Depends how it's done. Question him as a witness, concerned party, certainly, we can do that. Whether there's enough to arrest him, I don't know. We could, of course, if that's what you decide. And I think, nowadays especially, a lot of people would. Trouble is, you know as well as me, go down that road, first thing he's likely to do is get himself a lawyer, the lawyer advises him to say no comment, no comment ad infinitum and we're stymied, nowhere to go.'

'How about questioning him under caution, but no arrest?'

'Do that, we have to tell him he can walk back out at any time, not a thing we can do to stop him.'

'But if he decides to stay?'

'There's a good chance he's prepared to talk.'

'And if he goes?'

'He doesn't like our company?'

'Or he's got something to hide.'

Catherine watched for a gap in the traffic, sidled in, signalled and switched lanes. A short way along, she turned the volume on the radio back up again; some old song from the seventies, seventies soul. Sort of thing Jenny might have danced to at her wedding. For richer, for poorer; in sickness or in health. Till death us do part.

45

Barry Hardwick had nicked himself shaving, a fragment of the toilet paper he'd used to staunch the cut still sticking to his chin. After a day or so of brighter weather, the temperature easing itself pleasantly upwards, normal service had been resumed. Hardwick had his donkey jacket buttoned tight when he presented himself at the front desk, cap pulled down, scarf at his neck.

The duty sergeant had made an interview room available: the usual airless anonymity, the now usual technology. Introductions made on tape, the machine set in motion; a copy of the tape would be supplied at the interview's conclusion.

'What's all this about then?' Hardwick had asked before he was even seated. 'Some kind of – what d'you call it? – breakthrough?'

'We just wanted to talk to you about your wife's

murder,' Catherine said. 'Bring you up to date with the investigation. But I want to make clear that you are not under arrest and can leave at any time you choose. Is that understood?'

'Yes.'

'And you are happy to talk to us without a solictor being present?'

'Yes.'

'Very well.'

Catherine spoke in general terms about the progress they were making, avenues being explored, without there being a great deal to add to the telephone conversation they'd had after all the Michael Swann rumours had broken.

'It's nowt to do with him, then,' Hardwick said, 'that evil so-and-so, you're certain?'

'In the circumstances, we think it's unlikely.'

'Take some comfort from that, at least. Set the mind racin' somethin' rotten, I don't mind tellin' you.'

'We wondered,' Catherine said, 'if, since the funeral, you'd thought of anything else that might help us – something that's come back to you and that you think we should know.'

'Like what, for instance?'

'Anything, really. Anything you think might be pertinent.'

You could see Hardwick turning it over in his mind like cloggy soil. 'No, can't say that I have.'

'One thing we've been hearing about,' Resnick said, speaking for the first time. 'One or two trips Jenny had been making to London . . .'

'London?'

'Towards the end of the year it would have been . . .'

'She did . . . Let me think . . . Flying all over't shant, she were. But, yes, London, I dare say, along o' the rest.' He made a face. 'Didn't exactly fill me in on her social calendar, did Jenny.'

'How about people she might have met down there – you don't recall her mentioning any names?'

'No. No, but she wouldn't, would she? Knew I'd not be interested. Strike committee, that's who you should be talking to.'

Resnick nodded. 'We have, and we shall do again. But, as you'll know, the one person we'd like to talk to most . . .'

'Peter Waites.'

'Exactly, Peter Waites. Unfortunately, he's no longer around to ask.'

Catherine took a quick glance in Resnick's direction before directing her attention back across the table.

'We'd like to ask you about an incident that took place some time towards the end of November, an argument between Jenny and yourself in which you said . . .' Catherine glanced down at the papers on her desk. 'In which you said, speaking to your wife, "I'll kill you."'

'I said no such thing.'

'"I'll fucking kill you."'

'I never in my life said that. Not to Jenny, not to anyone. And anyone as said I did's a liar.'

'You didn't shout in your wife's face, threaten her, and then, in a fit of temper, punch a hole in the wall?'

Suddenly, Hardwick threw back his head and laughed.

'Is that what this is about? This incident, as you call it? Because, as it happens, I do remember, and save she were there, it was nowt to do with Jenny at all.'

'What then?'

'I'll tell you what. Just come home, hadn't I, home from pit, hoppin' bloody mad. These lads, Yorkshire lads – Barnsley, I dare say, Scargill's lads – tauntin' me all the way. Scab, scab, scab, you know what it were like. Well . . .' Looking at Resnick. 'You'll remember. Most of time I shut it out, either that or paid no attention, in one bloody ear and out t'other, only this time, I don't know why, this one lad – big lad with red face an' sticky-out ears – he really got to me, you know, under the skin, and I just wanted . . .' Hardwick shook his head. 'How I held back from lettin' him have some fist, I dunno.'

He took a breath, continued.

'So I get back home and I must've looked in a right state, 'cause Jenny she notices for once and says, what's up, and I start tellin' her and when I get to the bit about wanting to hit him I take a swing and swing a bit too far and 'fore I know what's happenin' I've punched a hole in bloody wall.'

He sat back as if pleased to have recalled the incident so clearly.

'And that's all there was to it?' Catherine asked.

'Yes, like I said.'

'And at no time did you say, "I'll kill you" or anything like it?'

'No. An' I'd remember if I did.'

'You're sure of that.'

'Sure as I'm sat here.'

Again, Catherine glanced down. 'We have a statement from a witness who remembers what happened differently.'

'Statement? What bloody statement? You can't . . . Oh, wait about, I know, it's Linda, i'n't it? She must've been there. Could've been. Part of bloody furniture, she were in and out so much. Good sort, an' all that, but if ever a woman liked the sound of her own voice . . . she'd've come up with some yarn just for the sake of not shutting up.'

'So when it says here that on the same occasion that you punched a hole in the wall, you threatened your wife with the words –' Catherine read them from the page – '"I'll kill you. I'll fucking kill you," that is untrue?'

'Yes.'

'No such words were uttered?'

'To Jenny? No, not then nor any other time.'

'So the witness is mistaken?'

'Mistaken is right. I told you, didn't I. Linda, if that's who it is, once she's got started, she'll say anything rather than shut up. Lets her imagination run away with her, I dare say. All them books. Allus got her nose in one, if she weren't gabbin' off. Leavin' 'em round the house all the time for Jenny, though I doubt she give 'em as much as a glance. Women's stuff, you know what I mean? Romance.'

He made it sound like a nasty disease.

Catherine slid one sheet of paper over another. 'There are two reports of your wife being seen with a black eye.'

'Oh, aye. Right bobby-dazzler it were, too.'

'You remember it, then?'

'Took one on picket line, didn't she? Like a rugby scrum up there sometimes. Caught somebody's elbow most like. Either that or summat got thrown.'

'Going back for just a minute,' Resnick said. 'This hole in the wall. I was wondering, what happened about that?'

'Happened? How d'you mean?'

'You got a builder in to fix it or what?'

Hardwick gave a quick, dismissive shake of the head. 'Did it myself, didn't I? Easy enough.'

Resnick smiled. 'Only time I ever put up any shelves, first thing I set on them, only light it was, whole lot came tumbling down. Try mending the hole in your wall, I'd like as not end up with something twice the size. Whole bloody wall'd collapse.'

Hardwick shrugged. 'Matter of knowing what you're doing, isn't it? That and a bit of nous.'

'And you do?'

'Come again?'

'Know what you're doing?'

'Yes. Pretty much.'

'Used to get in quite a bit of practice, I dare say. In the village. Once people knew you could turn a hand to things.'

'Helped out once or twice, yes.' He was starting to look anxious, uncertain where the conversation was going.

'The Petersons, their extension, ever help out there at all?'

'No. Never.'

'Quite a few people did, apparently. Hour here, half a day there.'

'And you think . . .' Hardwick leaned heavily forward, hands on the table like fists. 'You think I put my wife in her own grave, that what you're saying? That what you're accusing me of?'

'I'm not saying anything,' Resnick said evenly. 'Just asking a straightforward question. Did you at any time do any work on the Peterson house or did you not?'

Anger was writ large on Hardwick's face. 'You said I could leave, right? Whenever I wanted? No one to stop me.'

'That's right.'

He got to his feet and turned away; just five paces to the door.

Catherine looked sideways towards Resnick – arrest or not?

The interview-room door opened and, just as quickly, closed. Footsteps in the corridor outside, moving away.

'Don't worry,' Resnick said. 'He'll not go far.'

'Let's hope that's not famous last words.'

She could just see the expression on Martin Picard's face. *You had him and you let him fucking walk away . . .*

46

Jenny could tell from Peter Waites' face that things were bad, but not just how bad they were. By now, tales of men going back to work were legion and she could see herself that the numbers passing through the gates – spurred on by the Coal Board's offers of special Christmas bonuses for those who forsook the strike – were slowly but steadily increasing. There were rumours, even, of men returning in some of the more militant of the Yorkshire pits, a trickle mainly – in one case she'd heard, a solitary man, with pickets clamouring at the gates, had been smuggled in through the pithead baths.

And every return was something more for the NCB and the government to glory in; more ammunition, as Waites said, for those bastards in the London press to use in their determination to bring us down. Maxwell, that bastard Maxwell.

Not that we'll give in, not to the likes of him. Not ever.

Victory to the Miners. Coal Not Dole.

For the first time, she was beginning to doubt; to wonder how much longer they could hold on; beginning to hear the first sounds of uncertainty in her own voice when she spoke.

But the plans for the coming Christmas were in place and being fleshed out more all the time; two gigantic parcels of toys had arrived from France and there were more on the way. A fund-raising social had been arranged for the coming weekend: disco and bar, 50p admission and the first pint for every striking miner free, pass the bucket round towards the end, all donations gratefully received.

> *Jingle bells, Jingle bells*
> *Jingle all the way*
> *I'd rather be a picket*
> *Than a scab on*
> *Christmas Day*

Her own kids were excited enough about Christmas already, counting down the days, chanting them over breakfast. Seventeen, sixteen, fifteen . . . Scrabbling round the house, into every nook and cranny, they'd found the Woolworth stockings from the year before, and Mary had hopefully hung hers from the foot of the bed already.

Jenny's mum had been on the phone, anxious to arrange for the family to get together, if not on Christmas Day itself, then Boxing Day perhaps. But Jenny had put her off, imagining things might be difficult enough. 'We'll come over to you,' she'd said. 'New Year. That'd be best.'

'What do you think to this Keith business, then?' her mum had asked. 'Our Jill seems quite smitten, though if I'm to be honest – and you must promise never ever to repeat this – for the life of me I can't see why. And your dad didn't take to him at all.'

However much she might have been tempted to agree, some sense of loyalty to her sister led Jenny to say that, as far as she could see, Keith was all right. And if Jill was happy, well, wasn't that the most important thing?

It gave her pause for thought.

She and Barry, they'd been happy once, hadn't they?

They had, surely.

She's still thinking about this as she's walking home, worrying it through her mind, when a white van – the white, in truth, more smeared over with dirt and dust than not – pulls across the road just ahead of where she's heading.

Jenny slows her pace, then quickens it.

Two men jump out of the van.

She tenses, relaxes, tenses again.

'Hey!' Danny says. 'Thought we'd missed you.'

We?

The man with him, the one who'd been driving, is around the same age as Danny, possibly younger. Slim face with quite a prominent nose, skinny build; hair pushed up out of sight under a woollen hat with badges attached; pale eyes, rabbit-grey.

'This is Steve,' Danny says.

Steve cocks his head to one side, winks.

'Been looking for you all over,' Danny says. 'Tried the Welfare but you'd gone.'

He's cut his hair really short – done it himself, by the look of things, or had a mate do it for him – and on top of that, either starting to grow a beard or in sore need of a shave. For a moment, Jenny imagines the roughness of it against her skin.

From the state of their clothes, the pair of them, she thinks they've come straight from the picket line somewhere. Danny, she knows, taking a risk simply by being there.

'Thought maybe,' Danny says, nodding in the direction of the van, 'you'd like to come for a ride.'

Steve laughs at the word 'ride'. Looks at Jenny and slowly and deliberately pokes out his tongue and rolls it around his open mouth.

'Pig!' Jenny says and pushes between them, pushes past.

Steve laughs even more, a raw dirty laugh, and Danny tells him to fucking shut it and comes hurrying after her.

'Jenny! Wait! Wait up!'

He catches hold of her arm and she shakes it off.

'Jenny . . .'

'What?'

'Don't go off like that.'

'No?' But she stops.

'He didn't mean anything by it.'

'Like hell he didn't!' She moves closer, lowers her voice. 'You told him, didn't you?'

'Course not.'

'You bloody liar! Of course you did. Him and how many others? Talk of the bloody coalfield, am I? Standing joke?'

'No, no.'

He slips his fingers round her wrist and this time she lets them stay.

'I had to say something. He'd not've come here otherwise.' Desperate, he looks over his shoulder. Steve's still where he left him, whistling, rolling a cigarette. 'Look, we'll just go for a pint, eh? Me and Steve. Have to now he's here. Only fair. Then I'll come back. Your old man, he's on nights this week, right?'

How does he know that, Jenny thinks? But he's right.

'I'll come by later.'

'No.'

'Don't worry. I'll be careful. No one'll see.'

'Danny, you can't.'

Stooping towards her, he lowers his head for a kiss, just missing her mouth as she turns aside.

Moments and he's back at the van, climbing in, Steve poking his head through the window and giving her a broad wink before driving away.

She's trembling, praying that there's no one there to notice, but no one is. No one she can see.

At home, after checking the children are all asleep, easing Brian's thumb from his mouth, she changes into her nightie and, instead of getting into bed, curls up on the settee downstairs, half an ear towards the door, waiting. But he doesn't come.

47

The interview with Barry Hardwick over, Catherine had said she needed some fresh air to clear her head; Resnick had taken this to mean she needed a cigarette. Picking up coffee on the way, he tagged along, their direction towards the same piece of green space where they'd sat before, within reach of the canal.

The temperature had shifted upwards a degree or two since earlier, but it was cold enough still for their breath to be seen on the air when they spoke. Steam rose from Resnick's coffee when he prised off the lid. At the far side of the trees, the flour mills were shrouded in mist.

'These trips she made down to London – Jenny – you think there might be something relevant there?'

'Difficult to say. But whatever it was, I doubt she'd have gone without good reason.'

'A meeting, then? A rally of some kind?'

'Likely. But from what Linda Stoneman said, arrangements seemed to have been made pretty much last moment.'

'Filling in for another speaker somewhere?'

'Possible, I suppose.'

'But that's not what you think.'

'No way to be sure, of course, but I'm wondering if it could have been something to do with the movement of money. Cash money.' He shook his head in annoyance. 'I should've thought of that before.'

A dog walker went past, tailed by a Border Collie/German Shepherd cross doing its best to carry a branch three times as big as itself.

'You'd best explain,' Catherine said.

'Simple enough, really. Quite early on in the strike the union had its funds frozen. Just at the same time it was getting more and more dependent on financial support from outside. Other unions, you know, and not just in the UK. France, Russia, all over. Most of it smuggled into the country one way or another. As far as they were concerned, a case of having to. All secret, of course. Secret as can be. Surreptitious meetings, midnight assignations, banknotes hidden in the hollowed-out bottoms of suitcases. Like something out of what's-his-name? *Tinker, Tailor, Soldier* man?'

'Le Carré?'

'Le Carré. And, of course, rumours were rife.

Officers from my team would pick up a hint here, a hint there. Misinformation, some of it, of course. Throw us off the track. Not all. A matter of sifting through. Keith Haines, I remember – he had his nose to the ground as well – passed on some useful information a time or two.

'We had a tip-off once, might even have come through Keith in the first place, I'm not sure now. But anyway, we followed it up – a money shipment on its way from the Continent to Harwich by ferry, making its way from there to NUM headquarters in Yorkshire. We tracked it, intercepted it just outside Newark. Six thousand pounds under a blanket in the back of a Ford Granada. And that was just one we knew about, knew for certain. If even half the tales that came through to us turned out to be true, there'd have been that kind of money and more coming in all the time. A lot more. And heaven knows where some of it ended up.'

'So you think that's what Jenny might have been doing? Those trips to London? Acting as a sort of courier?'

Resnick hunched his shoulders. 'It's possible. I could have a word with Edna Johnson. She and Peter Waites were close, she might have an inkling. Other than that, there's someone I used to know quite well back then, worked for a while at the NRC. He'd be able to fill me in on a bit of background, if nothing else.'

Catherine stubbed out her second cigarette. 'You do that, Charlie. I'll see how things are back at Potter Street.'

At Potter Street, things were in a state of barely subdued excitement. Rob Cresswell, recently back from A & E, bandage around his newly shaven head, was sitting in the one good chair, basking in universal, if temporary, approval, not least from Vanessa and Gloria – Gloria, in particular – both women hovering close by in the expectation that he might suffer a sudden relapse and need their comforting attentions. Whatever checks they'd been making on the suspects thrown up by the earlier Donna Crowder investigation temporarily in abeyance.

Alex Sandford, meanwhile, was in the act of retelling the events of the morning for the benefit of John McBride and an assortment of officers from elsewhere in the building.

What it amounted to, Catherine discovered, was this. Having made two unsuccessful attempts to locate Joe Willis – a name passed down to them from the Swann investigation – at his last-known address in Kirkby, on both occasions with uniformed police from the local station in support, Sandford and Cresswell, acting on a whim and against McBride's instructions, had called back that morning without back-up, hoping to catch Willis sleeping. Which they had, persistent knocking and bell-ringing bringing a tired-looking

Willis to the door, a Leeds United sweatshirt hanging over a pair of droopy boxers.

No sooner had he recognised the two detectives for what they were than Willis had ducked back inside, hurling the door shut behind him, only Sandford's outstretched boot preventing it actually closing.

Grabbing a pair of trousers from the end of the bed, Willis had half-run, half-hopped towards the stairs, moving with surprising agility for a man of his age, and reaching the first-floor landing before Cresswell caught up to him; Willis lashing out and catching Cresswell hard enough to send him backwards down the stairs and head first into the wall.

Sandford had stopped to check that his partner was all right, giving Willis the chance to exit through a third-floor window and out on to the roof. When Sandford next spotted him, he was climbing down a rusty fire escape into a narrow ginnel that ran between the houses.

As long as he remained within sight, Sandford was confident of overhauling him. All that marathon training had to count for something.

When he finally caught up with him, just where the alley opened out on to the main road, Willis was no longer really running, more like jogging on the spot, shoulders and chest heaving, breath ragged and wheezing, mouth open. In danger, Sandford thought, of a heart attack.

From the sound of a police car approaching, Sandford knew that Cresswell had successfully called it in. Maybe they'd need an ambulance as well.

'All we wanted,' he told Willis, 'was to ask a few questions.'

''Bout that post office robbery . . . Basford . . . yeah, I know.'

'No,' Sandford told him, 'not that at all. Something that happened thirty years ago.'

Willis, still struggling to recover his breath, had looked at him with a mixture of dismay and disbelief. And when questioned later, he had not been able to assist in the investigation into Jenny Hardwick's murder by one jot.

Police had since found a cash box taken from the post office in the house where Willis had been staying, however, and had arrested a second man under suspicion of being Willis's accomplice, the pair of them having carried out the robbery armed with a replica pistol and a hammer.

'Good work,' Catherine said. 'And think yourself fortunate you've only got one sore head between the two of you.'

Once the euphoria had died down she would take the pair of them aside and remind them of what had happened not so long ago to two female officers who were lured into a trap by a wanted criminal and shot down in cold blood. On that occasion there had been nothing to suggest it was anything more than a routine incident they had been called to; no need, as far as they could judge, to call for back-up. But both Sandford and Cresswell had been explicitly told not to approach Joe Willis unless support was in place.

This time they had been lucky.

Next time, Catherine would make good and clear, they should obey orders to the letter or the outcome might be tragically different.

Home, for Edna Johnson, was a small ground-floor apartment in sheltered accommodation. A banner – white lettering on a maroon background, WOMEN AGAINST PIT CLOSURES – leaned against one wall. Photographs were dotted here and there, grandchildren vying for space with groups of jubilant, angry women, marching, singing, linking arms, holding hands.

'So,' Edna said, once they were settled, 'to what do I owe the honour?'

'Jenny Hardwick, just trying to fill a few gaps, plug a few holes.'

'Do what I can.'

'Last time we spoke, at the funeral, you mentioned visits Jenny might have made to London . . .'

'No might about it. London. Cardiff. A few more, I dare say. Union business, speeches. Never hurt to have a pretty woman on the platform.'

'And that's all it was?'

She looked back at him, saying nothing.

'Is it possible, I wonder, that she could have been acting as a courier? Collecting sums of money and delivering them up here to the Midlands? On up to Yorkshire?'

Edna took her time before answering. 'It's possible.'

'But likely?'

'Like I say, it's possible. There was money, right enough, and I doubt they were sending it through the post. Nor putting it in the bank, neither. Not the regular accounts, for certain.'

'Peter Waites, you and he were close.'

'We were.'

'You think he would have trusted Jenny sufficiently to send her on that sort of mission, what with the sums of money involved?'

Edna shook her head. 'If you'd known Jenny, you'd not've needed to ask that question.'

'He would, then?'

'He would. Which is not to say that he did. Not to best of my knowledge, at least. And if it did happen, I doubt Peter himself would have known too much about it. Whatever details Jenny might've been given, they'd've been for her eyes only. As far as I could tell, that's the way it was.'

A resigned expression on his face, Resnick nodded thanks.

'I'm sorry, Mr Resnick . . .'

'Charlie.'

'I'm sorry, Charlie, but that's all I can tell you.'

Resnick thanked her again, happy to spend another thirty minutes or so in conversation; he didn't know how many visitors Edna had on a regular basis, now that it was no longer so easy for her to get around, but he suspected, it was growing fewer with time.

Thirty minutes became forty and then an hour. Somewhere in the middle, Edna made her way into the kitchen and returned with two glasses of port and lemon.

'Not trying to lead me astray, are you, Edna?'

She laughed. 'I might, if I thought I could get away with it.'

As he was leaving, she touched him on the shoulder. 'Jenny's killer, are you any closer to finding him?'

'I'm not sure.'

'And this business with the money, you think that could be part of it?'

'It might.'

'Don't give away much, do you?'

Resnick planted a quick kiss on her cheek. 'Look after yourself, Edna.'

'You, too, Charlie.' She squeezed his hand. 'Not a bad bloke for a copper, I always said.'

48

A little over an hour to spare before his appointment, Resnick cut across Euston Road from the station, walked up Judd Street and through Russell Square, past the British Museum and on into Soho. Rain drifted lightly through the air.

Collar up, he entered Frith Street at its northern end, Ronnie Scott's two-thirds of the way down on the right-hand side. Ronnie's. Where he had seen Dizzy Gillespie; failed to see Thelonious Monk. Of the names on the bill now there were few that he recognised; few that he would have associated with the word 'jazz'.

Across the street, the Bar Italia was still in business, best cappuccino in Soho before the coffee boom and possibly still was. He signalled behind the counter and took a seat outside.

The last time he had been inside Ronnie's was a little over twenty years before; one of his favourite tenor players, Spike Robinson, fragile looking and stoop shouldered, doing beautiful things to George Gershwin, Irving Berlin, Jerome Kern. Before the final number, Resnick remembered, Robinson had dedicated it to the memory of another musician, the alto saxophonist Ed Silver, who had died earlier that week.

SILVER, Edward Victor. Suddenly at home, on 16 February 1993. Acclaimed jazz musician of the bebop era. Funeral service, Friday 19 February at Golders Green Crematorium, 1.45 p.m.

Silver and Resnick had been friends, up to and beyond the point when the musician had become a near-helpless alcoholic, unable to stand, unable to blow, threatening to take his own life if his liver didn't do it for him. Now Robinson was dead himself, and others too: Ronnie, of course, Max Roach, Stan Getz, Tony Burns.

He remembered Ed Silver standing in his kitchen, the night he had talked him out of taking off his own foot with a butcher's cleaver, looking mournfully round while they listened to the late Clifford Brown.

'*They're all dying, Charlie.*'

'*Who?*'

'*Every bugger!*'

And, of course, it was true.

Resnick shuddered involuntarily as if a shadow had passed over his grave. 'Now's the Time', that was the final number Spike Robinson had played.

Except you rarely knew.

He finished his coffee and continued south on to Shaftesbury Avenue; a taxi towards Victoria and to hell with the expense.

You only live once.

The hotel was in one of those largely unexplored streets behind the Catholic cathedral, old stone on the outside, plastic, glass and *faux* marble within. Matthew Prior was seated in a booth between the restaurant and the bar. At first sight, he seemed to Resnick hardly to have aged at all, but then, shaking hands, Resnick saw the lines around the eyes, the loose flap of skin beneath the chin. Still a full head of hair, some magic potion fending off the grey.

'Charlie, long time no see.'

His grip was still firm. Still a brightness in the eyes. His suit, dark grey with a faint stripe, custom made, and sombre tie suggested something successful in the City. Banking? A hedge fund manager, perhaps.

Resnick knew that for the past twenty years or so he had been a senior-level officer in British Intelligence. M15.

'Good trip down?'

'Fine.'

'Didn't mind trawling all the way over here? Lot on right now and at least this gives me a chance to stretch the legs. Would have suggested lunch otherwise.'

'It's good of you to take the time.'

A waiter was hovering at the entrance to the booth.

Prior placed a hand over the glass already in front of him, sparkling water, ice and lemon.

'Charlie?'

Resnick shook his head.

The waiter went away.

'So,' Prior said, 'the Miners' Strike. Funding of same. There's a novel there, Charlie, still to be written.'

'Perhaps just the outline, then.'

'Do what I can.'

A group of half a dozen diners went by on their way to the restaurant, chatting amiably, quite loudly, oblivious to others.

Out of habit, Prior held his tongue till they'd gone past.

'Basic facts, you'll know. I can fill you in a little more. In September of eighty-four, responding to an action that had been brought by two working miners, a High Court judge ruled the strike unlawful. As far as Mr Scargill was concerned, of course, this was a red rag to a bull. Denial of democratic rights and so on. It probably didn't take too much to persuade the national executive of the union to agree. Scargill was charged to appear in court and refused. Result, the

345

NUM were hit with a two-hundred-thousand-pound fine. When that went unpaid, on the twenty-fifth of October in the High Court, Mr Justice Nicholls ordered the sequestration of the union's funds. Assets, property, everything. Which meant, quite simply, no more money in or out. Everything was to be under the legal control of an official receiver appointed by the court.'

Prior paused for a mouthful of water.

More people went past on their way to early lunch.

'Now the union had already been moving some of its funds around – the Isle of Man, Dublin, Jersey, Switzerland, Luxembourg – but once it was out of the country, without the connivance of the banks it would be difficult to bring back in now without having it fall into the hands of the receiver. Same applied to the money they'd been drumming up from sympathisers overseas. The most obvious case being Russia, where, by dint of deducting a day's pay from all its working miners, the Central Committee of the Soviet Communist Party was sitting on a gift of a million roubles, getting on for one and a half million pounds, with no sure way of getting it into the NUM's hands.'

'So what happened?'

Prior's face coasted into a smile. 'Who knows? Possibly some of that money eventually made its way here, possibly none. What I do know, the government moved heaven and earth to ensure it stayed where it was. Pressure from the Foreign Office to the Soviet Embassy. Through top-level channels to Gorbachev himself.

'And then, of course, there was the Libyan fiasco, the less said about which the better.'

'But money was coming in,' Resnick said. 'Even if only in dribs and drabs. We picked up rumours about it, locally, all the time.'

'Where's there's a will, Charlie. People prepared, for whatever reason, to turn a blind eye. So, yes, of course, it happened. Sixty thousand pounds in hard cash, for instance, we know made its way into the country from Bulgaria and Czechoslovakia, the last leg of the journey by train to the NUM's headquarters in Sheffield. And, for quite a while, members of the CGT, the largest of the French unions, would come over to Folkestone regularly on the ferry carrying the maximum amount of permitted currency, hand it over to some courier or other and hop back again across the Channel on the same boat.'

'While you did what? Sat back and watched?'

A quick shake of the head. 'We passed on what information we had. Names, places. Times and dates when we had them, which wasn't so often. We had people placed to give us the inside track, but whoever was organising the money grew canny, didn't make it easy. And what the NUM had on their side was an almost endless supply of volunteers. Carrying round suitcases and cardboard boxes, some of them, containing more money than they could hope to earn in a lifetime. If it all reached its destination, who's to say? No one was exactly keeping accurate records and with all that money sloshing round . . . Well, I leave it to your imagination.'

He glanced at his watch.

'Is that what you're doing, Charlie, following the money?'

'Not exactly.'

He told him their suspicions about Jenny Hardwick couriering union funds; picking up donations in London from person or persons unknown and carrying them back to north Notts, where, in all likelihood, they would be handed over to a third party who would convey them the remainder of their journey.

'Eminently possible, Charlie. Probable, I'd say. Sitting in second class with anything up to ten thousand in a suitcase that last got used on a day trip to Skegness.'

'And if it didn't arrive . . .?'

'Who was to say?' Prior raised a well-turned eyebrow. 'If money went missing en route, they weren't exactly going to go to the police.'

49

Back home, Resnick fixed himself a sandwich, made coffee, fed the cat, found the CD of Spike Robinson playing Gershwin and set it to play while he relaxed in the armchair. He'd phoned Catherine from the train and it had been engaged; tried again after returning home and been shuffled on to voicemail both times. For whatever reason, she was lying low. No matter, nothing that couldn't wait till morning.

Somewhere in the middle of 'Somebody Loves Me' he closed his eyes. By the time 'How Long Has This Been Going On' had come to an end, the saxophone's breathy obligato sliding down over a bank of strings, coffee or no coffee, he was asleep.

Waking to silence other than Dizzy's gentle snoring, and mindful of the cat's arthritic bones, he lifted him from where he lay curled in his lap and placed him carefully back on the chair, switched off the CD and took himself to bed. No sense fighting the inevitable.

At three in the morning – five minutes past by the bedside clock – he woke with a start.

A car backfiring?

The same dream.

Nightmare.

His breathing was loud in the room. Adrenalin pumping. Face, shoulders slippery with sweat.

How much longer would this go on?

Barefoot, he crossed the room.

Outside, it was as dark as city centres deigned to get. Something moving in the street light's shadow; a fox trotting along the far side of the road, tail bushed out, oblivious to whoever might be watching.

Resnick let the curtain fall back into place.

Went back to bed.

After thirty minutes of twisting and turning, he got up again and went downstairs; poured away the unfinished coffee from the night before and made fresh. When he'd retired he'd been given a fat book of photographs by William Claxton, *Jazzlife*. Propping it across his lap, he turned the pages. Gerry Mulligan, in deep shade, at the piano, only his baritone saxophone, temporarily set aside, picking out the light. Donald Byrd, travelling uptown on the A train towards Harlem, touching the mouthpiece of his trumpet to his lips, while behind him in the carriage, a middle-aged white man, wearing an extravagantly banded trilby hat, turns to watch.

Looking in the wrong places, is that what they'd been doing? Himself and Catherine? Thinking to find a motive for Jenny Hardwick's murder in high emotion; an outburst of anger, lust, love. Maybe it was not that at all. Something colder, more calculating instead.

What had Matthew Prior said? *More money than they could hope to earn in a lifetime.*

Is that what you're doing, Charlie, following the money? He'd said that, too.

They hadn't – not pre-eminently – but maybe they should.

Bank accounts, credit card records stretching back thirty years – were they still available? It seemed doubtful and, even if they were, it would take more than just a phone call to access them, he knew that well enough. Nothing straightforward or simple, channels to go through, but worth the effort all the same.

But this was what he'd missed, he realised, the sniff of something catching fire, an idea, a new avenue to explore.

Restless, he showered, dressed and paced the floor.

Left with the first leavening of light.

McBride was in the office before him. 'Bit of luck last night.'

'Don't tell me. The Jags got the winning goal under floodlights, second minute of injury time?'

'Geoff Cartwright – RCMP have finally tracked him down. Place called Humboldt. Near Saskatoon? Recently retired from working for the city's compost-collecting programme. Officer I spoke to asked me to email over a list of questions. They'll set up an interview on Skype from the local RCMP station. Just a matter of fixing a time. Could be as early as this afternoon.'

'Our afternoon or theirs?'

'Theirs, our evening.' McBride treated Resnick to his crooked grin. 'Bloody Mounties. Always get their man, eh?'

'So it seems.'

Resnick had known an inspector in the Notts force who'd gone out to Canada and joined the RCMP. Brzozowski. Polish descent like himself. Good policeman, good detective. Resnick had liked him. Would have bet good money he'd more often than not got his man, too.

Good money . . .

'John, there's one more thing . . .'

He intercepted Catherine in the car park, enjoying a cigarette before the start of her day.

'I tried calling you last night . . .'

'I know, I'm sorry. Met a girlfriend and went to Sinatra's. Probably drank a little too much wine. Fell fast asleep almost as soon as I got home.'

'Me, too, more or less. And without the wine.'

'So how did it go? Meeting up with your spook friend?'

Resnick filled her in.

'Casts a new perspective,' Catherine said. 'Worth exploring, certainly. Tends to rule Barry Hardwick out, though, rather than in. Not exactly big-spender material.'

'Depends how much was involved.'

'Have to be enough to kill somebody for, if what you're suggesting is correct.'

'Ten thousand pounds – let's suppose, for sake of argument, that's what Jenny might have been carrying. That'd be worth – I don't know – two and a half times that now, possibly three. Worth taking a risk for, thirty thousand. Back then, especially.'

'But murder?'

'I've known people killed for a lot less and so have you. A bottle of cider or the price of a wrap.'

Catherine stepped away from the car.

'Derek Harmer, from the Swann investigation, the guy in Hull. He was in Full Sutton between eighty-three and eighty-nine. So that rules him out. Persons of interest passed on from the Donna Crowder inquiry, we've now got whittled down to four. It would be nice if whatever names Cartwright can give us were to match, but I'm not holding my breath.'

'This remove, he might not be able to remember names at all.'

Catherine smiled. 'Thanks, Charlie. Always on the bright side. What I like about you.'

'I knew there had to be something.'

She aimed a mock punch at his shoulder and together they went into the building.

Geoff Cartwright had weathered well; something in the Canadian climate or way of life had left him, even in the less-than-perfect Skype image, looking fit and healthy, a good few years younger than his actual age. His native accent, when he spoke, only occasionally breaking through that of his adopted country.

In response to McBride's emailed request, he'd earlier supplied a list of people he could remember working with him at 20 Church Street. Five names – after all that time it was all he could remember, all he could dredge up from a long-forgotten past.

'Come out here, you make a new life, that's what it's all about. Why you've come. Try hanging on to the past and somehow it's like you're marooned, you know. I've met people out here like that, Brits, a few – like they're in some kind of limbo. Easier for me in a way, I guess, no close family, not left alive, never married, no kids. Friends, I suppose, a few I missed, at first, anyway – Howard, for instance – look, you'll pass on my best – Howard and Megan, is it? – but you make new ones, don't you? It's what you do.'

There were three of them sitting round the screen: Catherine, Resnick, McBride.

Catherine asked him about each of the names he had provided; names that had already been passed into the system, were being checked against the National Police Computer. Cartwright added what detail he could, but it was precious little.

'Barry Hardwick,' she said. 'You knew him, I suppose?'

'Barry, yeah. From the pit. Jenny's husband. Gutted when I heard what'd happened to her. Lovely girl, she was. And the circumstances – course I never heard anything about it, never made the papers over here, first I knew was when the sergeant told me. Gave me a chill, I don't mind telling you, thinking when I was laying that last lot of concrete what was underneath. Jeeze! Doesn't bear thinking about.'

'Barry, though, did he ever lend you a hand? The work you were doing?'

'Church Street? No. No, never.'

'And you don't have any recollection of him hanging round the property at all?'

'No. Hey, listen, you don't think . . .'

'He and Howard, they weren't particular friends?'

'Not as far as I know.'

Someone behind him said something they couldn't properly hear, watching, and Cartwright turned his head to reply.

'Geoff,' Resnick said, 'there's something I wanted to ask.'

'Go ahead.'

'When I was talking to Howard, he said he and his family went away over the Christmas period, is that right? Is that how you remember it?'

'Yeah, yeah. Megan's folks, was it? Something like that.'

'And you stayed home, at the Vale? Worked on the extension?'

'Most of the time, yeah.'

'Most of the time?'

'Went up to see my old man. Just for the day. My mother, she'd already passed. He was living up in Seaton Carew, outside Hartlepool. Ended up staying over. Christmas Eve, it would have been, when I got back.'

'You're sure of that? It's all a long time ago.'

'Yeah, I'm pretty sure. Last Christmas I saw my old man. Not likely to forget.'

'And the work on Church Street, was that finished before you left to visit your father?'

'Not quite. I'd promised myself I'd get everything done and dusted before going, but in the event, never quite made it. Hard core down okay, insulation, and I ran out of time. Left boards across it overnight, reckoned I'd lay the concrete when I got back next day. Which I did.'

'And nothing had been interfered with while you were away?'

'Not as far as I could see.'

'But it could have been?'

'How d'you mean?'

'Would it have been possible, for instance, for someone else to have removed the insulation, dug up the hard core and then replaced it in such a way as you'd never know?'

Cartwright shrugged, pulled a face. 'It's possible, I suppose. Yes. As long as they knew what they were doing. Not difficult. And you think . . .' He shook his head. 'God, doesn't bear too much thinking about, does it?'

Catherine took her time. 'One final thing, Geoff, and thank you for your patience, but we have a list of names of our own. Only short, don't worry. I'd appreciate it if you could take a look at them, see if they ring any bells.'

'In relation to the building work, you mean?'

'That especially, yes.'

She typed in the names, pressed enter, and they appeared in the message box at the bottom of Geoff Cartwright's screen.

They followed his expression as he scanned the list quickly, then looked again at each one, giving it some thought before dismissing it and moving on. Thinking again, not quite decided, looking back.

'This name here, down at the bottom. Steven Rowland. There was a Steve put in a couple of shifts, I remember. Didn't think of him before.'

'But you think that could be him? Rowland?'

'Could be. Don't suppose I ever knew his last name. Just one of the lads out on strike, you know, looking for a bit of cash.'

'And he was what? Local?'

Cartwright shook his head. 'From the Vale? No? Sheffield way, maybe. Down from Yorkshire, certainly. Picketing, you know. Palled about with a ginger-headed lad, I remember. Can't summon up his name for love nor money.'

'And this ginger-headed lad,' Catherine asked, keeping her expectations under control, 'did he help out at Church Street, too, along with his mate?'

'May have done. Might well. I remember him being around, like I say, but any more than that . . .' He smiled. 'All a long time ago.'

Ginger-haired lad from Sheffield way: they could summon up a name even if Cartwright couldn't. Danny Ireland, had to be. How many red-headed Yorkshire miners were there likely to be in Bledwell Vale at the same time, after all? Danny Ireland, who had – how had Edna Johnson put it? – trailed round after Jenny like a needy dog.

Danny and Steve.

Catherine allowed herself a smile.

Steve Rowland had been brought in for questioning as part of the Donna Crowder investigation, initially because he'd been seen with Donna's boyfriend of the time, Wayne Cameron, driving him around town the evening she was murdered. When it turned out that he'd gone out with Donna himself previously, and that he'd once been named in an alleged assault against another former girlfriend, he had come into consideration as a possible suspect. But there had been no forensic evidence to link him to the crime, no proof that his car had been used again later that evening, and an alibi placing him at a lock-in at one of the local pubs till the early hours had proved difficult to break.

Maybe now it was time to look again.

It didn't take Vanessa so many minutes to come up with an address. He'd moved, but not moved far. The Rivelin Valley area of Sheffield. McBride made a quick call to the local nick: person of interest in an ongoing murder inquiry living in their area. Thirty minutes or so away along the A57.

50

Two days a week they run a luncheon club for the elderly and Jenny helps out when she can; hurrying home to collect Brian from Linda's and then maybe getting a bit of washing done before Colin and Mary get back from school; Mary, like as not, with Nicky in tow. Then it's setting her thoughts to what they were all going to eat later; seeing what kind of a mood Barry is in before letting him know there's a meeting at the Welfare that evening, will he just keep an eye on the kids before going out for a pint himself later? She'll get back as soon as ever she can.

Turns out, everything's fine. Hunky-dory.

Mary's got a gold star for a drawing she's done of a cat in class: big and black and beautifully shaded; so good, in fact, Jenny can scarce bring herself to believe Mary's done it all herself, except she swears that she has. Cross my heart and hope to die. And if Colin's scored even half the goals he claims, kicking around in the playground, Leeds United scouts will be knocking on the door any time soon.

Even Barry's in a good mood for once, talk of a Christmas bonus that might be wishful thinking on someone's part, but might almost as well be true. God knows, he thinks, they're due something for all the grief they've been taking, day in and bloody day out, months now. It's not been so bad for him, because of Jenny, he'd be the first to admit that. But some of his workmates – car tyres slashed, bricks through the windows, rotten eggs and worse stuffed through the letter-box. Got so he thinks scab might just as well be his middle name.

'Go on, duck. You go. Set world to bloody rights, eh?'

She needs no second bidding.

The meeting seems to go round in circles, Jenny feels, the same niggling points being argued about over and over. Not that there's been any doubt about the main items. Hasn't been for some time now. The kids' party will be held on the afternoon of Saturday the 22nd, starting at 3.30. Peter Waites has agreed to dress up as Santa, one of the others on the committee has promised to borrow his wife's fancy dressing gown and come as a Middle Eastern magician – more bad conjuring tricks, Jenny reckons, than Tommy Cooper

– and two of the lads are down to run the disco. Then it's Christmas dinner there at the Welfare on the day itself.

Thanks to the almost overwhelming generosity of others there'll be food and presents enough to go round.

Danny's standing just across the street when she emerges, duffel-coat collar up, cigarette cupped in the hand down by his side, street light just catching the colour of his hair.

Jenny hesitates for a moment, before turning sharply away.

Crossing the street after her, he calls her name. Not loud. Loud enough.

She lengthens her stride.

'Jenny, hang about, for Christ's sake . . .'

There's a narrow passage between two houses, leading on to an area of waste ground, a mix of grass and cinders, where groups of striking miners would have the occasional kickabout, and where, until recently, Sam Palmer had kept a shaggy, down-at-heels pony. The joke, when it disappeared overnight, was that Sam had butchered it himself and gone to the next village selling the choice cuts as best beef. Not so far removed from the truth not to be believed.

Just before the passageway opens out, she stops and leans back against the wall.

He's a little breathless when he catches up to her.

'What the hell're you running for?'

'I'm not.'

Tobacco smoke bitter and warm in his mouth, he kisses her and she kisses him back. His hand like a homing pigeon to her breast.

She can taste coal dust and dirt on his neck. Bares her breast for him and arches her back, her nipple hard in his mouth.

Her hand between his legs.

He takes the nipple between his teeth.

Fumbling with the zip of his jeans, she catches her little finger and he stifles her cry with the soft skin on the inside of his arm; takes her finger into his mouth and sucks away the blood, what little there is.

Despite the cold, she's wearing nothing more than skimpy pants beneath her dress.

She wants him to touch her and when he doesn't she takes hold of his wrist and guides him down.

Oh, God, she's wet.

Hands beneath her buttocks, he lifts her off the ground and she eases him inside her.

Minutes and they're done.

While he wipes himself, she leans back against the wall. The building seems to be shaking, but of course it's her.

Reaching out, she kisses him, hands on his neck, wants to hurt him, suddenly, without reason, fingernails gouging his skin.

'Fucker!' he says, eyes alight; thrusting against her, he kisses her hard in return.

And then, almost as soon as it started, it's over.

While he zips himself up, pulls his clothes to order, she's straightening her dress, lifting her coat from the dirt and brushing it down, combing her fingers up through her hair.

A cloud shifts across the moon and she can see the boyish grin on his face: the tomcat that got the cream.

'I must go,' she says.

'Hang on, I'll come with you.'

'No, not together. Just in case.'

'Okay.' He gestures towards the field. 'I'll go round by here.'

He reaches for one last kiss, but she's already moving away.

Stepping out of the alley, out from the shadow, she thinks she sees something away to the right, just out of the street light's orbit, someone standing there, watching, but when she looks again there's nothing. Nobody, still or moving.

Just her imagination, then . . .

Checking her watch, she realises she'd promised Barry she'd be home a good half-hour ago and hurries on her way.

51

Steve Rowland, like a good many of the miners who had supported the strike, had scarcely been in regular employment since the day the pit where he'd worked had, as Arthur Scargill had forecast, been closed with the loss of several hundred jobs. Painting and decorating, he'd done that for a while, the back of his van a jumble of stepladders, dust sheets, brushes, pots of paint; window cleaning, too; small-scale removals; worst of all, six bloody months in an abattoir across from the County ground in Nottingham.

'Get shot of their old strikers in here, do they?' he'd joked. 'Once they're past their sell-by date.'

A Doncaster Rovers supporter since knee high, he'd thought it was funny, a laugh. A quick fist had told him, that close to Meadow Lane, it was best to keep his smart-arsed remarks to himself.

Out of work and on the dole the best part of eighteen months, he'd finally got a job stacking shelves in a supermarket on the other side of the city. Part-time. Still had a van, a clapped-out Transit that should have been off the road by rights, and wouldn't start on cold mornings anyway, meaning he had to take two buses to get to work, a good fifty minutes each way. Added to which the hours, early shift especially, were such as to totally bugger any kind of social life you might have, though in Steve's case, as he'd be the first to say, that was hardly a consideration.

Never married, never even close, the last sex he'd had he'd paid for, regretting it almost as soon as the business was over, tart using her knickers to wipe between her legs, all the while lighting a cigarette.

There were a few faces he knew in his nearest local, people he'd pass the time of day with over a slow pint, moan about the weather, the useless bloody immigration laws, Manchester-fucking-United, the way the whole bloody country was going to rack and ruin. No one he'd really call a friend, a pal.

Not since Danny; not since Wayne. Both a long time ago.

Wayne, poor bastard, thrown through the windscreen on the motorway. And Danny . . . Danny he hadn't heard hide nor hair of since a postcard from Inverness and that had to have been fifteen years ago if it was a day. He had it still somewhere, dog-eared and fly-blown, stuck down the back of some drawer.

Great times they'd had, the two of them, during the strike, haring around those back lanes, the police, like as not, in pursuit; sticking it to them at the pithead gates, bastards from the Met waving twenty-pound notes in their faces, bragging about their overtime. One copper's helmet he'd knocked off with a half-brick, clean as sending over a coconut at Goose Fair that time they'd travelled down to Nottingham, Danny and himself, driving home in the early hours afterwards, half-pissed and happy, careful not to get stopped for speeding, no more able to walk a straight line than thread a sodding needle.

He missed him, that was the truth of it.

Thought of him not so long ago when that Jenny's body was dug up in Bledwell Vale. Fancied her rotten, Danny had. Never quite seen it himself. Married, three kids. Who'd want it after all that? He'd done his best to get Danny to tell him what she was like, mind – you know, doing it – but he never would.

'True love, then, is it?' he'd tease him, and Danny would tell him to fuck off and clip him round the back of the head.

But perhaps that's what it was. What it had been.

Aside from what he saw on TV, blokes moping around and making fools of themselves, Steve wouldn't know true love if it jumped up and bit him in the backside. Didn't want to. Messed with your head, that's what it did. Wayne, for instance, poor bastard, what it had got him into . . . but he didn't want to think about that either.

He was out by the van, the carburettor in pieces on an old tea towel, when the car drew up and the woman got out from behind the wheel, black as the ace of spades and tall. The man with her, broad-shouldered, bulky, the pair of them heading straight towards him. The woman, he didn't know, couldn't tell, but the man, the way he walked, a copper for sure.

A second car now, at the end of the street: blue and yellow squares of the South Yorkshire police.

'Steven Rowland?' She flipped open the small wallet she was holding in her hand. 'Detective Inspector Catherine Njoroge, Nottinghamshire Police.'

'Nottinghamshire, what's that . . .?'

He saw her eyes drifting past him towards the van.

'This isn't about the insurance? You've not come all the way for . . .?'

But he could read it in her eyes. The man's, too.

'We'd like to ask you some questions . . .'

He scarcely heard the rest. Two uniformed officers were approaching slowly now along the far side of the street, all the time theirs to take.

He felt sick.

'It's about her, isn't it? That's what this is.'

'Her?' Catherine said.

'Donna. Donna Crowder. Who else?'

An interview room was made available for them at the force headquarters on Snig Hill, one of the South Yorkshire team sitting in. Their case, but content for now to let Catherine make the running, the final kudos theirs not hers. Rowland had barely been cautioned before it had all come pouring out. How many times over the past years had he rehearsed this story? In his sleep or wide awake and staring out, isolated, into the dark? The words tumbling over one another now, a dam let loose.

'Slow down, slow down,' Catherine said. 'Start over from the beginning.'

She checked for the second time since his arrest that he didn't want a solicitor present. When she'd told him he could make one phone call, he'd looked back at her vacantly, not quite understanding. Who on the good earth would he call?

'We'd both been drinking,' he said, starting over. 'The night it happened. They'd had this row earlier, Wayne and Donna. 'Bout her goin' off clubbing in Sheffield with her mates. When we met up I could see he was still angry. Near got into a fight over nothing with this bloke in the pub. Bloke, he was someone I knew, let it go. Wayne settled down a bit then, seemed to. Went on somewhere else, somewhere else after that. Time I dropped him off, his old man's place, he was off again. Who did she think she was? What he wasn't going to do to her when he saw her next. Wanted me to drive round till we found her, meet her and her mates, maybe, off the last bus. Either that or go down to Sheffield. Forget it, I said, you'll never find her anyway. Course, thinking about it later, I wish I had. Gone with him, I mean. Things might've turned out different than they did.'

'What happened then?' Catherine said. 'After you dropped him off?'

'I went back to mine, started getting ready for bed – couldn't stop thinking about it. Wayne going off, half-pissed, going crazy. I'd seen him like that once or twice before. I got dressed again, drove down there. His old man's car had been parked up outside the house and it weren't there any more. Stupid bastard, I thought. Drove round for a bit, looking for him, bus station and that, then went out on to the Sheffield road.'

He stopped, rubbed the knuckles of his right hand along the tabletop hard.

'I didn't see him at first. Across the other side of the road where it runs along by the canal. Drove right past. Turned round first chance I got. He was just standing there, not doing anything. Just standing. At first I thought he was on his own, but then I saw her. Close by the canal, the canal path. Stretched out. You could see the blood, sort of leaking from the back of her head. The way she was laying there, you could see . . . see, you know . . .'

He blinked.

'There was this piece of wood down by Wayne's feet. Part of an old oar, paddle, something like that. Blood at the end. Dark. Oh, Christ, Wayne, I said, and I could see he was crying. Not making any noise, just like some kid, crying. Frightened, I s'pose. I told him to go and sit in the car. Checked to make sure she wasn't breathing, Donna, covered her as best I could. Waited till I thought Wayne had calmed down enough to drive and told him to follow me back into town. The piece of wood I took home with me and burned. Don't say anything, I told him, not to anyone. Never mentioned it to me again, not a word.'

52

'You ever get a tune stuck in your head?' Resnick said. 'No idea how it got there or why?'

Catherine smiled softly. 'Only all the time.'

He'd woken that day with it firm in his mind and been unable to shake it free. 'I Can't Get Started', Mingus at the piano, not his usual instrument, hesitant, stumbling, like a man searching for the exit in a darkened room. He knew how he felt. Things that would lurch into sight and then be gone.

Charlie Mingus, New York City, July 1963. The same month Philby had been revealed as the third man. Stuff that he remembered, useless, cluttering his mind.

They were in a café in an old industrial building on St James's Street: high ceilings, white walls; veggie food, but neither of them had been hungry; wanting just coffee, space, a change of scene.

They'd questioned Steve Rowland about his friendship with Danny Ireland during the strike, days that had started early morning, often before dawn, driving down from Yorkshire in Steve's van, Danny and maybe half a dozen others in the back, off to join the picket at Silverhill, Manton, Clipstone; asked him about the couple of afternoons they'd worked, Danny and himself, at the back of 20 Church Street, digging down around new drainage pipes, clearing the ground for where the foundations, the new concrete would be set. Wanting to know how close to Christmas had that been; how close to the date of Jenny Hardwick's disappearance, how far away?

When asked about Danny's relationship with Jenny, Rowland had reckoned it mostly went off inside his head. Had he ever known them to argue? Only one time he could remember: a bit of a row in the street; nothing important, at least it hadn't seemed so at the time.

The $64,000 question next: if Danny had ever ended up in a similar kind of situation as Wayne Cameron had with Donna Crowder, would Rowland have helped him out in the same way?

He hadn't needed very much time to consider his answer.

'Yes, prob'ly. Prob'ly would. But it's all – what's the word? Hypo-something.'

'Hypothetical,' Resnick offered.

'That's it, hypothetical. 'Cause he didn't, did he?'

Asking then for another Pepsi; all that talking, making him thirsty.

And did they believe him? Much as they might have liked not to, the probability was, yes, they did.

Catherine finished her coffee. 'Let me just go to the Ladies.'

Resnick waited out on the pavement. It was clouding over. The cold case team would be taking Rowland back through all the events surrounding Donna Crowder's murder, taking a final statement prior to talking to someone from the CPS, determining which charges to bring against him. Perverting the course of justice? Accessory to murder?

'"Sky is Falling",' Catherine said when she joined him. 'That's what I've been stuck with. Since I got out of the shower. Natalie Duncan. You know her at all?'

Resnick shook his head.

'You should. Comes from Nottingham. Great voice. You'd like her.'

When they got back to Snig Hill there was a message from John McBride. Danny Ireland's body had been found in a remote area of the West Highlands.

'Some climbers came across him,' McBride told them later. 'Been there several days by the look of things. Less than a quarter-mile, if that, away from shelter.

Climbers' bothy. Poor visibility, didn't see it. Likely never knew it was there. Either that or just too exhausted. There'll be a post-mortem, but from the sound of it, most likely cause of death was hypothermia.'

'Where does that leave us now?' Catherine said, shaking her head.

'About as lost as he was, poor bastard?'

Resnick turned away.

All dying, Charlie.

An echo, slight, beneath the piano music continuing to play somewhere deep inside his head.

53

Jenny met him in the pub close by the station. The instructions passed to her as she was leaving the Welfare, last minute, urgent. Peter Waites in the loop no longer. Not wanting to be. Instructions on a single sheet of paper, train tickets, cash in reserve, emergencies only. Where to go and when. What to do in case of something not working out as planned. Both paper and envelope she'd burned before hurrying along to Mrs Jepson and asking her to keep an eye on the kids until Barry was back off shift.

The man she's meeting, the same as once before. Thirtyish, glasses, sweating a little, top button of his shirt unfastened behind his tie. Ring on his wedding finger, dull, forgotten. She doesn't like being there on her own, not round King's Cross, worried what people might think. On the game. But the bar's crowded, thick with smoke.

'You'll have a drink,' he says. His accent's flat, normal, no accent at all.

'Best not.'

He pushes back his cuff to look at his watch. 'Plenty of time before your train.'

'No, really.'

The suitcase is on the floor by his feet. Dark brown with a strap.

'Suit yourself.'

The handle is smooth with use, still slightly warm from his hand.

'You know the arrangement?'

But already she's walking away. Self-conscious but doing her best to convince herself no one will notice anything out of the ordinary: a youngish woman, wisp of scarf, coat buttoned against the cold, making her way home.

At the entrance to the station, she buys a bar of chocolate, peppermint Aero, as a treat. A newspaper to read on the way.

She passes through the barrier, boards the train.

Not wanting to leave the suitcase with the others at the end of the carriage, she takes it with her to her seat. The man opposite offers to put it up on the rack for her, but it won't quite fit.

'I'll keep it here,' she says. 'By my feet.'

*   *   *

At Nottingham, the station seems dark, as if the lights are only on half-power. After the usual rush for the exit, people anxious to catch their bus, not wanting to wait too long for a taxi, she's left with a few last stragglers; a woman with kids, one that won't stop crying, no more than a baby; a man in a wheelchair, one of the station staff pushing him towards the lift. Wait on the platform and someone will meet you. They'll use your name, Jenny Hardwick. Just hand them the case, then it shouldn't be too long a wait for your next train. There had been money for the taxi to Bledwell Vale.

She looks up and down the platform. Walks along to the stairs and waits. Comes back. Someone coming out of the Gents, tightening the belt on his raincoat. She looks at him expectantly, but he walks past. Up the steps and away.

How long has she been there?

Five minutes?

It seems longer.

She could get a cup of tea from the buffet, but it's closed.

She paces, sits, paces again. The case is heavy but she doesn't want to let it be.

One of the station staff, hovering. 'All right, miss?'

'Yes, yes. All right, thanks. Just waiting for a friend.'

He nods and continues on his way.

Her throat is dry and she's sure he's not coming.

Something's happened. Something unavoidable. Unavoidably detained. She puts the case down, holds her face in her hands. The instructions, in the event of this happening, are clear. Do nothing to draw attention to yourself, take the connecting train, then a taxi to Bledwell Vale but an address not her own.

She checks the time on the screen overhead.

Platform 5.

Give it a few minutes longer, she tells herself. A handful of people come down the steps from the entrance, singly, together. A woman around her own age with dyed blue hair, laughing loudly at nothing in particular. A young man with a mohican. Two older men with briefcases, talking earnestly.

She hurries between them, up the steps, along and down, arriving moments before the train pulls in; finds a seat in the last carriage and closes her eyes. Inside, she's shaking.

When the taxi pulls up outside 20 Church Street, it's all she can do to prise herself from the seat. How easy to lean forward – sorry, she's made a mistake, give the driver her own address.

Instead she slides the suitcase out on to the pavement and follows suit.

The key is where she's been told it will be, beneath an empty plant pot to the right of the front door. Although it's late, there are lights behind several curtained windows further along the street. The Peterson house is dark. Gone off to visit relatives; no danger of them coming back. Let yourself in and wait.

How long, she wonders?

Not long. Just till he comes.

It strikes cold inside, as if they've been away for several days already. Not wanting to switch on the lights – no one's meant to be there, after all – Jenny moves carefully from room to room. In the kitchen she feels her way through several drawers until she finds a box of matches, then, some moments later, a torch. Shines it along the floor near where she's standing, around the walls. In place of the rear door, a thick sheet of polythene has been fixed in place; whatever work they've been having done, Howard and Megan Peterson, not quite finished.

There's a grey-trim phone in the hall.

She doesn't know who to phone, who to call.

She'll have to wait.

If nobody comes inside a half-hour, an hour . . . what then?

Cross that bridge, she tells herself, and not wanting to use up all its batteries, switches off the torch.

She sits on a straight-backed chair against the wall, the bulk of the room in shadow; the suitcase down beside the table where she left it.

She thinks she hears what might be footsteps approaching but they dematerialise as swiftly as they came. A car driving slowly along the street behind. Then nothing. She can't take her eyes off the case, a sudden desire to see what's inside.

That story she learned at school . . .

Pandora?

Just a myth.

For something to do as much as anything else, she picks up the suitcase and sets it down on the table in the middle of the room.

Shall I, shan't I?

She unfastens the buckle on the strap and slips it back. Her fingers are clumsy on the metal clasps, not easy working in the dark, and she thinks, of course, they'll be locked, why didn't I think before, but there's a key – a pair of keys, small and bronze – attached to the handle. Picking up the torch in one hand, with the other she lifts the lid.

My God! It's stuffed with money, fat with it, all kinds, all denominations. Twenty-pound notes, tight rolls of them inside elastic bands. But other money too. German? French? Different sizes, colours. She can't believe how much.

Switching off the light, she lets the lid fall back.

'Forty thousand, give or take,' the voice says.

She gasps, stifles a scream. Fumbles with the torch and lets it fall.

At the far side of the room, in the open doorway, a shape detaches itself from the greater dark.

Jenny struggles to control her breathing, the impulse to run.

'You terrified me,' she says.

'I'm sorry.'

Does she recognise the voice? As the speaker moves forward, she bends and scoops up the torch, shines it in his grinning face.

'I thought a quick knee trembler before we get down to the real business. Hard up against the wall. That's what you like, isn't it?'

She hurls the torch at his face, but he just sways aside and laughs; when he grabs her arm, she struggles and tries to wriggle free but he's too strong.

Screams but there's no one to hear.

54

Resnick's car resolutely refused to start. Easy enough to go back into the station, borrow a pair of jump leads, but easier still to accept Catherine's invitation of a lift back down to Nottingham. A miserable evening, the rain that had been threatening off and on for the last hour or so had finally started to fall. With a vengeance. Heavy goods vehicles on the motorway sent waves of water splashing across the windscreen, wipers at full speed. Catherine concentrating on the road, conversation at a minimum.

Resnick found himself thinking about Danny Ireland. A man he never knew, now never would. A haphazard path that seemed to have taken him from Doncaster to Leeds, from Goole to Aberdeen; work on the oil rigs, the ferries and then, as far as they could tell, no regular work at all until he turned up at a smelter north of Fort William, living in a room with a single bed, but choosing to sleep on the floor.

What had that been, that job briefly held? A last gesture towards civilisation? Or was that how he had lived, ten years or more? Picking up work here and there, enough to fund his next withdrawal from the world? And what was it, Resnick wondered, that had brought him to that point? Where the company of others was a contagion to be avoided at all costs? *Keeping the fuck away from the likes of you.* Had he done something so terrible that he avoided, at all costs, anything that might force him to acknowledge it? Or had the world – or someone in it – done something so hurtful to him?

Some went into a seminary, sought seclusion that way, took vows of silence, talked only to their God; some put a gun to their head, stepped out in front of a train, took what the judgemental referred to as the coward's way out, though Resnick knew it wasn't that; some simply walked away and kept on walking – keeping the fuck away – until the moment came, perhaps, when, for whatever reason, they could walk no more. Lay down and waited for the snow, the mist, the earth to cover them from thought and sight.

When Lynn had died there had been moments when he'd contemplated the second way out, longed for the third. Done neither. The thought of her telling him not to be so bloody stupid a necessary corrective.

They were leaving the motorway, joining the steady drift of cars towards the city centre.

'I don't suppose you fancy a drink?' Catherine said. He did.

She parked the car on the Ropewalk and they walked the short distance down towards the Old Market Square. Resnick maintained a fondness for the Bell, principally for the way you could walk in through that narrow entrance and find yourself more or less exactly where you were twenty or thirty years before. Catherine said she didn't care.

They found a seat in the back bar, Resnick settling for a pint of Greene King IPA, Catherine a glass of dry white, New Zealand Sauvignon. Conversations spun around them, customers walked in and out, some – a tidy few – looking over in Resnick's direction with a nod of recognition. The occasional raised eyebrow: what's he doing, lucky sod, with a woman like that?

Catherine was due to report to Martin Picard in the morning. A little over three weeks since the investigation had started and what did she have to tell him? One of their most significant potential witnesses had been found dead in the Highlands of Scotland. Not so much more.

She could see Picard's raised eyebrow now, his look of barely concealed contempt.

'Cheer up,' Resnick said.

'You are kidding.'

'Look at it this way – his way – Picard's way. What he wanted was a low-key investigation into a thirty-year-old murder. Quiet. Discreet. No feathers ruffled. All right, there was all that business with Fleetwood and Michael Swann, but like most things in the headlines these days, twenty-four hours later, it was as good as forgotten.'

'I don't know, Charlie.'

'If the case remains open after a few weeks, Picard said, no skin off anyone's nose.'

'He said that?'

'More or less.'

'Then why am I letting myself get worked up into such a state?'

'Because, whatever Picard or anyone else says, it's your case. And you want a result.'

Catherine braced back in her chair. She wanted a cigarette, but not enough to go and stand in a shop doorway along the street, sheltering from the rain.

'Do they do food here?'

'Did the last time I asked.'

'Because I really want another drink, but if I drink any more without food it's going to go straight to my head.'

'I'll get us some menus,' Resnick said, pushing back his chair.

Catherine ordered a club sandwich, Resnick steak-and-ale pie. So as not to talk any more about the case, she asked him about his family, and he told the story, in so far as he understood it, of how his parents, along with countless other Poles, had made their way to England in the late summer of 1939, fleeing the German invasion.

'We're not so unalike, then, Charlie, you and I,' Catherine said. 'Exiles under the skin.'

A hen party made a final sally through the bar, funny hats, party poppers, whistles, slogans, skirts up around their behinds. Across the street, a contingent of men aged between twenty and forty – shaven heads, shirts worn outside their trousers, more than the odd tattoo – had emerged from Yates' Wine Lodge and were serenading the occupants of the police car parked at the bottom of Market Street.

Resnick and Catherine turned along St James's Street and past the Malt Cross in the direction of the Castle. A short way along the Ropewalk, Catherine lost her footing and grabbed hold of Resnick's arm for support.

'Sorry, Charlie. I must be drunk after all.'

'Easy done.'

Outside the building, she fished inside her bag for the keys. 'Quick cup of coffee?'

Reading his hesitation, she smiled. 'Relax, Charlie. Coffee just means coffee, okay?'

'Okay.' Said with a self-conscious grin.

The flat was a little impersonal, he thought; by which, in all likelihood, he meant not filled with clutter. Neat and tidy. Modern. Not to his taste, but wasn't that only to be expected?

'You want it with milk or black?' Catherine called from the kitchen.

'Better make it black.'

There were stains on the wall closest to the kitchen, not quite washed away; as if someone had thrown a glass of wine in anger, he thought – and thought again about the bruising that had discoloured Catherine's face, the man who had confronted her in the street.

'That man,' he said, when she brought in the coffee.

'Abbas?'

'Yes. You seen anything of him lately?'

Catherine shook her head. 'Back in the City somewhere. Busy setting up another takeover or two, I imagine.'

'That's what he does?'

'Venture capitalism, I think that's what it's called.'

She pressed play on the stereo. Guitar, bass, lazy sort of tempo, trickle of piano, a woman's voice.

'Is this that Natalie someone you were telling me about?' Resnick asked.

'Natalie Duncan. No, this is someone else.'

She sat down next to him on the settee. Listened.

Brushed against his arm once reaching for her cup. A mistake. He asked her a question or two about the flat, if she was just renting, things like that.

She mentioned Lynn. That saved him. Saved them both.

'Are you going to get a taxi or . . .'

'Rain's stopped. I'll probably walk.'

'I can call for one if . . .'

'It's okay. There's bound to be one or two by the square if I change my mind.'

Taking her cigarettes and lighter, she walked him down the stairs and out on to the street. The pavements were still a little dark from the rain, a little damp, but otherwise it was a clear night, fresh, not over-cold.

'Well, I'd best be off.'

'Tomorrow, then.'

'Good luck with Picard.'

'Thanks. You want a lift in afterwards?'

He shook his head. 'It's okay. I'll catch the train.'

Watching him walk away, she lit a cigarette, inhaled deeply, holding down the smoke. Above the Castle, the clouds were gathering around the moon. A light across the street went out. And then another. Muffled laughter. She continued to stand there, smoking, thinking about what had just happened, what hadn't happened, about the various stupid things she'd done with her life, mistakes she'd narrowly avoided, mistakes she'd made.

Turned back inside.

He was waiting for her on the landing, his body crashing into her the moment she turned the key in the lock.

55

The impact sent her flying, arms flailing, all balance gone, cannoning into the edge of the door before falling to the floor. His body on top of her, pressing her down, crushing her, making it impossible, almost, to breathe. Something sharp then pressing hard between her shoulder blades, down into the small of her back – an elbow, a knee – and before she could lift her head, he had seized hold of her by the ankles and half-dragged, half-swung her through into the living room and over towards the settee, bouncing her off the furniture, the walls.

Then leaving her. Stunned.

Lifting herself carefully, slowly on one arm, Catherine blinked the blood from her eyes.

Her left eye.

Heard the flat door slam.

Abbas was nowhere to be seen.

He'd gone.

Gingerly, she leaned back, closed both eyes, and, a moment later, trembling, began to cry.

'Catherine?'

She jumped at the sound of his voice, stifled a scream.

'Catherine,' he said, concerned. 'I do believe you're bleeding.'

'Why are you . . .?'

'Doing this?' A smile. 'It's no more than you deserve. Fucking that old man.'

'He's not . . .' It hurt her to speak.

'Not what?'

'Not old.'

'Wrong answer.' He slapped her hard across the face. 'What you should have said, I wasn't fucking him. You fucking bitch.'

'I wasn't . . .'

His hand was at her throat. Squeezing hard, he tightened his grip, leaving Catherine unable to speak, unable to breathe.

'Can't help it, can you? Like animals in the fucking fields. You bitch. You black fucking bitch! You passed me over for that. That!'

Rearing suddenly away, he relinquished his grip, and she rolled, choking, to one side, fighting for breath. And when she rolled back, he was standing over her, impassive, staring down, and she could see the anger, the hatred, still simmering in his eyes, and knew it wasn't over.

It had just begun.

Reading her fear, he laughed.

'What? You think I'm going to rape you? Is that what it is? That's what you're frightened of?'

Stooping, he brought his face down close to hers. His voice a whisper. 'You really think I'm going to soil myself inside you? Inside that?'

A look of disgust on his face, he arched back his head and spat.

'Abbas,' she said. 'Please . . .'

Without warning he punched her in the chest. And again. Again. The belly, the head, the breasts. Even after she had lost consciousness it continued. Went on until he was exhausted, knuckles swollen and starting to leak a little blood of their own.

Eyes like pinpoints, shining in the dark.

Oh, Catherine . . .

There was something about the way she lay there, head lolling sideways, one arm outstretched, the other cradling her breast, that he thought rather beautiful.

Stepping over the broken furniture, he went into the kitchen and lit a cigarette.

Gradually, Catherine opened her eyes. Correction, one eye. The left one was stuck fast. Turned slowly, inch by inch, on to her side. Her front. Even that much caused her pain. Summoning up all her reserves she began to crawl.

Through the partly opened blinds, the dull ghost of the city rose up into the sky.

There was something wrong with the side of her face, her jaw.

Not just the bleeding, something else.

Her bag was wedged between an upturned chair and the wall.

With an effort she managed to tip its contents out on to the floor.

3.57: the time by her phone.

She realised her one good eye had closed again and had to will herself awake. Fingers fumbling a little, uncertain, uncontrolled. The phone slipped from her hand and she nudged it closer, trapping it against the wall. Her breathing seemed alternately shallow and harsh, each breath like a saw working against her chest.

With difficulty, she rested her ear close by the phone, heard it ring and ring.

'Hello?' Disoriented, tired.

'Charlie . . .'

By the time Resnick arrived, the ambulance he'd called for was already in the street outside, paramedics on their way up the stairs. At the first glimpse of her he had to look away.

Quickly, without seeming to hurry, they checked for a pulse, took readings, manoeuvred her on to a stretcher, strapped her in. Resnick gently squeezed her hand, lowered his face towards hers to hear what she was saying.

'I'm a nuisance, Charlie.'

'Damned olive oil.'

It hurt like hell to smile. 'Not this time, Charlie.'

Although he knew, he needed her to tell him who it was to be sure.

When she had and he straightened and stood away there were tiny bubbles of blood breaking against his ear.

'Okay to go?' the paramedic asked.

'Okay.'

Andy Dawson didn't take to being woken in the small hours. 'Charlie, this better be fucking good.'

'A man named Abbas Rashidi. My guess is, staying at one of the better hotels. Easier for you to check than me.'

'And this is because?'

Resnick told him.

'I'll get on it.'

It took a little while. Mr Rashidi had ordered a taxi to collect him from his hotel and take him to East Midlands Airport, 5 a.m. sharp. Andy Dawson picked up Resnick outside Queen's Medical Centre at a quarter past.

'How is she?'

'A mess.'

'But she's not . . .?'

Resnick shook his head. 'She'll be okay. It just might take a while.'

There were three early flights: Dublin at 6.30; Berlin at 6.45; Paris at 6.50. When Dawson had checked, there were seats still available on each one.

As they left the ring road, a second car pulled in behind them.

'Just in case,' Dawson said. 'Couple of lads who punch well above their weight.'

Resnick sat with fists clenched and pressed against his knees. Seeing nothing through the windows as they hurtled past. Trying to forget what he'd last seen of Catherine's face.

He'd like nothing more, he thought, as they neared the airport, than to have to haul Abbas off a plane, frogmarch him away from the line waiting to board. But he was in the executive lounge, sipping an espresso, breaking apart an almond croissant with long deft fingers. When Resnick and Dawson approached, he seemed to tense for a moment, and then, recognising Resnick, relaxed.

With two plain-clothes officers built like brick shithouses guarding the door behind him, Resnick prayed for Abbas to make a run.

No such luck.

'Abbas Rashidi,' Dawson said, 'I am arresting you on a charge of causing grievous bodily harm with intent, in pursuance of the Offences Against the Person Act of 1861. You do not have to say anything, but it may harm your defence if you do not mention when questioned something which you later rely on in court. Anything you do say may be given in evidence.'

A mocking smile slid across Abbas' face.

'She'll never go through with the charges,' he said to Resnick quietly. 'You know that, don't you? It'll never get to court.'

The only way Resnick could stop himself from punching him and punching him hard was to walk away.

56

Bruises to most of her body aside, Catherine had a dislocated jaw, seven broken ribs and a ruptured spleen; it seemed increasingly as if she might lose the use of her left eye. The gash at the front of her head had taken twenty-three stitches, another seventeen to the wound in the scalp; one half of her hair had been shaved away. As a look, she didn't think it would catch on. Either that or its brief day had passed.

It was forty-eight hours before she was wheeled out of intensive care, fit enough, just, to join the general population, a semi-private room in one of the general wards.

Her parents came and sat by her bed, bewildered and hurt. When her father set off on a diatribe about police work and its dangers, Catherine told him, politely, that police work had nothing to do with this.

It was thanks to police work that she was alive and not dead. Soon after that, they left.

'Sky fell in on me this time and no mistake,' she said when Resnick came to visit.

'Martin Picard sends his best wishes, hopes you get better soon.'

'Now you are joking.'

Resnick grinned.

Catherine hitched herself up a little in the bed. If it ever got to the point where she could move without it hurting in half a dozen places, she'd know she was on the way to recovery.

'What's happening to the investigation?'

'McBride's stepped up for now. Picard's made noises about taking over, but so far we've not seen hide nor hair.'

'They'll let it die, won't they?'

'Probably. Remain open, on file. Move on.'

'We should have done better.'

'We did what we could.'

'You think?'

'If they'd decided to throw everything at it, bags of resources, that might have made a difference. But even then . . . thirty years, too long a time.' He sat up. 'You gave it your best shot.'

'Just not good enough.'

It lay between them, the ghost of failure, still there after Resnick had left.

When McBride came a day later, his hands were awkward with a box of badly wrapped chocolates, all fingers and thumbs.

Seeing her face, he cried. The first time in years.

'That bastard,' he said, 'just give me five minutes with him alone.'

Waking from a shallow sleep that afternoon, Catherine was surprised to find Jill Haines sitting upright beside the bed, best frock, best coat, fresh flowers from her garden resting neatly in her lap.

'It was in the paper,' she said. 'On the news.'

'It's nice of you,' Catherine said. 'Nice of you to come.'

She was conscious of the other woman fidgeting in her seat.

'I should have come before,' Jill said eventually.

'It's only been a few days.'

'No. Before. Before any of this happened.'

Somewhere inside Catherine's brain, wheels started to turn.

57

It was a near-perfect spring day. Spring turning into summer. Open land, criss-crossed with channels as far as the eye could see. Two fields over, a line of men, twenty or so, was making its way, bent backed, across the ground, picking some crop he couldn't clearly identify. All it needed, Resnick thought, an overseer on horseback, a dog or two, chains.

He drove carefully up the lane, window down; his car working again, for now at least, fingers firmly crossed.

The two black Labs came trotting out to meet him, sniffing his hand.

Keith Haines was in the nearest of the greenhouses, a faintly bemused expression on his face. 'Whenever Jill's away I always think there's stuff I should do – keep things on track till she gets back – but then I can never figure out what it is.'

'Away?' Resnick said.

'Three days' residential. Sussex somewhere. Landscapes, I imagine. The usual. But if it gives her pleasure . . .'

He looked sideways through the glass; little to see but his own reflection, some small distortion.

'Let's go inside,' he said.

Resnick noticed again the slight sideways stoop, the almost-shuffle when he walked.

'Small stroke,' Haines said, following Resnick's gaze. 'Few years back now.' He shrugged. 'Could have been worse. Basket case by now.'

Without asking, he fetched a couple of beers from the fridge. Decanted them into glasses.

'Bass, Charlie. Pale ale. Still brewed in Burton, believe it or not. Miracle it's not China like everything fucking else.'

He eased himself down into his chair, slowly shaking his head.

'Getting old, Charlie. Old and crabby. You and me both. Someone'll do us a favour, one day, take us out and have us shot.' He raised his glass. 'Cheers, anyway . . .'

'Cheers,' Resnick said.

'First time Jill saw this,' Haines said, pointing at the label on the bottle, 'fair wet her knickers. It's in some painting, apparently. Famous. Folies-Bergère, one of those. Whoever did it – Monet, Manet – stuck a bottle of Bass slap bang at the front. Product placement, isn't that what they call it nowadays? Probably slipped the bloke a few francs when he was setting up his easel, something of the sort.'

Resnick took another swallow. Time his to take. Happy to let Haines talk.

'Something about the strike,' Haines said, 'that's what you said when you called. Something you wanted to check, see if I remembered.' He tapped the side of his head. 'Memory like mine, porous don't come into it. I'd not hold out too much hope.'

'You'll remember this,' Resnick said.

'Oh?'

'Cash, quite a lot of it, coming in from abroad.'

'Newark,' Haines said, brightening. 'October time? I'd heard a whisper, pot of money coming in. Rotterdam or somewhere. Ferry, any road. Could've been nothing, of course. Idle chat. Rumours going round back then, well, you know, like fleas on a cat's back. Came to you with it, all the same. Must've seemed more to it than most. My thanks, got to ride with the big boys. There for the intercept. Newark ring road. I can see it now, expression on that bloke's face. Excuse me, sir, but would you mind if we take a look inside the vehicle. What was it? Six thousand in neat little bundles, all over the back seat. Unbelievable.'

'Not the only time, of course,' Resnick said.

'How d'you mean?'

'You said yourself, rumours flying round. Caseloads of cash. Awash with the stuff.'

Haines nodded. 'There's this story, isn't there. True or not. Scargill and two of his mates. Pile of cash on the table. Donations. Huge. What? Twenty thousand? More than that, maybe. Scraped together by some poor bastards in the Ukraine, somewhere of that sort. Here, Scargill says, and divides it into three. Take it. Keep it safe. Never seen again. One of 'em, at least, used it to pay off the last of his mortgage. You believe that?'

'No, not really.'

'Me, neither. Good story, though.'

Resnick set down his glass. 'There was another occasion, Keith. Just short of Christmas. Bledwell Vale. Some other snippet of information you'd come across, overheard.'

'What about it?'

'Just wondering when you decided not to pass that on? Keep it to yourself.'

Haines looked beyond Resnick's shoulder, as if, perhaps, he was expecting someone else to come in.

No one did.

'Like you said, Charlie, there were always stories. Exaggerated, most of them. Christmas, especially. Famous for it, of course. Frankincense and fucking myrrh.' He laughed, short, abrupt.

'Some of them true,' Resnick said.

Haines took a long, slow draft of ale. Tasting it go down. Hoppy. Bright. Whatever he might wish for now, it was not going to happen.

'Twelve thousand,' he said eventually. 'Twelve thousand and seventy-two pounds, that's how much there was. I took the case, split the money, buried it in three different locations. Paid it in gradually, careful as I could.' He made a small sound, part sigh, part something else. 'Helped to buy this place. Down payment and a bit more. Jill, she came up with the rest.'

'And Jenny?'

'Far as she was concerned, I was the one meant to be taking it from her, moving it on. Who could be more above suspicion, after all? Village copper.'

'So, what? She just stood aside, let you take it?'

'Of course. Surprised, mind. She was that. But then when I explained . . .' He shrugged, one shoulder higher than the other.

'You left her there.'

Haines nodded.

'Alive?'

'Alive? Of course, alive. Jesus, Charlie, come on. Whatever happened afterwards, believe me, I never knew. Not till . . .'

'You thought she'd done a runner, that's what you said. Your report.'

'That's right. Thought maybe she'd dipped into the case already. Did occur to me. Helped herself, like.

No way of knowing how much was there in the first place. Didn't mention it at the time. Not after what I'd done. But, Charlie, no, when I walked out of Church Street, Jenny, she was alive as the day she was born.'

Resnick settled back in his chair. Ever since he'd arrived, Haines had been over-anxious, over-keen to talk. 'Comes easy after a while, I suppose,' Resnick said. 'Easier, anyway.'

'What's that?'

'Lying. First you tell it to yourself, somewhere inside your head and then, eventually, out loud. Try it on others. Your wife, for instance. All the while you're speaking, trying to read the expression on her face, see if she believes you. Bit like you were doing with me a few minutes back. But she didn't, did she? Jill. Not ever. Deep down.'

'Don't talk such bloody . . .'

He made as if to get up, but Resnick reached over, rested a hand on his arm.

'She came in – Jill. Made a statement. Information we thought might be of interest. There were complaints, apparently, before the two of you got together and after.'

'Complaints? What bloody complaints?'

'We've checked out a few, those we can. Young women, married mostly . . .'

'Don't be so bloody daft!'

'Claiming you put them under pressure . . .'

'Pressure? What kind of pressure?'

'Pressure to give sexual favours. Husband driving a car when uninsured. Taking paid work while claiming benefit. Breaking bail conditions. Be nice to me and I'll make sure it all goes away.'

'This is fucking ridiculous. Pie in the fucking sky!'

'You might've tried that one on Jenny, I suppose. When you wanted her to fall into line, do whatever you were asking. Danny Ireland, for instance, reported for breaking the conditions of his bail.'

'Don't be so fucking stupid!'

'What happened, Keith? Didn't she care what happened to Danny? Not enough to get down on her knees? A quick hand job? Or was the thought of it just too disgusting? Her sister's intended.'

All the colour had drained from Haines' cheeks. He closed his eyes; when he opened them again, Resnick was still sitting there, waiting.

'At first she just laughed,' Haines said, speaking slowly, not looking at Resnick, addressing a spot on the floor. 'Laughed in my face. And then, when I tried to . . . to get her to change her mind, she flew at me, scratching and slapping, and I pushed her – that's all it was – I pushed her back, against this plastic, this plastic across the doorway, and she went right through and hit her head when she fell . . . hit her head on these slabs, paving slabs, they were there, waiting . . .

right . . . right on the edge of one. Didn't even cry out, just lay there, and I panicked, I don't mind saying . . . got out of there as fast as I could . . .'

His eyes fixed on Resnick now, imploring. 'I went back. It must have been, I don't know, an hour later.'

'For the money.'

'To see how she was. I thought maybe . . .'

'You went back for the money.'

Haines' mouth was dry, the words sticking in his throat. 'When I got back no doubt but she was dead. She hadn't moved, not one inch. I think she must have been already dead when I left her. I don't know, but that's what . . . that's what I like to think now.'

He wiped a hand across his open mouth; took a swig of ale and swilled it round, spat it back into the glass.

'There was this sort of trench by where she lay. Whoever'd been working there had filled it in with hard core. Covered it with some sort of insulation.' Desperately, he sucked in air. 'I dug it all back out and . . .'

It was all he could say. A convulsion shook him and he clenched his arms tight across his chest. Shuddered and gripped the sides of the chair.

Resnick started to reach out towards him, then stopped. Sat there pitying him; not pitying him at all.

'What . . .?' Haines said. 'What happens now?'

'Everything you've told me,' Resnick said, 'it wasn't

under caution. It'd be inadmissible in court. I could get you to make a note of what you've said, but even signed and dated, just the two of us here, not take much for some clever barrister to have it thrown out, no problem. So what happens, what happens next, it's up to you. You can drive back with me now and make a statement at the station, that might be best. Proceed from there.'

Haines didn't answer, not immediately, leaving Resnick wondering if he'd taken in all that had been said.

'I think,' Haines said eventually, 'yes, come along with you, that's what I'll do. Better the devil you know, eh?'

'Fine by me.'

Haines got less than steadily to his feet.

'I'd best go to the jakes first . . .' He laughed. 'Wonder I didn't shit myself already. Then grab a coat.'

'Keith . . .'

'Yes?'

'You'll not try anything daft?'

'Like do a runner, you mean? How far d'you reckon I'd get, my condition?' He grinned. 'Come and stand outside the door if you'd like.'

Resnick shook his head. 'Don't be too long about it.'

The shotgun was in the first of two sheds near the

garden end: single barrel, 12 gauge, kept there in wait for any stray fox or weasel, anything that succeeded in burrowing beneath the wire. One of the dogs had followed him out and he nudged it away with his knee before closing the door. The box of cartridges was on the shelf above.

He took a breath.

Whatever happened, Jill would look after the dogs.

He was fingering a shell, awkward, down into the chamber when the shed door swung back open.

'Rabbit or two, Keith? That what you're thinking?' Reaching across, McBride took the weapon from Haines' faltering hands. 'Some other time, eh?'

Resnick was waiting at the car. McBride's and one other parked further back down the lane, out of sight.

For a moment, Haines looked into Resnick's face, then away.

Only his breath seemed to be moving, hoarse and ragged, through the quiet air.

58

Six weeks later, Resnick picked up the phone and it was Catherine Njoroge. Would he be able to drag himself away from whatever important work he was doing for long enough to meet her for coffee, her treat?

He said he would.

Work for him was much the same as before, a civilian investigator still, though now with an office on the upper floor. On a clear day he could see out beyond the dome at the top of the Council House and imagine the fields beyond.

Keith Haines had been remanded in custody, his trial date not yet fixed.

Spurred on by his part in the arrest of Abbas Rashidi, Andy Duncan had pleaded successfully for a further year in harness. The student, whose injuries had been such a concern to Resnick and himself, had made a better-than-expected recovery and was convalescing, prior to resuming his studies at some near future date. Rashidi was still awaiting trial, having assembled a prodigious and expensive legal team to support his expected plea of not guilty.

Resnick had just negotiated an empty bench at the edge of the square when he saw Catherine walking past the stone lion on permanent guard outside the Council House, a takeaway cup in either hand.

If he hadn't known that her natural stride was more forceful, stronger, he might not have noticed much different about her at all. The same black trouser suit or similar, a silver instead of purple ribbon in her hair. And the eyepatch was, beyond any doubt, a stylish addition.

'Flat white, I hope that's okay?'

'Fine.'

They sat for a while in near silence, comfortable, despite all that had happened, in one another's company, watching the good folk of Nottingham go about their daily business.

'I handed in my resignation yesterday,' she said.

Resnick took a beat before replying. 'You don't think that's a waste of a good copper?'

'Come on, Charlie. Whoever heard of a one-eyed detective?'

'Depends how much they can see.'

Catherine shook her head. 'I'm going back to uni. To study law. It's probably what I should have done all along. Needless to say, my father's beside himself with joy. Sees me as some kind of lost sheep come back to the fold.'

'You'll go here or . . .?'

'Manchester.'

He nodded. Dredged up a smile. 'I can just see you standing up in court, sweeping all before. Black robes and that eyepatch, made for each other, I'd say.'

'You're a pal, Charlie. A good friend.'

'I like to think so.'

They continued to sit, chatting easily about this and that, nothing of great importance.

'I've just realised,' Resnick said suddenly. 'What's different.'

'What's that?'

'All this time outside, coffee, and you haven't had a cigarette.'

'I've given up.'

'New leaf.'

'Something like that.'

With a glance towards the Council House clock, she got to her feet. 'Are you going back or . . .?'

'I'll sit here just a bit longer. Finish this.'

'Okay.'

'You'll stay in touch.'

'Of course.'

He didn't watch her walk away.

He might wander up to Music Inn, he thought after a while. There was a new Monk album he'd seen advertised, concerts in Paris and Milan. 'Off Minor', 'Straight No Chaser', that kind of thing.

Why play the right notes . . .?

You know the rest.

AFTERWORD

So, Resnick's last case. When I sat down with my friend, the late Dulan Barber, sometime in 1988, and began putting together the bits and pieces of Charlie's character, it would not have occurred to either of us that he would still be around some twenty-five years later. If only just. But after twelve novels, some sixteen short stories, two television adaptations and four radio plays, to say nothing of various e-books and audio versions, he's still standing. More accurately, sitting, and appropriately, on a bench overlooking Nottingham's Old Market Square.

Which is where I propose to leave him, nursing a cup of takeout coffee and hankering after a fresh helping of Thelonious Monk. In one early draft, not ever properly committed to paper, I did what is I suppose the obvious – what many readers might have expected – and killed him off. No Reichenbach Falls. No return. But it just didn't feel right.

So at the end of *Darkness, Darkness* he's still alive, Charlie, and though in some ways he's central to the novel, this time he's more and more a witness, observing rather than influencing the action; understanding, perhaps, less and less of the world moving fast around him. And in that, I suppose, Charlie and I, we're alike. Writers are witnesses after all, and as we get older our vision, however much we might fight against it, clouds over.

By the time this book is published, I shall have inched closer towards the end of my eighth decade than I shall be from its beginning. And there are things I still want to do. Things that don't seem to involve Charlie.

He'll be okay. He's got a flat white and yet another version of 'Blue Monk' to keep him warm.

In the writing of this book, in particular those sections relating to the Miners' Strike, I'm grateful to a number of people who were involved in the strike in differing ways for their comments and observations – in particular, Sylvia and Gordon Abbott, Peter Coles, Peter Jarvis and John Morgan. My thanks, also, to Graham Nicholls, for his perceptive reading of the manuscript.

For a detailed overview of the strike and its political

and social background I'm indebted to the following: *Marching to the Fault Line – The Miners' Strike and the Battle for Industrial Britain* by Francis Beckett and David Hencke (Constable, 2009); *The Enemy Within – The Secret War Against the Miners* by Seamus Milne (Verso, 2004) and *Strike – 358 Days that Shook the Nation*, a *Sunday Times* Insight Book written and edited by Peter Wilsher, Donald Macintyre and Michael Jones (André Deutsch, 1985).

For more detailed and personal observations of the strike, I'm grateful to *The Miners' Strike Day by Day – The Illustrated Diary of Yorkshire Miner Arthur Wakefield,* edited by Brian Elliott (Wharncliffe Books, 2002) and *The 1984–1985 Miners' Strike in Nottinghamshire – 'If Spirit Alone Won Battles', The Diary of John Lowe*, edited by Jonathan Symcox (Wharncliffe Books, 2011); also to *Queen Coal – Women of the Miners' Strike* by Triona Holden (Sutton Publishing, 2005), *The Cutting Edge – Women and the Pit Strike*, edited by Vicky Seddon (Lawrence & Wishart, 1986), *Never the Same Again – Women and the Miners' Strike*, by Jean Stead (The Women's Press, 1987) and *Hearts and Minds – The Story of the Women of Nottinghamshire in the Miners' Strike, 1984–1985*, by Joan Witham (Canary Press, 1986).

I gained a great deal of insight from watching DVDs of Mike Figgis's film of Jeremy Deller's *The Battle of Orgreave* (Artangel Media), *The Miners' Campaign*

Tapes (BFI) and *Dole Not Coal – The 1984–85 Miners' Strike, The Striker's Story* (Compress Media).

Conscientiously, I avoided reading any fiction which uses the strike, to a greater or lesser degree, as subject or setting – though I will admit to sneaking a look inside David Peace's excellent and incomparable *GB84* (Faber & Faber, 2004) whenever inspiration sagged. It was in the course of several conversations with David at *Quais du Polar*, the annual crime fiction festival in Lyon, that he convinced me to go ahead with the book which became *Darkness, Darkness*, and for that I'm truly grateful.

Without publishers and editors there would be no Charlie Resnick, no books. It was Tony Lacey at Viking Penguin who first said yes to Charlie and set him on his way. In the US, Marian Wood, then at Henry Holt, guided him through the first ten books with acuity and enthusiasm, and, in France, François Guerif at Rivages has been steadfast in his active support. Writers need agents, too, and I'm grateful that in Carole Blake and latterly Sarah Lutyens I have been blessed with the best combination of professional guidance and unbridled enthusiasm.

My thanks, finally, to everyone at Random House – be it sales, marketing, design or editorial – all of whom have worked hard to make this and earlier books a success – and to Mary Chamberlain, whose conscientious copy editing, book after book, has helped me to avoid the worst errors of misdating and slovenly punctuation.

Anyone who knows anything about publishing will know how very fortunate I have been to have had Susan Sandon as my editor for the past nine books; it was she who held my hand and Charlie's to the end, encouraging, cajoling, applying just the right amount of pressure when the time was right. Susan, thank you!

Lonely Hearts

John Harvey

Shirley Peters is dead. Murdered. Her body is found twelve hours later in her own house. Just one of the many sordid domestic crimes hitting the city.

Tony Macliesh, her rejected boyfriend, is the obvious prime suspect and he's just been picked off the Aberdeen train and put straight into custody.

But then another woman is sexually abused and throttled to death. And suddenly there seems to be one too many connections between these seemingly unrelated crimes.

Because Detective Inspector Resnick is sure that the two murders are the work of one sadistic killer – two lonely hearts broken by one maniac. And it's up to Resnick to put the record straight – and put the bastard where he belongs.

'Harvey reminds me of Graham Greene – a stylist who tells you everything you need to know while keeping the prose clean and simple'
Elmore Leonard

arrow books

Cold in Hand

John Harvey

Two teenage girls are victims of a bloody Valentine's Day shooting; one survives, the other is less fortunate . . .

It's one of a rising number of violent incidents in the city, and DI Charlie Resnick, nearing retirement, is hauled back to the front line to help deal with the fallout.

But when the dead girl's father seeks to lay the blame on DI Lynn Kellogg, Resnick's colleague and lover, the line between personal and professional becomes dangerously blurred.

As Lynn, shaken by this very public accusation, is forced to question her part in the teenager's death, Resnick struggles against those in the force who disapprove of his maverick ways. But when the unimaginable occurs, an emotional Resnick takes matters into his own hands. No one could have foreseen where this case would lead, and this time Resnick will need all his strength to see justice done . . .

'Reveals modern England in all its most depressing messiness while engaging the reader with characters whose warmth and humanity give real pleasure'
Times Literary Supplement

arrow books